SHOW ME SOMETHING

AUBREY BONDURANT

Photograph and cover design by Sara Eirew
Text copyright © 2017 by Aubrey Bondurant
ISBN: 9781977708960

CHAPTER ONE

$\mathcal{I}$ studied my reflection in the full-length mirror of my temporary apartment bedroom and sighed heavily. As I took in my stressed out, tired face in the mirror, I felt years older than twenty-nine. Why had I agreed to go to this fancy cocktail party tonight?

The short answer was because my friends had invited me, and I couldn't possibly say no. After all, they'd rallied to move my son and me up to Connecticut when we'd suddenly needed to leave Charlotte. I didn't want them to see me unhappy or think I was ungrateful for their support.

But dressing up had never been my thing. I was more of a Keds and jeans kind of girl. As if to drive the point home, when I stepped into the only somewhat fancy dress I owned, it was tight around my midsection. Unfortunately, it was becoming difficult to rationalize the extra pounds stemming from pregnancy now that my son was over two years old.

One more thing to add to my Juliette 2.0 plan. Lose these last ten stubborn-as-hell pounds. Oh, and stop cursing so much. But did internal cursing really count toward having to put money into the swear jar? Hm. Determination to be made later.

1

After slipping the garment off, I shimmied into some Spanx, tugged them up, and hoped this would suck in my stomach and make my hips appear slimmer. When I put the black dress on again, I was pleased that my zipper strained a little less. Shapewear. Seriously, the best invention ever. Well, maybe a close second to my seat warmers. Because who didn't love a warm ass while driving?

Next, I contemplated whether to wear my shoulder-length, blonde-in-desperate-need-of-a-root-touch-up hair up or down. But why bother the contemplation? It would go up in a ponytail like it always did these days. Lastly, I put on some concealer along with some mascara. As I inspected the result, I had to fight the self-doubt creeping up.

Who was I kidding by attending a party while my life was in shambles? It would be better to skip tonight rather than fake my way through. I was just about to take the dress off and bag on going when I heard a knock on the bedroom door.

My mother's smiling face poked in. She'd made the drive with me from Charlotte, North Carolina, home for us, and had helped me get settled over the last couple days. She was essentially an older version of me with her tiny frame and big brown eyes. "Don't you look pretty."

"Thanks, but I think I've changed my mind. I should stay here and spend time with you and Tristan, especially since you're leaving tomorrow."

She wasn't having it, using her infamous mom-guilt voice. "No, you're not, Juliette Marie. The party is literally two flights of steps up, and I'm not letting you back out of it. You're a wonderful mother, honey, but it's not all you are. You deserve a night out with your friends, especially today of all days."

Ah, yes. Ten years ago on this date, at the age of nineteen and while full of hope and a heavy dose of naïveté, I'd said *I do*. And now I was celebrating my wedding anniversary seven hundred miles away from the man with whom I'd pledged to spend the rest of my life.

Yeah, happy anniversary, asshole.

I tried unsuccessfully to bite down on my resentment. Both my two-year-old son and I had been forced to pack up and leave town a few days ago because an investigation had revealed my couldn't-be-my-ex-soon-enough husband was a dirty cop. I'd been told he was about to be arrested for a litany of crimes. Thankfully, I had filed for divorce months ago and had full custody. At least for now.

My son. Tristan. He was the light of my life. And fortunately, he was completely oblivious to both his father's indifference to him and criminal behavior.

Ugh. I needed to stop focusing on Rob otherwise it would put me in a bad mood. It wasn't an easy task considering I held onto a lot of anger. I was especially furious that he'd put his son in potential danger. But I forced myself to tamp it down. Keep it all internalized. Over the last few months, I'd perfected the art of putting on a brave front despite going through personal hell. What were a few more months?

My mom hugged me tightly and I knew she got it. After my father left us when I was six, she'd raised both me and my sister by herself. She'd remarried once we were older, but I remember her devoting every hour outside of her job to her girls. I only hoped I could be half the parent she had always been.

"Maybe you're right. I should go and forget for a little while."

We both heard the knock on the front door, and my mother smiled. "I'm sure that's one of your friends ensuring you don't back out, too. I'll get it."

Haylee's voice and a tap on the door sounded a minute later. "Hey, Juliette, can I come in?"

Haylee was twenty-four, a new mom, a law school student, and quickly becoming one of my best friends. It was due to her generosity that I was living in this apartment building. She was as nice as she was beautiful. Although she'd married the multi-millionaire owner of the company I worked for, it hadn't changed her one bit. She was still as down-to-earth and sweet as she'd always been.

"Sure," I responded and watched her walk into my bedroom, already dressed for the party.

She was wearing a stunning, most likely vintage, print dress with vibrant purples and greens. She looked like a cover model, which incidentally she'd once been for Cosmo Life magazine.

I didn't have a jealous bone in my body, but the effortless way she was put together hardly quelled my insecurity over my too-tight dress and hair in a ponytail.

"Ooh, I love your dress. You look gorgeous," Haylee complimented.

I shrugged it off. "Thanks. But you're the one who looks amazing." And she did, with her long brown hair left soft and down and her stunning wrap dress setting off her curves. "And don't think I'm swinging this way, but your boobs are, like, incredible."

She laughed. "One of the benefits of nursing the baby would be my added cup size. Great to look at but not as nice to touch, unfortunately. Matter of fact, the next order of business before I go up to the party is to pump."

I didn't share that mine had never returned to their original shape and size after a year of nursing, opting to exercise a rare filter on my speech and hope she wasn't as unlucky with her post-nursing body. "Do you want something to drink? I have milk, Diet Coke or water."

"No, thanks. I just wanted to make sure you still intended to come tonight."

My phone buzzed in that moment, and I held up the text message from our mutual friend, Sasha.

"Don't even think about changing your mind about the

party. I will find you and force-feed you a martini if necessary."

"Looks as though you weren't the only one worried I'd back out. To tell the truth, I'm tempted to stay in. Things in my life are a little crazy currently, so attending a party seems, I don't know..."

Haylee lifted a brow. "Who would judge you? Not this crowd, that's for certain. And if you're not up to it tonight, there's a luncheon tomorrow you could go to instead."

I shook my head. "Thanks, but I need to take my mom to the airport."

"That's right. I forgot. If you don't want to go tonight, I certainly won't guilt you into it. That being said, I do have someone I'd love for you to meet."

Wasn't there a rule that you couldn't be set up on your wedding anniversary while waiting on your soon-to-be ex to get arrested? No? There probably should be. But more significant than that issue, the thought of being intimate with someone new conjured up a whole other level of insecurity. I'd only ever been with Rob. Even that had been a long time ago.

"Although I appreciate it, I don't think I'm quite up for it tonight."

A flush crept across her pretty face. "Oh, no. I'm sorry. I didn't mean to imply that kind of setup. Although what I'm about to suggest is probably equally as presumptuous, if not more so."

"I'm not easily offended, so hit me with it."

She smiled. "Okay. There's a therapist by the name of Doctor Mark MacNally—Dr. Mac we call him for short. He's a PhD, not medical, doctor, by the way. Turns out he'll be attending the party tonight. He's amazing. He's helped me deal with my depression over losing my parents. And he's also been great to talk to about my marriage. Thanks to him, we were able to navi-gate a year full of changes. Although he may specialize in grief, he's really good with all things. I'm not implying you need someone to talk to, but if you do want to with all that's happening—I'd be happy to introduce you."

I was surprised. Not that she was suggesting I speak with a therapist—hello, my life lately practically begged for one—but rather that she was so open about her own struggles. From the outside, it appeared she had it all, much like my friend Sasha. Incidentally, Sasha had also confided to me she'd seen a professional for her anxiety disorder. Maybe there was something to be said about this whole counseling thing. I found myself genuinely curious.

"How does he help? Do you simply talk the entire time, or does he ask questions?"

"Both. He goes off your cues. Talking to him, at least for me, is cathartic. He directs my thoughts and doesn't judge. Obviously, your friends and family will be there for you, but if you're anything like I am, you don't want to feel as though you're a burden. That's why it's nice to unload on someone who makes it a profession to listen to people."

I appreciated that she got the type of person I was. "I think me being up here is enough of a burden." Especially since I was staying rent free in the building her husband owned, and I was being allowed to 'work from home.' "But I wouldn't mind meeting him. Maybe I'll get a sense then if I'd be comfortable talking with him professionally." Perhaps he could help me put a plan in motion for my reinvention.

"Great. I'll be sure to introduce you. And you're not a burden at all. Matter of fact, Josh is happy that someone else is living here, especially since he works in New York during the week. His friend Mark has an office in the building, but he doesn't live here or hang out much."

Considering this apartment building was only a short walk from the Yale campus where Haylee went to school, was four stories high, and had multiple units, I'd been surprised to see it unoccupied. "Yeah, I noticed there weren't any other tenants. Why is that?"

She sighed. "At first it was because Josh wanted to remodel all of the rooms before renting them out. But after the renovations were finished a few months ago, he was leery about who to rent to."

"Ah. He worries about who might be sharing a building with his wife and daughter."

She laughed. "Bingo. Even if I suggest only women move in, he's worried about the men who may visit them. And I don't think a doorman to screen people is common practice here in New Haven. Although I think Josh is sometimes overprotective, I appreciate he's thinking of safety. For the record, I'm happy to have another mom I can talk to and hang out with during the week. I'd never tell him, but I get lonely. Monday through Thursday, I miss him."

The bright spot in this situation was that I got to spend time with Haylee over the next few weeks. "I look forward to hanging out with you, too. And I definitely appreciate all you've done. Not only did you furnish the apartment, but you also showed me around town and are including me in everything."

"So, does that mean I'll see you up there soon? As a special tonight, they're making pomegranate martinis."

I smiled. "You had me at martini. See you up there."

THERE WAS one thing I knew straight off when I stepped onto the rooftop that was beautifully decorated for the party with white lights and small, high-top tables: I needed liquid happiness. Which meant locating the bar. The September night was crisp, especially compared to North Carolina. But outdoor heaters were located in several places around the wide-open space under which guests could mingle.

Simply sniffing the ruby-red pomegranate martini handed to me by the bartender started to give me a buzz. That's how low my tolerance for liquor had plummeted over the last couple years, driven down by pregnancy, nursing and, you know, keeping my shit together as a single parent.

But I wasn't a quitter. Matter of fact, I was determined to get my tolerance back up to a respectable level. Now this was the type of goal I didn't think I'd have a hard time sticking with. I'd train hard if I had to. Someone cue the Rocky music.

On more serious matters, I'd given some thought to what Haylee had said earlier about her therapist, Dr. Mark something or other. But I was nervous about spilling my guts to a stranger. I might be outspoken when it came to giving my opinion or over-sharing, but dealing with emotions and vulnerability was a different matter. If I ever did, it was often masked by sarcasm and a heavy dose of self-deprecation. That was my thing. But perhaps meeting the therapist tonight would give me a better sense as to whether or not I could be comfortable talking with a stranger. Actually, it might feel good to get some things off my chest to someone I didn't have to see the next day if I didn't want to. A safe zone, if you will.

I was relieved to see a familiar face and smiled when Brian Carpenter came up. He was both my boss and one of my best friends. Although people would be hard pressed to realize it, I was intimidated and feeling far out of my element here tonight.

"Hey, there. You look beautiful," he complimented, kissing my cheek.

"Thanks." He was always so polite. "Where's your better half?" Sasha Brooks was his fiancée and another one of my best friends. We all had worked together in the Charlotte office of Gamble Advertising for years.

"She stopped off in the ladies' room but will be up in a moment. So, are you getting settled in?"

"Yeah. I got a mani/pedi this morning with the girls, and it was great. The apartment is great, too. And, well, you know, Haylee and Josh are—"

"Great," he offered with a chuckle, but then got serious. "I'm sure this is all a whirlwind, but I hope you realize you've got a lot of support and are surrounded by good people who think the world of you. I know it'll be tough being away from your mom and the office, but it's only temporary until shit settles."

I smiled, not wanting him to think for a moment that I was ungrateful, especially since contacting Haylee about moving up here had been his idea. "I know and appreciate it. I'm sure the time will probably fly by."

As I drained my glass and then grabbed martini number two, I spotted Sasha coming toward us. She hugged me and then took her fiancé's hand. They made a stunning couple, I mused: Brian with his boy-next-door handsomeness and Sasha, striking with her straight black hair and flawless complexion. I'd called it eight years ago that they'd make a great pair when Brian had first met her at the office. There had been sparks flying a mile wide. But it hadn't been until last year that they'd finally gone for it.

Sasha was dressed as impeccably as always, with her sky-high heels and designer dress that accentuated killer curves. But under the image of perfection beat the heart of a true friend, someone I knew struggled daily to battle her anxiety disorder. It went to show not to judge anyone by what you saw on the surface. Take me. I was all smiles despite feeling completely out of place.

"How are you? You look amazing," Sasha commented.

"Thanks. It's definitely been a long time since I've had a reason to dress up. Matter of fact, I'm working on my drinking tolerance and could use some help to get it back to a respectable level."

Brian frowned at my idea, but Sasha grinned. "Let's grab the other girls and get you started."

I HAD SURPASSED BUZZED straight into drunk status about an hour later. That I still managed to walk upright in heels made me proud. So did the fact I'd kept my mouth shut. Unfortunately, in intimidating situations such as tonight, my nervousness was known to cause me to over-talk. Often without a filter and always with too much information. But tonight, thankfully, I'd kept my guard up and my mouth shut.

Wanting to take a few minutes to sober up before going downstairs, I sipped on a glass of water and made my way to the other side of the roof. There it was quiet with a number of unoccupied chairs.

While watching all of the happy couples tonight, I felt refreshed to see such bliss was possible. But if I was being honest, it was also a little depressing. Not that I'd ever let on, but even when Rob and I had first been married, he hadn't watched me across the room as though I was the best thing to ever happen to him. But the men here tonight looking at their significant others that way was a sight to behold. Gah, maybe I did need to talk to a professional.

I took a deep breath, surveying the view the rooftop afforded me of the quaint college town. Upon turning, I caught movement as a man with dark hair and glasses stood up in the corner.

"Sorry. I didn't mean to startle you. I'm Mark. You must be Juliette."

Oh, wow. The good Dr. Mac was much more attractive and younger than I'd envisioned, with dark brown hair that was slightly wavy, a strong jawline, and great eyes framed with sexy black glasses. "Yes, I am. Nice to meet you." After a pause, I just decided to get it out there. "I take it Haylee spoke with you about me."

He looked at me curiously. "Uh, yeah, a little bit. You're up from Charlotte and have a young son, right?"

If he was trying to put me at ease by mentioning my pride and joy, it was working. "Yes. His name is Tristan, and he's two years and four months old."

He gave me a warm smile. "Isn't this the point where you whip out your phone to show me a picture?"

"Oops. I guess I'm not in mommy mode, what with the vodka. Do you mind if I sit? I'm not used to being in heels for this long."

"No, not at all. Here, take this seat over here by the heater."

I grinned appreciatively and took the spot he vacated. When he looked at me expectantly, I cocked my head to the side.

"The, uh, pictures," he reminded.

"Oh, shit—" I sighed at yet another slipped curse word and another dollar for the swear jar. "Sorry, I had a bit to drink, which appears to affect my profanity filter and short-term memory." I fished out my phone and scrolled to a recent photo of Tristan. He was smiling at me with his big brown eyes and blondish hair.

He chuckled. "You don't need to apologize. And he's a handsome fellow. He definitely looks like you."

"Thank you. You know you're easier to talk to than I thought you'd be."

A furrowed brow conveyed his confusion. "Why would you say that?"

"Before I say more, you're bound by a privilege thingy, right?" Would I be able to spill my deep, dark stuff to such a handsome stranger? God, he kind of looked like Clark Kent. Nerdy hot.

"Well, yes, but you'd have to become a client first. Do you need help with something?"

Uh-huh, like an orgasm.

Wow. Where did that thought come from? And damn if the thought didn't lead to me make the mistake of glancing at his hands. Strong hands with long fingers. Was I really so pathetic that studying a man's hands was turning me on?

Yes, yes I was.

Because his amazingly capable-of-giving-a great-two-fingered-orgasm-looking hands were inspiring all sorts of sexual fantasies. And clearly, being inebriated had given me a one-track mind.

"Juliette?" he prompted, taking a seat across from me.

Jesus, I needed a cold shower, stat. Refocusing, I put out a disclaimer. "See, the thing is I'm not sure if I'd be comfortable with a professional or not. I mean, you're the expert, but I don't know if this is my thing. I hope you understand. It's nothing personal toward you."

"Uh, okay. Maybe if you told me the problem, I could decide whether or not you should talk to someone. It doesn't need to be me. It depends on the type of issue you're having. We all specialize in different fields."

"Right. That makes sense." Just because the guy was a therapist didn't mean he specialized in my brand of crazy. "Haylee seems to think you'd be good for me to talk to. She credits you with ensuring she and Josh made it to where they are now."

His handsome face turned pink under the twinkling lights, but he appeared genuinely pleased to hear the compliment. "That's nice to hear. They are both great people, and I'm lucky to call them friends."

"Yes, they are. So here's the thing." I took a deep breath and dove straight into the deep end.

"My soon-to-be ex-husband is a piece of shit. Maybe I should feel bad saying those words out loud because he's Tristan's father, but this is a man who chose drugs over both me and, even worse, his baby son. One, I can get over; the other, not so much. Haylee said you specialize in grief counseling and depression, but those aren't my issues. I'm kind of known as being upbeat and not letting anything affect me—ya know. So I'm not sure if you're the correct person to speak with since this might not be your specialty, but it kind of feels good to get this off my chest, so maybe your field doesn't matter as much as my being comfortable enough to talk to you."

"I think you have me confused—"

I held up a hand, not actually listening to him. I was on a roll, convinced that drinking and therapy really went hand in hand. "Turns out that, in addition to Rob becoming a shitty husband over the last few years and, if possible, becoming an even shittier father, he's also a shitty cop. One who is about to be arrested on a slew of charges."

Damn. And there went two, nope, now three more dollars into the swear jar.

"And once he's charged, all those people he put in jail, even the real criminals, could appeal their cases. Both my private investigator and divorce attorney—cuz I have one of each now—worry that Tristan and I could be in danger once they release his name. And the thing is that, although I hate him being a drug addict and soon-to-be felon, those facts help me in the long run to keep full custody of my son." I took another sip of my water. Despite his stunned expression, I was not even close to being finished.

"Anyhow, I realize being an only parent isn't easy, but I pretty much have been a single mother all along. And I can't regret being married because I wouldn't have Tristan. Obviously, once upon a time I loved his father, but then he changed, almost overnight, which I presume can be attributed to the drugs. At least that's what I tell myself."

"Juliette, I'm not—"

"No, let me finish. Haylee is convinced we'd click. Although I thought at first she was trying to set me up with you on a date."

"What?"

I laughed. "Don't worry. She meant to set me up with you to talk. I don't think I'm ready for the other. Hell, after this experience, I don't have a clue how I could ever trust someone again. Sometimes I just feel broken. Too broken to ever have a relationship with anyone normal, someone who wouldn't run the other way upon hearing my baggage."

I was off on a tangent, but I couldn't seem to stop voicing all of my insecurities.

"I've only ever been with Rob, you know, sexually. And if I'm being honest, it wasn't all that great. Not that I have anything to compare to, but he should at least be better than my vibrator, right? I can't believe I said that out loud, but who better to talk to about this kind of stuff, I guess. Although if you think about a vibrator, maybe it's not fair. I mean a man's fingers can't buzz like something battery operated. But can you imagine if they could?"

I barely took a breath, the words erupting now with unstoppable momentum, random, drunken thoughts mixing with real insecurities which had been building for years.

"Anyhow, the thought of being with another man physically is paralyzing. But I'd love more kids. Someday down the road. And I think I'm a pretty good mom, despite what my ex might say. Hell, I'm even happy to waive child support if it means he'll stay out of the picture permanently."

"You'd let him off the hook for paying child support for his own kid? That shouldn't happen."

His indignant response made me smile.

"It's the only reason he may not fight me for joint custody, so he wouldn't have to pay. And although doing it alone sucks, the thought of having another man in my life or in Tristan's petrifies me completely. What if I pick another loser? Honestly, I should probably stop thinking about a relationship and maybe date casually at first. Don't you think? Maybe eventually I'd meet someone, but what if I'm not any good at sex, either? What if I simply want a guy to skip the foreplay and fuck me in the dark, then leave the next morning before I wake up? Or does that idea mean I'm completely cuckoo for cocoa puffs? Which incidentally is such a great cereal. Instant chocolate milk to drink after you're done eating it. What's not to love, really?"

I studied him for a moment and realized he was even cuter when he was blushing slightly.

I took a sip of my water. "Haylee didn't mention: are you single?"

"Uh, I—"

Holy inappropriateness Juliette. "Oh, fuck me. I mean, not literally. In case you were thinking that 'cause it was on the heels of asking you about your status— I'm so sorry. I didn't mean to hit on you. And I wasn't propositioning you, either. And after talking about the vibrator and sex, what you must think of me."

I wasn't aware how I'd gotten onto the subject. And did I blurt out that I wanted to be fucked in the dark without foreplay? Oh. My. God. Even for me, knowing my propensity for TMI, that was over the line.

"Um, I'm hoping that because you're a therapist you've heard more embarrassing stories? I blame it on the martinis and the shots Sasha had me do, or maybe it's my sex-starved brain cuz it's been way too long." Oops, I was talking about sex again.

"Actually, you know what, since I should be honest, especially with you of all people, I blame it on the fact that there a lot of truly happy couples in love here tonight. And when you're not, well—I realize that sounds completely pathetic, but witnessing it makes me a combination of envious, hopeful, and sad. If that makes any sense."

"More than you realize," he said with sincerity. "But look, as I was saying before, I'm not—"

"No, no, I know what you're going to say. I'm all over the place, and my issues aren't the kind you deal with. I'm trying to work on myself. I have a 2.0 plan. I want to start a new chapter of my life with my son. Because although I may appear confident, even to my friends, the truth is—" I lowered my voice to a whisper, leaning into him.

He appeared as though he was waiting on my words, while I once again suffered from drunk brain interruptus.

"Sorry I forgot what my train of thought was. So if you're not my kind of therapist, maybe you can recommend another one? One who maybe isn't as good looking as you? No offense, but I kind of pictured an older guy without the sex appeal." Based on his shocked expression, I realized I'd reached capacity for information overload. Verbal diarrhea strikes again.

"Uh—"

"I'm sorry. When I drink, I get a tad bit loose—loose lipped, that is, not loose like slutty. Sweet baby Jesus, I'm making it worse. Just—stop—talking—Juliette." I gave him a wan smile and stood up unsteadily. "I think I've probably done enough damage here and ironically ensured that now you need a therapist."

"Mark. Hey, I'm glad you finally got to meet Juliette." Brian's voice and footsteps approached.

I looked over at him, unaware that my boss also knew the good doctor.

"Uh, yeah, we just met," Mark said, standing up and putting his hands in his pockets awkwardly.

"It's weird that after all these years you two haven't crossed paths before," Brian commented, sipping on his beer and glancing between the two of us.

My face scrunched up in confusion. "Why would we have met before?"

"Because Mark and I went to college together, along with Josh. That was back in the day at Harvard. Been friends forever, so I know I've talked about him a ton over the years. You've probably patched through his calls at the office. He works for Gamble Enterprises as Josh's attorney."

The color drained from my face and my head swiveled as if

in slow motion. I met Mark's uncomfortable gaze and felt an out-of-body experience of the worst kind of humiliation.

The tiny—starting-to-sober-up—part of my brain registered all of the times he'd kept trying to interrupt me.

Right on cue and driving the humiliation home, Haylee came over with an older man and smiled at all of us. "Juliette, this is Mark MacNally, or Dr. Mac as we all call him. Dr. Mac, this is Juliette."

Holy fuck. I'd completely spilled my drunken guts to the wrong Mark.

CHAPTER TWO

$\mathscr{T}$he next morning I awoke slowly, wishing I'd gotten drunk enough to have forgotten everything from the prior night. After the revelation of my slip-up with Mark the lawyer, not Mark the psychologist, I'd excused myself to have a proper freak-out in the bathroom. Then I put on my big-girl panties and faced everyone for a few more minutes before saying goodnight. I hadn't dared make eye contact with the handsomer of the Marks, nor did I bother to do more than say hi to Mark the therapist—who happened to be twenty years older than hot Mark, with a graying beard and non-orgasm-fantasy-inspiring fingers.

I groaned, just thinking about all of the personal stuff I'd vomited up all over the first Mark. He probably thought I was the biggest sex-starved whack-a-doo on the planet, someone who needed a therapist now more than ever.

Sighing with regret, I shoved the whole situation to the side when I heard Tristan's laughter coming from the other room. Because here's the thing I was quickly learning about a hangover and little ones: they don't mix. Yet even with a pounding head, I couldn't wait to spend time with my son.

Of course, the closeness I felt with him had caused a lot of the tension in my marriage. I worked full time; therefore, my weekends were a chance to catch up on all of the wonders I'd missed during the week with my baby. But Rob had never shared that view. Instead, he'd try to guilt me about not paying enough attention to him. When that didn't work out, he'd leave the house completely. Funny how I'd be relieved when he would. Maybe I could have spent more time on my marriage, but I doubt it would have helped. From the moment I'd gotten pregnant, Rob had started to withdraw and developed a mean streak. It was as if he'd had a midlife crisis and decided to wake up one day and resent me and the ball and chain I'd supposedly put on him.

I found a travel sized pack of Ibuprofen and brushed my teeth before heading into the living room. There my pride and joy was drinking milk and cuddling with his grandma.

His eyes lit up when he saw me, and he smooshed a kiss against my face when I leaned in for a kiss. "Hi, Mama," he said in that cute little toddler way, making me melt.

"Hi, baby. Did you have fun with Grandma last night?"

He nodded and then pointed toward his train while making choo-choo noises.

"Did you enjoy the party?" my mom asked as I sat on the sofa with my bottle of water I'd grabbed from the refrigerator.

"A little too much, by way of martinis and a couple shots of something. My drinking tolerance is for shi—uh, shizzles." I quickly amended the last word, still working on my potty mouth. I probably owed a good twenty dollars toward the curse jar from last night.

"Are you all packed?" Reality was starting to settle in that this afternoon my mother was flying back to North Carolina, and I'd be on my own.

"Yep. After your sister has the baby in a couple of weeks, I'll come back up here over a long weekend. Maybe Halloween."

Although I was aware of the likelihood I'd have to be up here for at least a couple months, hearing my mother confirm it was tough. "Yeah. That sounds great."

Three hours later Tristan and I dropped Grandma off at the airport. We then headed to the local grocery store, a place Haylee had been nice enough to show me a couple days ago. While I was perusing the aisles, a thought occurred to me. Since Brian and Sasha were still in town, I'd cook a big dinner tonight. They were all at a charity luncheon today but had said they'd come by later and we'd all order dinner. How better to both convey my thanks and do something I enjoyed than to cook a big meal instead. Matter of fact, I'd invite Haylee and Josh as well.

The challenge became apparent, however, when I pulled into the parking lot and had seven bags to carry up three flights of stairs—along with my toddler. Suddenly I missed pulling my Explorer into my warm garage with only eight feet separating the car from the kitchen. Tristan wasn't at an age to leave by himself, so I piled all of the bags on my left arm and took him by the hand.

I made it two flights before the pain of the plastic handles cut off circulation. Meanwhile, Tristan decided sloth speed was in order for climbing steps. After setting half the bags down on the first-floor landing, I scooped him up and walked the remaining steps to my apartment. Desperate for some sort of 'kid-friendly cage,' I quickly popped open his Pack 'n Play and set him inside of it with a few of his trains.

"Give me two minutes, Tristan. Please. Only two."

As I rushed down the stairs like a mad woman, my brain filled with absurd visions of my baby falling out of his temporary prison while I selfishly tried to rescue the ingredients for enchiladas, I turned the final corner and ran smack into Mark. That is, the way-too-hot-to-be-a-lawyer-and-definitely-not-a-therapist Mark.

"Shit. I'm sorry. I just—I'm in a hurry 'cause Tristan is upstairs."

I'm sure it only came out a jumble of words as he merely steadied me and then bent down to pick up the bags.

"You go, then. I got these."

I hesitated only a moment before racing back up the stairs while throwing a "thank you" over my shoulder. Of course, when I went inside, I found that Tristan had barely moved a muscle. He was intent on his trains rather than teetering precariously on the edge of danger.

Meanwhile, I was completely out of breath, my little sprint calling attention to how out of shape I was. At the sound of footsteps, I turned.

"Where would you like these?" Mark asked, stepping over the couple of bags I'd already dumped on the floor.

"On the counter would be great." While he did as I asked, I moved the first load into the kitchen as well.

"Are you here to visit Haylee and Josh?" Although I tried to make small talk, I could feel my face flush as I remembered last night when I'd completely word-vomited all over the man.

"Uh, no. I have an office across the hall."

"Oh. Right. I think Haylee mentioned that." The thought of seeing him here often was both unsettling and exciting. The fact that he was dressed in a nice charcoal gray suit was doing nothing to ease my brain from leaning towards the latter.

"Mama." Tristan's voice broke my pervy thoughts of our neighbor just in time, giving me the reality check I needed.

"Hey, baby. Did you drop your train?" I walked over to where he stood and focused on the toy he'd dropped out of the pen and onto the floor. "Here you go. Do you want to watch Thomas on TV?"

He clapped his hands together. "Yes."

I picked him up, put him on the couch, and started his favorite DVD of all time, one with Thomas the Train. That should buy me at least twenty minutes to get the groceries put away and start on food prep.

Turning toward Mark, I expressed my appreciation. "Thanks again for the help with the groceries. Any interest in dinner tonight?"

From the panicked look on his face, he probably thought I was hitting on him like I had the night before.

So I clarified. "Sasha and Brian are coming over later. I sent a text to Haylee and Josh to invite them, too. In case you were contemplating a restraining order about now regarding my invitation."

That earned me a small smile. "I wasn't. In fact, I was hoping you weren't angry with me over last night."

I'd started to unload the contents of the bags, but stopped to quirk my head to the side, completely confused. "Why on earth would I be upset with you? I was the one who firehosed you like a drunken tsunami with embarrassing information that Would. Not. Stop."

He smiled fully. Wowsers, it was not making his hot factor any easier to ignore. And now I was staring at his hands again. Dammit. I really needed to get some batteries for my vibrator. Thankfully, I'd thought to pack it.

"I should've worked harder to stop you."

I shook my head. "Believe me. There was no stopping the Mack truck that needed to get all of that shit off my chest." Great. I was another dollar in. There was no way I was going to count the internal curse words, or I'd be broke.

Crossing over to the stool where I'd plunked down my purse, I took out of it the single plus the twenty which should cover last night's curse words. Then I walked back over to the refrigerator where I reached up and stuffed the bills into an empty animal crackers tub on top.

"What's the money for?" he asked, appearing curious.

"It's for the swear jar. It's only a matter of time before Tristan starts imitating all my words, and I can tell you now, I don't want to be the mom of the two-year-old who introduces the word *fuck* to all the other toddlers in the daycare class." Groaning at yet another slip, I crossed back over to my purse, pulled out another dollar bill, and put it up with the others.

"Uh, right. Yeah, that wouldn't be good. What will you do with money?"

"Take him to Disneyworld. I like the irony of me saying *fuck* a lot funding a trip to the happiest place on earth. Plus, that way I don't begrudge putting the money in." And now another dollar. Crap. I was out of cash, so I started a tab on a sticky pad on the counter.

"Right. I should probably go."

He looked as though he was on the verge of backing out of the room slowly, like he was in a cage with a wild, unpredictable, foul-mouthed animal.

I had to bite down on a giggle at the thought, else he spook. "See ya around, then. Thanks again for the help."

"Sure. Anytime." But his gaze honed in on the bags of cheese I was taking out, followed by some avocados. "What are you making, by the way?"

"Beef and chicken enchiladas. Are you sure you won't come for dinner? It won't be for another four hours, so you have time if you have some work to get done first."

He was about to answer when Haylee came to the still-open door. "Hey, Juliette. Oh, hi, Mark." She glanced between us curiously, causing him to look even more awkward.

"I was leaving. Nice seeing you again, Juliette. Take care, Haylee."

"Wait. Are you coming for dinner?" Haylee stopped him steps before his clean getaway. Her eyes flicked to mine. "That's okay, isn't it?"

"Of course. I just invited him."

"Oh, well, in that case, you're joining us, right?" Haylee asked him.

Mark, meet the spot she was putting you on. While I was

more of an observer of someone put on the spot than a rescuer, after considering last night and the fact I'd already put the guy through a full therapy session, I gave him an out.

"It's all right. He has to work, but maybe a raincheck for another time."

He appeared relieved, but it was short-lived because Haylee sighed. "Okay, but Abby would sure love to see her Uncle Mark. She lights up when you hold her."

Oh, boy. Baby guilt. Home girl didn't mess around.

And it was clear Mark had a soft spot for her daughter. "You know, I should be done with my work by, um, did you say six o'clock?"

I nodded. "Yep. Six o'clock."

"See you then."

The door shut, leaving me to laugh at Haylee's satisfied smile. "The Uncle Mark pretty much did him in."

She smirked. Like Mark, she was still dressed from the luncheon, in her case in a beautiful pink dress. "I can't help it. He's like family and would spend all his hours working if I didn't guilt him into the fun stuff."

"Does he live local or in New York?"

She walked over and gave Tristan a big smooch. "He lives here in New Haven, although he does travel sometimes. His office is a one-bedroom apartment across from you, so you may see him from time to time."

"Is he, um, single?" God, my subtlety needed work.

The way she stood up from where she'd bent down to talk to Tristan, with her eyes wide, caused me to clarify.

"I didn't mean it that way. I guess I was only curious about him. I've always known he was Josh and Brian's best friend since college and that he's Josh's lawyer, but nothing more. I'm sure I've talked to him on the phone a bunch of times when he's called the office, but last night at your party was actually the first time I met him in person."

"Huh. It's surprising you've only just met, but I suppose he doesn't get down to Charlotte a lot since he works mainly with Josh's acquisitions and real estate deals. And, to answer your question, he's single. But, uh, he doesn't date."

"That doesn't beg for a backstory or anything, does it?"

She laughed before sighing. "Brian and Josh know a lot more than I do, but he lost his fiancée a number of years ago during law school. But do me a favor and don't mention it to him. He's very private and I don't want him thinking we're talking about him. At the same time, I didn't want you to maybe think…"

That I had a chance.

I finished the sentence in my head. It wasn't just the tragedy regarding his fiancée which had me thinking he would never date me. First, I'd pretty much ensured that would never happen with my embarrassing TMI session last night. Second, he was a successful attorney living in Connecticut, which was pretty far away from Charlotte, my real home. And third, I wasn't in a position to look for anything romantic. "I wasn't thinking that. I tend to be genuinely curious about people."

"Actually, you might be good for getting him out of his shell. Anyway, I came down with the intention of asking if we can bring anything tonight. It's very sweet of you to offer to cook."

I smiled. "I love doing it. If you want to bring drinks, you could. Otherwise, I have everything else covered with enchiladas."

She came over, surveying the ingredients. "Wow, I can't wait. Someday, if you have time, I'd love to watch you cook. Maybe pick up a few pointers."

That gave me an idea. I might never be able to pay her and Josh monetarily, but I could definitely return their favors in dinners and cooking pointers.

"Anytime." I meant it. "See ya at six."

TRISTAN NAPPED WHILE I CLEANED, not that there was much to do. I was quickly finding out that a thousand square feet was easy to keep tidy. I'd been able to unpack and organize some things, so at least I wasn't living out of suitcases. We'd driven up with my SUV packed full of clothes and toys. Thankfully, Haylee had furnished the two-bedroom apartment with comfortable furniture, including a crib for Tristan. She'd also provided things like sheets and towels, saving me the trouble of having to pack or buy them.

Two pans of enchiladas were about to go in the oven when the first knock came at the door. Brian and Sasha arrived with smiles and Mexican beer. It wasn't long before Josh, Haylee, and their four-month-old baby girl, Abby, joined us. The final knock brought an awkward-looking Mark, who had changed into jeans. Jeans, I might add, that when he bent down to pick up baby Abby, encased the man's ass quite nicely.

"Ow," I squealed. I was putting the pans in the oven and had hit the rack with my finger while preoccupied with said ass.

Sasha glanced up from the fridge, where she was grabbing sour cream. "You okay?"

I ran my throbbing thumb under cold water in the sink. "Yep. All good." And let that be a lesson to me. *Stare at the ass, and you're bound to get burned.*

The evening was fun. I couldn't begin to count the number of compliments I received on the meal. But what I loved most was the way everyone was with Tristan. They all took time to engage with him and ensure he was getting extra attention. When eight o'clock rolled around, however, it became the witching hour, bedtime for both Abby and Tristan and everyone ready to say good night. I was adamant that the pile of dishes be left alone, not allowing anyone to touch anything.

"I have nothing but time and a great big dishwasher," I argued, giving Sasha and Brian hugs and making them promise to send work my way come Monday. I was the office manager in the Charlotte branch of Gamble Advertising. I might be working remotely, but I wanted to continue to earn my money.

"We'll be traveling, so why don't you take a week off?" Brian offered.

"And do what? You know I need to be busy. Josh, do you have anything I can help with?" I knew he had a completely competent admin in Nigel, a man who'd worked for Josh for many years, but maybe there was some task I could work on.

"I just thought of what would be a good project and would take at least a couple weeks of your time, if not more."

I was all ears. "What's that?"

"Organizing Mark's office. Since he works for the company, that would make it a work project. If you're up for a challenge, his files are a mess."

My eyes met Mark's. I could already see the fear set in. Whether he was afraid of anyone touching his stuff or that I would now have an excuse to be near him, I wasn't sure.

"My stuff is fine," he grumbled, making both Brian and Josh burst out laughing.

In good old ribbing fashion, Brian then teased, "Your office is like an episode of hoarders. You hold onto everything."

"Legal documents are important," Mark defended, without any heat. Being with the other two men over the years had clearly led him to develop a thick skin.

But I enjoyed the idea of having something to do and piped up, "If you have the cabinets, I have lots of time."

Brian vouched for me. "She's organized the entire office, man, so you'd be in good hands."

Yeah, he would. Thankfully, the indecent thought stayed internal. "I'd love to do it, so I guess let me know."

Mark gave me a smile which was noncommittal, at best. "Sure."

Everyone finished up saying goodnight, and with my front door shut, I focused next on getting Tristan to bed. Later there would be plenty of time to do the dishes and clean the kitchen. Then if I had time, I really wanted to get signed up for online classes. It might take me ten years to get a degree, but I was determined to do it. And if I had to choose between exercise and school on how to spend my free time up here, well, it was school, hands down.

After changing my sleepy boy into his PJs and setting him down in his crib, I took a moment to caress his face and read him a quick story. By the time I was done, he was out.

I slipped out of his room, shutting the door quietly and then froze at the sound of dishes clinking. Turning toward the kitchen, I saw Mark gathering up dirty plates.

"And here I thought the crime rate was low in New Haven. But I was unaware of the growing trend of dishwashing break-ins."

His eyes met mine while he flashed a sheepish grin. "Sorry. The door was still unlocked, and I felt guilty about leaving you with the dirty work after you did all the cooking."

"That's very sweet, but with Tristan down, I have all the time in the world."

"Good. Then you can dry."

He threw me a towel, obviously unwilling to give up on the task. "Your phone keeps buzzing, by the way."

I glanced over and expelled a frustrated breath at the phone lit up on the counter. Rob's parents had been calling all day with escalating messages. Their son had been arrested earlier today. And according to my attorney, the charges included drug trafficking, tampering with evidence, witness intimidation, and possession. The latest message from his mother had been that it was my duty to put up the twenty-five thousand dollars for his bail. How quickly they seemed to forget we were divorcing and I owed Rob nothing.

Putting that aside, I focused on the man in front of me instead. "Thanks for helping."

"Yeah, well, I have time on my hands, too. And about the organizing of my office: I don't want you to feel obligated."

"I don't at all. If anything, I'd be grateful for something to keep me busy." I noticed while standing next to him that my five-foot-two inches only came up to his chest. And when his dark blue eyes focused down on me, I had to force my thoughts to the dishes instead of on how much I wanted to climb him. Jesus, since when had I been so affected by a man?

"Okay. In that case, I'll buy some cabinets and get them set up. You could start in a couple of days, but only if you're sure."

"Believe me, if I didn't want to do it, you'd know."

To that I got a chuckle. "What will you do with Tristan during the day?"

"Haylee has been generous enough to offer to share her nanny, Natalie, who watches Abby. I need to work out logistics, but I think if Natalie can watch Tristan for five hours in the morning, I can then put him down for a nap here. That'll give me a full work day."

What I didn't mention was needing to discuss the cost with Haylee. I might be willing to accept some charity in the form of this apartment, but I was absolutely insistent on paying for my portion of childcare. Of course, the amount would impact the number of hours I could afford. Unfortunately, I already had a lot of financial obligations. I was not only on the hook for our mortgage solo—Rob hadn't bothered to pay toward it in months—but I was also still paying for childcare in Charlotte since I didn't want Tristan to lose his spot. But if I was here more than a couple of months, I might have to reconsider paying double and un-enroll him for now.

My phone was once again buzzing on the countertop, interrupting my train of thought.

"Are you planning on answering that?"

"No." Then, because he raised a brow and I was, for the most part, an open book, I shared: "It's my soon-to-be ex's parents.

Rob was arrested this morning, and they want me to put up money for bail. One, I don't have the cash without selling the house, and two, I wouldn't give it to him anyhow. The messages started friendly, but, uh, they aren't real nice now. So there's no way I'm answering."

"You should get a new phone number."

I sighed. "Yeah, probably."

"It would be the safe thing to do, in case they know anyone who can track the phone's location to you here."

The blood drained from my face as the thought hadn't occurred to me.

He stopped the water and dried his hands, quick to reassure me. "I'm sorry. I didn't mean to scare you. I'm probably overreacting, but with your ex being a police officer, it might be the most prudent course of action."

There was something surprisingly sexy about hearing him say smart words such as *prudent*, but it didn't detract from my worry. "Yeah. I didn't think about that. Plus I'm tired of having my inbox full of nasty messages as if I should be responsible—"

I stopped midsentence, hardly believing I was unloading on the man yet again. He didn't need to know I'd listened to every one of their messages, telling me I should be ashamed of myself for not being a better wife to him. "I'm sorry. You got enough of an earful last night."

He turned back toward the sink, shaking his head. "Don't apologize. I'm a good listener."

"Oh, yeah. Last night make you want to drop the law and become a therapist?"

He laughed fully. Something told me this wasn't a man who did so easily. "Not quite, but, um, if you want help with a phone tomorrow, I'll be around."

"Thanks, but I have it covered." Although it was tempting to have someone to lean on, I was used to being independent and needed to do these types of things for myself. "Can I talk you into taking some of these enchiladas home with you?"

"I wouldn't say no. It's been awhile since I've had a good home-cooked meal."

I grinned, putting some of the leftovers into a container. "Well, then, turns out you have the right neighbor."

CHAPTER THREE

$\mathcal{B}$y the time Tuesday afternoon rolled around, I'd grown comfortable with Natalie watching Tristan along with Haylee's daughter, changed my cell phone number, and run out of things to do from home for Brian and the Charlotte office. I'd registered for two online courses, but until the materials arrived—hopefully tomorrow—I couldn't get started. In the meantime, I was bored.

Sure, I could've used the time to start exercising or plan out healthier meals so I could finally lose those last few pounds, but everyone knew you only started a diet on a Monday. So, maybe next week. Plus, I needed to be busy, busy. Which is why couch surfing the television didn't appeal, either. With things currently so uncertain in my life, I needed a distraction. And maybe, together with all of that, the fact I hadn't seen Mark in the last couple of days had me knocking on his door across the hall.

He didn't disappoint, opening the door while looking sexy as hell with his glasses and tousled hair.

"Sorry, I didn't mean to interrupt, but uh, if you're still willing to let me organize and file…"

"Sure. Although you might change your mind when you see all of it."

He opened the door to what was a replica of my apartment minus one bedroom and with boxes everywhere. And that was the highlight, because what wasn't in boxes were in stacks of folders placed on the floor, the kitchen counter, and on half of the lone desk against the wall. In addition to the desk and computer chair, there was also a well-worn sofa in the living room. That made up all of the furniture. I wondered if he had a bed in the bedroom, but most likely the space was full of even more boxes.

"Don't hold back. What are you thinking?"

I walked further into the room, my eyes wide. "You can ask Brian. I tend not to hold back. And this—Well, this is a colossal mess. But it's also a challenge. And it's just the type of thing I was hoping for."

"Okay, but if it becomes too much or you change your mind, I'll understand. You really work for Brian and only for Josh indirectly, so I feel a little awkward having you do this for me."

I smiled. "Why? In the end, we all work for the same company. Plus, it gives me something to do. I'd be eternally grateful."

He shook his head as if he couldn't believe it. "Okay. In that case, let's get started in the bedroom."

Uh.

It took approximately ten seconds before his face turned crimson, and he started sputtering. "I didn't mean—"

My laughter bubbled up. "Relax. Even if it's been awhile, it takes more than a heap of messy files to get me into bed."

My playful teasing only served to turn him a brighter shade of red. His embarrassment was unnecessary, though, because after walking into the bedroom, I saw it was sans bed. But it did have three large wooden filing cabinets four drawers tall. "See?

Now there's no mistaking you really do want me only for my filing abilities."

This time he smiled. Perhaps my warped sense of humor was finally wearing on him. Brian and I could crack these types of jokes all day. Then again, my boss was like an older brother and not as reserved as Mark. Yeah—introverted people struggled to get me.

"Are you sure you don't mind?"

He truly was adorable when he got serious. "Promise, I don't. Now stop asking. I don't want to bother you while you're working, so let me know what time works best."

———

MARK and I agreed my hours could be flexible in doing the filing since my schedule would always depend on Brian and the office and whether they needed something first. But I was used to a packed day and didn't think it would be a problem to juggle both tasks. On Wednesday afternoon, then, with nothing better to do, I used the key Mark had given me to go inside his office and tackle my first stack.

Since the age of twelve, I'd always worked. I started by babysitting for the next-door neighbor. Thinking back, I'm not sure why she thought having a twelve-year-old take care of her toddler was a good idea, but at least my mom had been only one door down in case there'd been an actual emergency.

By the time I was fifteen, I was bagging groceries at my local supermarket. And by nineteen, I was the receptionist at Gamble Advertising. That's when I met Brian. His sense of humor meshed immediately with mine and I eventually made the transition to his administrative assistant. Although I'd been promoted to the office manager position a few years ago, I'd retained the responsibility for Brian's administrative needs. Not only was he one of my best friends, but he was also low maintenance, and I enjoyed keeping him organized.

All of this is why I viewed Mark's office with determination. The man, although hot, was in fact a slob. This room could be featured in an episode of hoarders as the legal paperwork special.

Deciding to help pass the time with some tunes, I slipped some headphones in. Meanwhile, I put the video monitor showing Tristan's sleeping form in his crib in front of me, knowing it would light up if there were any sounds from his room.

It might not actually count as a workout, but after two hours on my hands and knees organizing stacks of papers, it certainly felt like one. I was bopping to some country tunes, oblivious to everything but the task in front of me when a touch on my shoulder scared the ever-loving crap out of me.

"Oh, my clucking God." I ripped the earphones from my head and sat back on my heels, watching Mark's face quickly flush.

"Sorry. I was calling your name but then realized you had earphones in. Did you say clucking?"

I grinned, setting a few more folders to the side. "Yeah, it's my new adaptation of the other word. I call it mommy cursing."

He blinked twice, clearly waiting for more of an explanation.

"Yesterday I said fuck accidentally while Tristan was listening. So I had to cover real fast, which led to making clucking sounds like a chicken. And thus far, it's stuck."

Two more blinks. "What other words have you modified?"

"Mm. I'm still working on the list, but shizzles seems to have made its way into my vocabulary lately. And I managed to call a woman that cut me off the other day in traffic a 'be-ach ball.'"

He threw back his head with laughter, taking me completely off guard. I giggled in response.

At that moment, Josh walked into the apartment. He tilted his head to the side at the scene, and I guessed this side of Mark wasn't typical.

"What's so funny?" He glanced between us.

Mark abruptly stopped, looking embarrassed. "Juliette's mommy-cursing modifiers. Guess you'd better make some notes for your little girl."

Josh smiled. "Indeed. I see you haven't wasted any time in getting started on Mark's files."

"Well, I didn't have anything else happening today, and I kept thinking of this room. I figured with Tristan down for a nap, I'd get started."

Josh had an amused expression. "And Mark is letting you?"

"She was rather persistent about it," Mark mumbled, appearing as though he regretted his decision.

"Don't you dare go complaining after I've been on my knees the last two hours, hoping to impress you with my skills."

It took a moment. That space in time where you watch someone absorb your words and realize the expression on their face is not the one you'd expected. So you rewind your words through your head and realize what was actually said. "Oh, crap, that didn't come out right."

Josh bit his lip, which I think was an effort not to laugh, and then cleared his throat. "Uh, I'm just going to, uh, not touch that one. Mark, you ready?"

Mark, who seemed to permanently sport adorable pink splotches on his handsome face when I was within a ten-foot radius, backed up slowly. "Yeah. Um, thanks for working on this mess and see you later."

"Sure. See you then."

He couldn't seem to get out of there fast enough.

Again.

Cluck. My. Life.

IT HAD TAKEN the rest of the week, but Mark was now officially organized. Judging from the expression on his face, he could hardly believe it looking around his space.

"This looks amazing. But how do I find things?"

I led him into the bedroom to show him. "Everything is sorted by year." I pointed to the four cabinets. "The far one is the oldest, and the closest one is the most recent." I opened one of the drawers to show him the files. "Everything is labeled with a color for the year and then a bar code which I haven't input yet. But eventually it will be on your computer, so if you were searching for the—" I glanced down at the file name. "2015 Cancun Hotel deal and everything related to it, it would be assigned this number."

"So if I input that name into the computer, it'll tell me it's filed under 2015?"

"Not only that. It'll also show you it's the orange color code, file cabinet number two, drawer two. As you can see, all these folders are tagged with orange, and they're in drawer number two. But like I said, I'll need another week to get all of this info into the computer. Physical mess first, impressive computer online filing system second."

He walked over to another set of drawers and pulled one open, running his hand across the top. "I don't know what to say. I don't think I've ever had a system, let alone things simply filed. Thank you."

I beamed. I might not have a college degree, a fancy title, or an impressive vocabulary, but I was a filing ninja. "You're welcome. By the way, the active deals, the ones that were on your desk, are still there, but now they're put in folders." I stepped back into the living room. "And this accordion file is full of miscellaneous stuff, mostly receipts. Judging from the majority, you eat out a lot."

Boom. He was blushing again. He put a hand behind his

neck, gripping there and looking embarrassed. "I don't cook much."

"In that case, if you're interested, I have pulled pork cooking in the crock pot for dinner. Along with that, I've got potato salad and coleslaw already in the fridge."

"Do you make big meals every night?"

"No. Mainly on the weekends. And since today is Friday, I'm cooking for Haylee and Josh, too. I don't have many methods of paying them back for allowing me to live here, but this is one way. Oh, and I have apple pie." Because if I was starting a diet on Monday, I was eating whatever I wanted this weekend.

"Okay. Um, what time should I come over?"

I couldn't hide my surprise. "Really?"

"Did you not mean it?"

I shook my head. "No, of course I did. How about six? Does that work?"

"Sure. Um, can I bring wine or something else to drink?"

"I prefer beer but only if you're getting some for yourself."

His grin came easily. "Sounds good, but it won't be the light stuff."

"Thank God. See, I knew there was a reason I liked you, Mark." I flashed him a smile and let myself into my apartment prior to going upstairs to pick up Tristan.

HE WAS RIGHT ON TIME. It made sense, considering there was something about him that screamed punctual. When I opened the door, the blush which seemed to permanently stain his cheeks was already there. I wondered why he subjected himself to me if he was embarrassed before I even opened the door.

Then again, based on the man's fast-food receipts, perhaps any embarrassment was worth it for a home-cooked meal. "Hi.

Come on in and pardon the Legos on the floor." Tristan had been busy building while I'd been working in the kitchen.

"Sure. Are Haylee and Josh coming down with the baby?"

Oh, dear, of course he'd thought there'd be others here. "No. Sorry. Haylee went to New York this weekend unexpectedly. Something about needing to see her friend Will before he moves. But I did drop off the meal at their place for when they return."

And there went the deeper blush. "I wonder where Will is moving to."

I shrugged, not knowing a whole lot about Will except that he was an Aussie model who'd worked with Haylee over the years. I knew they were good friends and that his leaving had her upset. Appreciating how deeply this group cared for their friends, I wasn't surprised she was sad to see him move away. Meanwhile, I took the six-pack of bottles out of Mark's hand and admired the imported lager.

"It's not too late to back out, but you do sacrifice a beer."

He chuckled. "No, no. And glad you approve. Um, do you have glasses? I can pour."

Huh. Yeah pour. Not chug out of the bottle as I was about to. "I think there are two pint glasses in the top cabinet next to the fridge."

He poured while I brought down two adult plates and one for Tristan. I then watched Mark kneel down to talk to Tristan about the tower he was creating.

"Want some help?"

My son nodded enthusiastically.

Mark seemed equally happy to sit down and began building him a castle.

All was comfortable until three minutes in when Tristan said the dreaded word. "Dadda."

"Uh." Mark had a complete look of panic, which of course put me into a fit of giggles.

Finally calming myself enough to speak, I knelt down to

caress Tristan's face. "No, baby. This is Mark." I then turned to Mark. "Don't worry. He said the same to Brian and to Josh."

He grinned and picked up my smiling boy. "Are you telling me I'm third choice behind Brian, of all people? Tristan, we need to talk about your taste."

I was thankful he didn't ask about the sad reason my son kept asking any adult male who was around him more than five minutes if he was his daddy. Tristan was desperate for a father figure. Wanting to keep it light, I took my son from Mark and put him into his high chair. "Time for dinner, handsome."

Turning, I watched Mark peruse the food on the countertop.

"What kind of potato salad is this?"

"Bacon ranch. And the pulled pork is the Texas type with barbeque sauce, instead of the vinegar type, which is more Carolina. Shh, don't tell anyone, though. They'd revoke my state card."

"Don't worry. I won't. Especially since you had me stop all cognitive thinking at the words bacon and ranch."

I grinned, thinking he was funnier than I'd given him credit for. "Good."

We chatted throughout the meal without any awkwardness. Mark complimented my food, and Tristan ate most of what we did.

"He's a pretty good eater."

I wiped my son's hands and face and then let him down to play with the Legos for a few more minutes before his bath. "Most of the time. I try to give him a simple version of dinners, but during the week we tend to eat a lot of breakfast foods for all meals. Especially when I'd come home after work. Guess you could say we both like pancakes and yogurt. Save room for apple pie, by the way."

Mark patted his flat stomach, which had me wondering what was beneath the Yale sweatshirt he was sporting. The distraction had me completely miss his words.

"Sorry, what was that?"

"I wondered if you'd had a chance to explore the city or get out and about Connecticut?"

I shook my head. "No, but tomorrow I figure we'd make the hour drive to Mystic. I heard there's an aquarium there. And, of course, there's the pizza it's known for."

He helped clear the dishes. "Just the two of you?"

"Yeah. Why? You don't think it's safe?"

"It's perfectly safe. It's a nice drive, too."

I dished up the pie à la mode and coerced Tristan back into his high chair for apples and a scoop of vanilla ice cream.

"This is amazing." Mark's expression of pure bliss made me jealous of the fork between his lips.

"Thanks. If ever I wonder why I can't lose those last ten pounds, I can remind myself of this. I love dessert."

I glanced up from my dish to see him frown.

At the same moment, Tristan splatted his chubby hand full of vanilla ice cream directly into his own hair. It was hard not to laugh at the shocked look on his face when the cold hit him.

"Buddy. It goes in your mouth, not on your head. Come on, let's get you in a warm bath and washed up." I lifted him up out of his chair and put him on my hip. Glancing toward Mark, I made sure he didn't think I was dismissing him. "Um, please don't feel like you have to rush. I just need to get him cleaned up."

"Okay. No problem."

Déjà vu when I brought out a now-clean Tristan from the bath and saw Mark in my kitchen doing the dishes.

If I thought my attraction toward him might only be physical, he went and upped the ante by grinning at Tristan. "Are you an airplane?"

My son looked down at his PJs and a laugh bubbled up from inside him once he noticed what I'd dressed him in. All planes.

"Do you mind?" Mark held out his arms.

I shook my head. Then I watched as Mark scooped him up and had him flying through the living room, telling him to stretch out his arms like the real thing.

He stopped after two laps around the living room and put Tristan on the couch beside him. "So, about tomorrow and Mystic. If you want the company and a tour guide, I could come with?"

Huh. "Sure. If you don't have any other plans."

"I seldom do on the weekends, unless I'm traveling. What time did you want to leave?"

"Nine o'clock too early?"

"Nope. I'll see you then." He handed over my smiling son. "Good night, Tristan. Good night, Juliette."

I GROANED at the state of my bed. Clothing was strewn everywhere. Why was I stressing about what to wear to a freaking aquarium? Of course, it was because Mark was coming with us. What was happening to me? Twice in one week I wanted to do more than throw my hair up into a ponytail and swipe some Chap Stick over my lips. As much as I didn't want to believe I wanted to pursue something with him, my internal voice called me a clucking liar.

Hearing Tristan's voice calling for me, I realized my time was up. I settled on jeans, a sweatshirt and—you guessed it—my hair up in a ponytail. Scowling at my roots, I realized it was about time to do a touch-up. Deciding I was done fighting the inevitable, I swiped on my peppermint Chap Stick. Nothing said sexy more than minty, non-chapped lips.

It wasn't as though Mark had ever given me the slightest indication he was interested in anything. True, he'd been kind and friendly, but most likely he was just being nice. I thought back to his innocuous statement that he seldom had weekend plans unless he was traveling.

Mark might have asked if we wanted company today simply because he was lonely. I knew that companion myself all too well. But the difference in our lives was grinning at me twenty minutes later from his high chair while he gobbled down Cheerios. At least I had Tristan.

Tristan, who made a mess of Cheerios everywhere. Times like these I wished we'd gotten a dog. I could use someone cleaning up the dropped food on the floor. I'd thought briefly about it, but with Rob's short temper and extreme mood swings, I didn't think I could take on the responsibility. It would mean one more soul over which I'd have to keep a watchful eye.

The knock came, and I opened the door to a clean-shaven Mark. All thoughts about my ex-husband flew out of my head. God, was he handsome. And holy shizzles, did he smell good. It took everything in my being to keep from burying my nose in his shirt and sniffing him thoroughly. I opted to err on the side of non-crazy-town and resisted the urge to climb him like a spider monkey in heat.

"Hey," he said.

Thankfully, my automatic response kicked in. "Hey." Oh, yeah, I'm sure he could hardly contain himself from responding to the sexual confidence exhibited by my verbal prowess. I rolled my eyes internally and let him in.

"Did you eat breakfast?"

"No, not yet. But Tristan is finishing up. I'll pack some snacks and his sippy cup; then we'll be ready to go."

"We could grab bacon sandwiches at this place about fifteen minutes from here if you like."

"Sure. Sounds good." I finished packing my backpack with all of the essentials in case of diaper changes, blowouts, meltdowns, hunger, thirst, and first aid. "Um, we'll have to take my SUV because of the car seat."

"No problem. If you want me to drive, I can. But I'm also a good passenger."

His laid-back attitude was refreshing, especially since my ex had been overly irritable about every little thing. "Since you know the way, it would be great if you drove."

After getting Tristan settled in the back, securely strapped into his car seat, we visited a drive-thru for breakfast and took off toward Mystic. Turned out once I got past the whole embarrassing-Mark-with-every-little-thing-that-came-out-of-my-mouth, he wasn't as painfully shy as I'd first assumed. In fact, there was an adorable sarcastic side to him which both surprised me and made me laugh throughout the day.

The aquarium was a hit, and afterwards we got a Mystic pizza to go, something we took to a park where we found a bench. We all sighed with the flavor and oozy cheese, and Mark held up his soda to clink it toward mine. "Cheers to your first proper introduction to Connecticut."

"I appreciate you taking the time today. Did you grow up here?"

He shook his head. "No. I grew up in Vermont. For undergrad, I moved to Boston. That's where I met Brian and Josh. After that, I moved up here for law school."

"And decided you loved it enough to stay?"

Something sad passed over his expression before he nodded. "Pretty much."

"You have a house?"

"Yeah. It's about ten minutes from the apartment building. Speaking of which, what's happening with your house? Is anyone looking after it?"

I shook my head. "Not really. Alarm is set and the locks were changed a couple months ago. With Rob being in jail now, I'm not sure if the divorce proceedings will be delayed. Unfortunately, I can't sell the house until we agree on the division of assets."

Mark's expression was sympathetic. "Did he have the arraignment?"

"Yep. Pleaded not guilty, which isn't surprising. Now I guess it goes to trial. In the meantime, the judge did remand him to custody, so at least he remains locked up. Unless they can raise the twenty-five thousand for bail."

"Are his parents still bothering you for it?"

"No, not since I changed my number, but Brian said they came by the office asking for me. They seem to forget I filed for divorce. Not only that, but he has a twenty-one-year-old girlfriend now. Why don't they bother her for the money?"

"I'm sorry." His eyes held a sincerity that left no doubt he meant it.

I made quick work of wiping Tristan's hands once he was done with his pizza and then held out his sippy cup. "No. I am, for once again airing my dirty laundry."

"It's what friends are for. Although we only met a short time ago, I'd like to think we're becoming that."

Funny how words so sweet would be somewhat disappointing.

I'd been friend zoned.

Of course, I couldn't blame him one bit. In fact, at this point, why in the world would I entertain the idea of anything more? It was a complication I definitely didn't need. At least, that's what I told myself as we packed up and headed back.

Mark wouldn't hear of letting me schlep a sleeping Tristan upstairs and took him from me. Considering the kid weighed thirty-two pounds, I was happy to let him. I followed, carrying only the bag and leftover pizza. I fought the emotion of seeing my baby asleep on the strong shoulder of a man who had shown him more attention and kindness in one day than his own father ever had in his young life.

"Should I put him in his crib?" Mark whispered when we went inside.

45

"Sure. I might be able to get another hour of nap."

Watching while Mark gently put Tristan down, I had to swallow the lump in my throat at the vision of such tenderness.

We both tiptoed out into the hallway, where Mark awkwardly put his hands in his pockets. "So, thanks for today."

I smiled. "That's my line. Um, I'm making a cheesecake tonight. You know, if you're, like, around later." Great, I was officially one 'like' away from being as stunted as a sixteen-year-old girl.

"I actually have some work to do."

"Yes, of course. Thanks again for today, though. Maybe we could do it again sometime." OMG. I couldn't seem to stop. Suddenly I was in a hurry for him to leave. I wanted to be alone in order to beat my head on something hard. Stupid. Stupid. Stupid.

"Uh, sure. Okay, then. See you around."

"Mm-hm. Yep. Sure thing." I followed him toward the door and leaned against it once it was shut, feeling like an idiot.

Clearly, flirting was a perishable skill, and mine had expired long ago.

CHAPTER FOUR

*N*ever make drastic hair decisions after ten o'clock at night, two beers in. If there was a lesson to be learned, that would be an important one.

I'd taken Tristan to the drug store after he'd awakened from his nap and come home with a box of color, one boasting a beautiful woman with luminous, light reddish-brown locks. I'd hoped to change my hair closer to my natural color—although who could honestly remember what it had been twelve years ago before I'd gone completely blond.

But instead my hair turned an unfortunate shade of pink. I couldn't blame Ms. What's-Her-Face, the name of the brand. The truth was I'd lost track of time while making a cheesecake and also should've done the test patch as the directions suggested. And now the bitch on the box was mocking me with her perfect locks, as if to say, *"Don't ask if your life can suck more. It can, indeed."*

Ugh. I'd only wanted to get rid of the blond hair my ex had loved on me since high school. Evidently, he had a thing for blondes considering his little girlfriend was platinum. Besides, nothing said reinvention quite like changing your hair color in the middle of the night, making it the exact opposite of what your ex would have wanted. I should've known better, though, than to do it on an emotional whim. A salon would've done the job right.

Deciding there was absolutely nothing to be done unless New Haven had a hair coloring delivery service, I went to bed with a wet head and hoped it would look better in the morning.

It didn't.

Matter of fact, in the harsh bathroom light, my hair, now dry, appeared even worse. I could see a line of what could be assumed was the correct color on my roots, but this faded into a horrible pinkish/brown hue when it reached the previously bleached portion of my tresses.

Any minute I had a toddler waking up which meant my options were limited regarding going anywhere to try to get the problem fixed. At least I had an Oreo cookie cheesecake to console me until I could do something about my hair. Perhaps later today I could take Tristan to the drugstore to get another box and go another round during his nap. For now, I shoved my offensive locks into a Charlotte Hounds cap and went about getting my adorable toddler out of bed.

While he was watching cartoons, I opened up the first math book I'd held in over eleven years. I was excited to get started on my classes, however thirty minutes later, I was ready to cry. I'd never been at the top of my class and if I'd imagined that the years had improved my math skills, the first assignment was proving me wrong. After shutting the book in frustration, I took out my English book. At least this subject seemed less intimidating.

Later that day while we were sitting down for lunch, a knock on the door got me excited it could be Mark. Then I remembered the state of my hair. Thankfully, it turned out to be a smiling Haylee at the door. Along with Abby in her baby seat, she was balancing two Starbucks in a drink tray. It was impressive.

"I come bearing coffee. Well, tea for me, but Sasha tipped me off that you're a caramel latte kind of girl."

I laughed. "I am. Thank you. Come in if you have time."

"I do. I just got back from New York. Had dinner with Will last night. I hate that he's moving back to Australia. Plus, I think he's had something going on with Catherine, which means he'll be leaving her behind, too."

"Sorry to hear he's leaving, and wow. How's Catherine taking it?" She was a good friend of both Sasha and Haylee. I'd met her last weekend during our spa morning. Considering how sweet she'd been in giving me advice and wisdom about life post-divorce, I instantly felt sad for her about Will.

"Josh said she's pretty torn up. But she sent an email about throwing a Halloween party. That'll be her birthday, too. In it, she wanted to make sure I extended the invitation to you. She really hopes you can come."

"To New York City?" I'd never been.

"Yep. We can trick-or-treat in the morning. There's a trunk-or-treat thing for the little ones, where cars gather in a parking lot. That way, we can catch the train in time for the party."

I knew this group of friends all did a lot of events, but the logistics sounded overwhelming to me. "Um, I think my mom is coming up that weekend."

"Perfect. She could babysit. You can either go back that same night or stay in a hotel. Or she could come with Tristan if you prefer. If she wants to attend the party, then we have a babysitter in the city we've used a couple of times who is terrific."

"Um, I'll think about it." Traveling to New York sounded like a lot. "Before I can go out in public, I've gotta schedule a rematch with Ms. What's-Her-Name to fix my hair."

"You colored your hair?"

"Attempted a change. Let's just say it doesn't look like the box."

"I'm sure it's fine. Let me see."

I lifted the hat from my hair and watched her eyes widen along with her mouth, which formed an O. "Um, it's not that bad."

I giggled. "Liar."

She smiled in return. "Okay, it's not great. What happened?"

"I lost track of time. And I think I needed to leave it longer on the blond parts than the roots, but it's kind of a moot point now."

"You're in luck. I have a classmate whose mom does hair out of her house. She's cut mine and does highlights for a couple of the girls I know, if you're interested in having her correct it."

That sounded better and cheaper than a salon, which would probably charge a fortune. Plus, there were no guarantees another box off the shelf would fix the problem. In fact, I could make it worse. "Definitely. I think having someone who knows what they're doing might be smarter than using another drugstore box."

"I'll send my friend a text now to see when her mom can fit you in this week. If there's anything universal in girl code, it's an SOS signal for a hair crisis."

I laughed, thinking that was true. We each took a seat at my dining room table to chat more comfortably. "Thank you. Meanwhile, how's school going?" I knew Haylee was a smarty-pants. She'd gone to Stanford and was now attending Yale law school. But she was also a mother a few months in, so juggling the two couldn't be easy.

As evidenced by her sigh, she was feeling the strain. "It's okay. I'm doing well in my classes, but I find myself distracted. I want to finish and I do want a law degree, but being separated from Josh is tough. We try to cram everything into the weekend, but it's tough. Not that he complains. He's been absolutely terrific and supports my dream of becoming a lawyer."

I sipped my coffee and then was candid. Because frankly, I

didn't know how not to be. "Priorities change once you have a child. It's simply fact. Is law school still what you really want?"

She seemed to contemplate the question. "You and Dr. Mac are the only ones to come right out and ask me that. Josh is afraid it'll come across as unsupportive, and I guess I'm afraid to ask myself the question because I worked extremely hard to get here."

"Sometimes we women are so invested in something that we lose sight of what we're getting out of it. Glutton-for-punishment syndrome I call it."

And yes, I was speaking about my marriage. How many times had I considered leaving until I thought about the thirteen years I'd invested in him?

"I'm not saying you should quit law school, especially if it's your dream, but have you thought about modifying the situation? What about transferring to a school in New York so you can be with Josh during the week? Are there any good ones?"

She nodded. "Yeah, Columbia and NYU. I was accepted into both of them. Bigger class sizes, but at this point, I'm not sure I care. I'm not looking to sign with a top law firm. Matter of fact, I find myself wanting to be more a part of Josh's brother's charity, which is now taking off. It would be nice to be with my husband during the week. He isn't keen on raising Abby in the city, but it would be temporary. I just feel bad with him buying this building up here for me to stay in, and we have a nanny, and—"

I stopped her there. "Haylee, he bought this building to keep housing costs low so you would choose a school near him back when you were dating. As for Natalie, she's wonderful, but eventually you're planning to move anyhow. You need to do what's best for your family."

"You're right. Although I want to discuss this with Josh, he'd only say, 'whatever you want.' Of course, I'd need to make certain the transfer is possible."

"So do that first. Then you have your options. Simply

applying and telling him you got in will probably give you his raw reaction to you moving to New York."

"The school wouldn't be so different from here. I'd miss the beautiful campus, but not as much as I miss Josh during the week. He'd continue to travel, but he's cut down quite a bit already."

From the excitement in her voice, I could tell she was already halfway toward making the decision. "You sound happy about the possibilities, which I think tells you something."

"I've been counting the days until the end of law school so we could move. So why do it if I'm miserable?"

"Exactly."

"Have you met with Dr. Mac yet?"

I couldn't help but blush in remembering my first encounter after I got him mixed up with the other Mark. "Uh, not yet. And I know I should. I will. I really don't have any excuse."

"I don't mean to pressure you. Whether you see him or not is completely up to you. But he inquired about you the other day and wanted me to tell you he's open if you ever wish to call him."

I knew I needed to make an appointment, but my avoidance kept me in blissful denial that I was struggling. Sometimes not dealing with emotions seemed a whole lot easier.

Haylee suddenly grabbed her vibrating phone. "Oh, it's my friend calling about your hair."

I listened while she described my unfortunate hair-color-from-the-box incident and was relieved when she asked, "Does tomorrow morning work? You can drop Tristan off with Natalie, and her mom can meet you at nine o'clock at her place. It's about six miles from here."

My nod could not be more enthusiastic. "That would be amazing."

Haylee confirmed the time and paused, covering the phone

with her hand. "Do you mind if I chat with her about our paper? It's due later this week."

I waved her off, not minding in the least. "Of course not." Getting up, I poured more milk for Tristan and then heard another knock on the door. Since chances were it was Mark, I remembered my hat. Didn't want to scare anyone else with the state of my hair.

"Hi." I hadn't expected to see him again this weekend. The fact that he appeared fresh from a shower, looking handsome in jeans and a flannel, practically had me giddy. I was a sucker for him in jeans.

"Hi, yourself. You, uh, going to a ballgame?" He pointed to the hat.

"No. Got into a fight with a chick on a box of hair color, and she kicked my butt."

He quirked his head to the side in a familiar way. It practically said, 'what the hell is this crazy girl talking about now?' "Pardon?"

Wow. Even his manners were a turn-on. "Um. I attempted to color my own hair and it turned out kind of punk rock meets sad stripper." Jesus. Sometimes I truly couldn't help myself with the crap that came out of my mouth.

But he only grinned. "Do I get to see it?" There was a twinkle in his eye which had me grinning back.

"No way. This hat stays on until tomorrow morning. That's when a woman Haylee knows will fix it for me."

"Hm. You know I really want to see it now."

He made a fake move for my hat, making me giggle.

"Nuh-uh. And you're a gentleman. As such, you should respect a woman's desire to hide a bad, bad dye job."

His hand reached out and tipped the brim. "Who says I'm a gentleman all the time?"

Zing. Right. To. My. Girly. Parts.

Only to be interrupted by Haylee's cheerful voice approaching from behind me. "Hey, Mark."

She looked a cross between amused and curious, glancing between us both. I wondered how much she'd overheard.

Mark—no shocker—got awkward. "Oh, hi, Haylee. Um, I was coming by to let you know that I'm heading to the store. And see if you needed anything. Either of you."

Now it was my turn to cock my head to the side. The one-eighty from flirtatious hunk of a guy to stuttering uncomfortable man was staggering. It was, however, completely endearing. "I'm good, but thank you."

Haylee smiled. "I'm good, too."

"Great. Um. Okay, then. Have a nice rest of the weekend."

I gave him a small wave, wondering how differently things might have progressed if Haylee hadn't been here. "You, too."

The moment the door was closed, my friend arched her brow. It was clear she wanted details.

"What?"

She laughed while I walked back over to Tristan to get him cleaned up and down from his high chair. "I do believe that's my question for you," she remarked.

I shrugged. "He's nice and evidently came by to see if I needed anything from the store."

She met my eyes and seemed to be waiting for more. When nothing came, she relented. "I guess I was hoping there might be something to him randomly dropping by on a Sunday."

"But I thought you said Mark didn't, you know, date anyone."

Now it was her turn to shrug. "He hasn't. But never say never."

"I, for one, think you couldn't find more opposite people than Mark and I. The likelihood is he's only being a nice guy and good neighbor." He'd gone to Yale law school. I couldn't make it through my first online math assignment.

"Are you open to dating?"

I thought back to my ideal, 'doing it in the dark scenario' and smiled. "I'm not sure, to be honest. The thought of getting back out there is terrifying. But if you're asking if I'm still pining over my ex, the answer is no."

I'd spent the last three years falling out of love with him a little more each day. However, I had no clue how to overcome the damage to my self-esteem.

"What if, instead of dating, you simply get out and meet some people? More casual, less pressure that way. I was invited to a mixer at school next Tuesday. Although spouses are invited, Josh won't be here since it's during the week. Even if he was in town, it's not his thing. I think it makes him feel old to hang out with law school students."

I laughed out loud. Josh was ten years older than Haylee. His wife was an exception when it came to maturity, but something told me other college kids probably weren't.

"I'm not sure I'd have much in common with your fellow students, either."

She shook her head. "And I do? I have a husband and baby. In any case, I've never really fit in with peers, so it would be a favor if you went with me."

I recognized this could be an opportunity. If I went out and met people, it would help me work on the courage to exit my comfort zone. Matter of fact, this had Juliette 2.0 written all over it. "Sure, but only if I can get this mess of my hair fixed first."

HUH. I didn't look bad as a brunette. Haylee's hairdresser had to do some serious coloring with a darker brown than I'd originally intended in order to cover the debacle. She'd then lightened it with highlights, breaking up the flat brown with blond streaks. I loved it. I wasn't the only one, either, judging by

Haylee's reaction when I walked through her door to pick up Tristan.

"Wow, Juliette. Your hair looks awesome."

"Thanks to you hooking me up with Molly. She was fantastic and probably charged only half of what a salon would've, to boot."

"I'm glad it worked out. So, I'm heading down to New York on Thursday after school since I happen to have no classes this Friday. Natalie said she could still be available on Friday if you need her. But if you don't, she planned to take a three-day weekend."

As if I'd be the reason Natalie didn't get a long weekend. "No, no. My schedule is flexible. And pretty empty. In fact, I have to beg Brian almost daily to send me work. Other than putting Mark's files in the computer, I don't have a lot happening." I wasn't ready to tell anyone I'd started online classes, especially since math had been brutal thus far.

———

THE NEXT MORNING I let myself into Mark's office and started with the digital filing of his folders. It was smooth sailing now that I had everything organized, made even easier by the bar scanner I'd had them ship up from the Charlotte office.

"You have an actual scanner gun?" Mark's voice came from the doorway.

This time I hadn't been wearing headphones and could hear him. "Sure do. They let me borrow it from the office down in Charlotte. Makes it quicker."

"Great. So, you got your hair fixed. It, uh, looks browner."

An involuntary eye roll told him how I felt about his compliment. "Yeah, that's cuz it is."

But instead of turning red like he normally would've, he

grinned. "Sorry, my compliments are kind of rusty. It looks nice."

I returned his grin, trying not to read anything into his lingering gaze. "Better. Now then, why did you get weird when you realized Haylee was in my apartment the other day?"

This produced his trademark blush. I suppose part of me might feel bad, but it had been bothering me. "If you don't want her to know we've become friends—at least I thought that's what we were becoming—then I guess I get it."

His eyes got big. "That's not it. What kind of asshole would I be? I just—It's that—"

I waited him out.

"I don't want her to think anything romantic is going on. And before you get an idea my aversion to having Haylee know we hang out is about you, it isn't. Whenever I get around any female, they all want to set me up. I realize Haylee's intentions come from a good place, but I don't want her getting any ideas."

"I don't think she has any considering when I asked what your deal was, she said you didn't date."

"You were asking about me?"

"Um, maybe."

"But you're still married."

Now it was my turn to have my entire face heat in a rare display. "Separated, actually. Anyhow, if you need to use your office, I can come back tomorrow. Or if I'm not disturbing you, then I'll carry on." I couldn't get back to scanning fast enough.

"Juliette, I didn't mean it that way. I'm sorry."

"It's fine. You're not wrong. I am technically still married."

He winced. "It wasn't a judgment on your marital status, only a surprised reaction that you might be ready to move on. I know this entire thing can't be easy on you. To be honest, if anything, I admire you'd be able to think about getting out there again."

Implying, with a big neon sign, that he was not. Since I believed he was sincere, I immediately lost my irritation.

He went on. "And you're right: we were becoming friends before I might've blown it twenty seconds ago. I really do apologize with the way that came out."

"I'd be pretty hypocritical to hold regrettable blurted words against anyone. So apology accepted."

He smiled slightly. "Any chance I could bring dinner by tonight? After all your cooking, I'd like to return the favor. Plus, no apology would be complete without an 'I'm sorry' pizza and brownies."

He was adorable, plus maybe I could start my diet next Monday. "Deal."

As MARK DISHED up the pizza that evening, I realized things seemed casual and easier between us. Maybe there was something about this morning which had made it such. For me, I think it was that I now knew without a doubt there was no chance with him. He'd friend zoned me with a big permanent marker. It took the pressure off. And perhaps it was a sign that, until I was divorced and had put Rob and the mess which was my current life behind me, I wouldn't be able to move on to anything more. But in my defense, could I help it if I was lonely for a man's attention? Especially a man as nice as Mark.

"What do you think of the pizza?" he asked.

"It's great. Tristan sure likes it." He was already on his second piece.

"He's going to be big. Is his dad tall?" He grimaced and then apologized. "Sorry, I didn't mean to bring him up."

I refused to let the question bother me. "It's okay. I have to remember my son deserves to know his father. That means I can't take offense at innocent questions about him. And in answer to your question: Rob is six feet tall. I heard my father was over six feet. Hopefully, I didn't dilute the gene pool with being only five foot two."

He grinned. "You are kind of tiny."

"Height, yes. Waistline, not so much, but is it any wonder?" I took another bite of ooey, gooey cheese pizza.

He set his slice down, frowning. "You're not fat."

"No, but I'm heavier than I should be. Anyhow, maybe after this stress is over, I can concentrate on working out and eating healthier. For now, I'm not depriving myself of good comfort food."

"Speaking of the stress, does your husband remain in jail?"

Ugh. I hated thinking of Rob as my husband about as much as I loathed Mark referring to him as such. "How about we call him Tristan's father? It makes me resent him a little less when brought up that way. And yes, he's still in jail, although they are trying to raise bail. So that situation might not remain for long. I'm told his trial date is set for March. That seems so far away."

"It's pretty typical. The prosecution and defense need time to prepare their cases. Has anyone contacted you about testifying?"

"Yes. But I've made it clear I won't be part of the defense. They'd like me to tell some fantasy about how he was a good father and husband. As much as it pains me, I'll be part of the prosecution where I'll help show the pattern of destruction started at home."

"I'm sorry you have to go through all of this."

I got up, needing to be busy, and brought the brownies over to the table. There I cut off a small square for Tristan. "It won't be easy, but my only goal is to ensure he doesn't get custody."

"Do you think he'd go after him?"

"Maybe. To punish me. Who knows? But it'll be a cold day in hell before I'd let him near my baby. Not with the lifestyle he's adopted, which includes dealing drugs. Anyhow, um, if you're interested, we have *Inside Out* tonight for our movie."

He took the hint in my subject change. "It sounds like a horror film."

I giggled, happy for the distraction. "I never considered that, from the perspective of the title. It's not horror but cute and Disney. But if you want to pass, I understand."

"I'm down with movie night. Shall we, Tristan?"

I watched as Mark unbuckled him from of his chair and lifted him up, afterward taking him to the living room. While I cleaned up Tristan's chair, I saw my laughing boy completely mesmerized by Mark while he was down on the floor learning the names of his trains. I realized how important it was for my son to have positive male influences in his life. I might try to be all things to him, but at the end of the day, he needed to have men to look up to, as well.

"Okay, movie time."

CHAPTER FIVE

*A*lthough I might miss home, I certainly was keeping busy. Math continued to give me trouble, but I'd made a perfect score on my first English assignment. Perhaps these were only online courses, but they meant I had taken the first step toward bettering myself.

On Wednesday Haylee came over for dinner where I taught her how to make chicken-fried steak and my mom's gravy. Then after her classes on Thursday, I dropped her and her daughter off at the train station to travel down to New York to see Josh. Haylee was so excited that I knew her decision to transfer to a closer law school would be the right one for her family.

All in all, I'd thought it had been a great week until later that night when Tristan fell ill with a fever of one hundred and two degrees. Everything he'd eaten for dinner made its way out of both ends making me thankful he was still in diapers. Meanwhile, I hoped he hadn't passed it on to Haylee's baby. Fevers and stomach bugs were scary enough with two-year-olds, but with babies, well, it was even worse.

I texted to give her a warning and settled in for the long night ahead of me. Thankfully, this wasn't my first rodeo. The initial panic when I'd been a new mom during his first year had been replaced by experience. I knew what to do, and my stomach was prepared now for the horrors of cleaning up after him.

Motrin to bring down his temp, a tepid bath, and a little bit of apple juice later, and he was asleep in bed with me. Unfortunately, it wasn't long before he awoke again, throwing up what little he had left in his tummy. A changed bed, clothes, and a cleanup later, he was back asleep. While he lay back in my bed, I hurried to put the dirty sheets in the wash. I only had two sets, which meant I needed to ensure one was on standby.

Everything was a blur as Thursday night bled into the next day, and I tried everything to keep him hydrated. By Friday afternoon, however, his fever seemed to have broken. His little chubby cheeks were back to peach instead of red, and his eyes appeared clearer. I was grateful this seemed to be a limited, twenty-four-hour bug.

Breathing a sigh of relief, I snuggled him close. "Are you hungry, baby?"

"Yes. Waffles, pease."

"Waffles for lunch sounds good. And you need to take a bath." In addition, I needed to wash everything he'd touched and hope to God I wouldn't come down with his virus.

By the time I'd put waffles on a plate for Tristan and poured his juice, mixing it with water, my stomach served notice. It was too late.

Having a sick kid was scary. Being sick when your kid was starting to feel better was pure torture.

Realizing I was on borrowed time before it hit me fully, I stripped both our beds, ran his bath, and started a load of wash. Next I put him in the bath, then cleaned the kitchen and vacuumed. But before long, I was on the couch and curled in a blanket, trying to warm myself from the chills which threatened to take over.

In the meantime, Tristan acted like his normal toddler self, watching cartoons, sucking down his sippy cup, and chomping on Cheerios.

"Mama, play. Play."

"Give me a minute, buddy." I got up and puttered to the kitchen in search of some adult Tylenol, wishing I had some. Something told me it would be a long night.

The knock at the door surprised me, but not as much as Tristan running toward it in an excited way.

"Mark, Mark?" my son asked. Evidently Mark had made quite the impression on Tristan.

"Uh, I don't know yet." Glimpsing out the peephole, I saw that, sure enough, it was Mark. "Back up a little and no hugs or kisses yet. We don't want to spread germs. Okay?"

"'Kay."

He had no idea what I was saying, so I kept a hold of his hand to keep him contained.

"Hey," Mark greeted when I opened the door. He immediately glanced down toward Tristan and then back up at me, his expression looking concerned. "You guys okay?"

I felt like a complete scrub. But the man had already witnessed me embarrass myself verbally. That he should now view my less-than-flattering appearance was just icing on the cake.

"Yeah, but don't come any closer. Tristan is on the up side, but I think my battle with this nasty virus is only beginning."

"You don't look good. At all."

It was official. Maybe I had in fact hit rock bottom. Had I even managed to brush my hair today? I didn't think so. The thought had me giggling, bordering on hysteria.

His face turned pink and as always it was adorable. He was probably trying to figure out whether to back away slowly from the crazy girl or pat me on the head and say, 'bless her heart.'

"I didn't mean—You know what? I only meant you look as though you're sick."

63

I gave him a lopsided grin. "I know. I just lost my grip on sanity for a moment. Now go save yourself and move far away from this hazmat situation."

Tristan tugged at my hand. "I wanna play with Mark."

"I know, sweetie, but maybe some other time when we're both feeling better."

"How about I come in and entertain him, and you can take a nap?"

My face must've betrayed the deep desire to fall into bed before my mind could intervene. "No, no. I couldn't ask you to. You'll get sick."

He was already entering my apartment and taking Tristan's hand. "If I get sick, then you can return the favor by waiting on me. But for now, you need a break, Jules."

It could be the fever, but the image of 'waiting on him' suddenly popped in my mind in the form of a slutty nurse's outfit and giving him a sponge bath in a very naughty way. Add to that he'd called me Jules, and I was standing there a bit stunned. One minute I was wondering how I'd manage tonight, then the next my handsome neighbor tells me to take a nap as he leads my son over to his Legos to keep him entertained.

"I can't ask you to do this." My voice caught on the last word, and tears welled up at the unexpected kindness.

He dumped the bag of Legos and ruffled Tristan's hair. "Hold tight, bud, while I get your mom settled." He turned toward me.

My eyes got big when his hand felt my forehead.

"Jesus, you're burning up. Do you think you have the flu?"

"Tristan's only lasted twenty-four hours, so it's mild if it's the flu."

"Did you take something for the fever?" His hand trailed down to the side of my face in an intimate gesture.

I shook my head, feeling a tear run down my stupid face despite my best effort against it. His kindheartedness was completely undoing my defenses. "I don't have anything unless I want to start chugging the toddler version."

He cracked a smile, pulling his hand back. "Let me run across the hall. I think I have some."

He returned within minutes with two Costco-sized bottles of pills in hand. "I have Tylenol and Motrin. Not sure which is better."

"I can piggyback them like I did with Tristan. Take Tylenol now, then Motrin the next time."

"Good. Take some. What do you have to drink?" He crossed to my kitchen and pulled open the fridge door to survey the gallon of milk and diet Coke. I didn't have anything else.

"Diet Coke is fine."

He handed me one. "What about your stomach? When is the last time you've eaten?"

"Last night, but I don't think I can do it. Tristan barely could, either. Um, he has cut up fruit in the fridge along with yogurt and noodles if he gets hungry for dinner. Cheerios in the cabinet. But please don't give him any of the sugar."

He opened the cabinet and raised a brow at my stash of Frosted Flakes, Pop-Tarts, and gummy candy. "I take it he doesn't share in your, uh—"

"Sugar addiction. No. And you can pretend you didn't see my dirty little secret."

There he went turning red again. "Lips are sealed. Now then, let's get you into bed."

I quirked a brow watching him roll his eyes despite blushing at the way that had sounded.

"I seem to put my foot in my mouth a lot around you."

Smiling, I assured him. "With me looking this way, I'd have to question your sanity not to mention your timing. And I put my foot in my mouth all the time."

"It's kind of cute when you do."

Yeah. Cute. Like a puppy. Terrific. "I feel guilty asking you to babysit, especially because you'll be exposed to whatever this crud is."

His handsome face got stern. "Let's make something clear. You're not asking. I'm offering. You're an amazing mom, but you need to take care of yourself, too."

Oh, cluck. My lower lip wobbled, and tears clogged my vision. "Thank you." It barely came out as a whisper.

"You're welcome."

I turned and made my way into the bathroom, letting the tears finally hit me. What was it about being sick and turning into an emotional mess that went hand in hand? It was as though all the balls I'd been juggling had completely crashed down around me. Then Mark, probably the nicest guy I'd ever met, drops in and is not only terrific with my son, but also offers to let me take a nap. I'm not sure what I did to deserve his compassion or that of any of my other friends over the last few weeks. I did appreciate it, though, and considered myself one lucky girl.

The shower made me feel semi-human, and the Tylenol helped with the aches and pains. When I then puttered out into the living room, I had to smile at the scene of Tristan in Mark's lap on the couch with a sippy cup in hand. They were watching Mickey Mouse Clubhouse.

Mark caught my eye and grinned. "We're bonding over our mutual love of Pluto. Although if he asks, I don't know if I can explain why Goofy is a dog who can talk while Pluto cannot."

I smiled at the way his mind worked. I hadn't ever considered this Disney dog conundrum. "I think you may be safe from that question today."

"You need to go lie down. Don't worry about us boys. If anything comes up I can't handle, I'll come get you."

"Okay. Wake me in a couple of hours, and I'll put Tristan to bed."

"Will do."

SHIVERING, I opened my eyes to a darkened room. I was completely soaked through my T-shirt and sheets. Glancing toward my bedroom window, I realized it was pitch black outside, too. Frantically, I looked toward the clock. Holy crap. It was after eight o'clock. I'd been out for four hours.

When I stood up too quickly, I had to fight nausea from the movement. I managed to fumble with the light and walk out my door down the hall.

Mark was in my kitchen, wiping down the counter.

"Why did you let me sleep?"

He glanced over, his brow furrowed with concern. "Because you needed it. I put Tristan to bed about twenty minutes ago."

"But you didn't have to." I was getting emotional over nothing, but I couldn't help it.

"I know I didn't. Here's the monitor. He's curled up with his stuffed doggie."

I swallowed hard as I studied the monitor screen. I'd always been the one to put Tristan to bed. Oh, my mom had done so, too, but only a handful of times. "How was he feeling?"

"Great. He ate some Cheerios, and yogurt, and we played Legos and then trains. He broke the red one, though. I'm hoping I can superglue it back together." He came around the counter and put his hand on my forehead. "You need some more meds and to get back in bed. Christ. You're soaked with sweat. Do you have a thermometer?"

I nodded. "Yeah. One of the ear ones in the bathroom cabinet."

He was gone and back in a flash and then wasted no time in punching the button on the electronic thermometer and holding it out for me.

After a few seconds, I pulled it out of my ear and blinked at the number. One hundred three degrees.

He took it without asking and frowned at the display. "Maybe I should take you to the emergency room."

I shook my head. "It's only spiked up. I'll take Motrin and be better." Although my uncontrollable shivering wasn't exactly convincing either of us.

"Why don't you go take a shower? I'm going to strip your bed and get some fresh sheets."

Although I hated the thought of him doing this task for me, I couldn't fathom coming up with the energy to do it myself. "Okay. Did Tristan go right to sleep for you?"

"Yep. I changed his diaper, put him in his PJs, and found a new toothbrush for him in the drawer. I figured the old one might be the one he used while sick. Read him a story—actually two because I'm a sucker. Then he rolled over, like 'peace out, dude. Time for sleep.'"

I had to be delusional to get completely turned on by the way Mark had been so capable. Yes, indeedy, capable was the new HOT, especially when you were used to doing everything on your own. "Thank you."

He uncapped the Tylenol bottle, handed me two pills, and then poured me a glass of water. "I want you to drink the full thing. You're probably dehydrated. In fact, when you're done with your shower, I'll run out and get some Gatorade and chicken broth. I'll only be a few minutes."

"Thanks again." What else could I say?

He came around the counter and tipped my chin up with his finger, surprising me with such a familiar gesture. "Stop thanking me. It's what friends do."

Right. But I bet friends wouldn't have the same thoughts running through their heads that I was in this moment with him so close. Deep breath and focus back on reality. "Yes, well, my friends have had to do a lot for me lately. Although I'm eternally grateful, it sucks always being on the receiving end."

He smirked and dropped his hand. "Just remember that when you're fixing me chicken soup in a few days, and we'll be fine."

"Deal."

ANOTHER SHOWER FELT HEAVENLY, but it also made me light-headed. The last thing I needed was to pass out naked and have Mark find me that way. After slipping on fresh pajamas, I frowned at my reflection. Holy nightmare. I looked like death puked up, well, death. Good thing Mark and I were only friends. And I didn't care what my *friend* thought of my appearance. Yeah, right.

Staring in the mirror was doing nothing for my self-confidence as I tried to look at myself through his eyes. Then I thought, nope. Not going there.

I pulled out the blow-dryer, intent on getting some of the dampness out of my hair. But within minutes my nausea came back full force, together with a heat rush right to my head. I turned the dryer off and splashed cold water on my face. Feeling like I might be sick, I opened the cabinet door below the sink in search of some Pepto. I'd thought I had some in here somewhere in a travel bag. When I unzipped the pouch of the bag, however, it was full of tampons. Desperate for something to help quell my stomach, I dumped the entire contents of the bag and finally found the small bottle of stomach-relief pills in the bottom. After shaking a few out, I swallowed them with a bit of water and then sat at the base of the toilet with my cheek on the cool porcelain of the tub. I sure was thankful I'd earlier scrubbed this bathroom top to bottom.

Please don't get sick. Please don't get sick.

My watering mouth wasn't exactly an encouraging sign, but it didn't stop my half prayer, half mantra. As if I could give my stomach the pep talk necessary to stay put. Upon hearing a soft knock, I glanced up to see Mark's face pop in.

"Jules, you all right?"

I nodded, unable to verbalize a response.

He didn't hesitate to take action, grabbing a wash cloth, wetting it with cool water, and then placing it on my forehead. His gaze next hit the floor.

My glance tracked his, and I realized what he'd found. The twenty-plus tampons strewn about as if the box had exploded.

I glanced up at the ceiling, asking the universe *why me?*

"Um, do you want me to give you privacy?"

Great. Now he was probably thinking that, on top of being sick, I needed an entire box of tampons to stop my monthly flow. "No. I was searching for Pepto. The feminine hygiene products are only to push my humiliation to the brink of ridiculous whenever I'm around you."

"You're humiliated around me?" He frowned at my admission.

"Repeatedly, but not by anything that's your fault. If anything, I'm shocked you haven't permanently hid from me."

That pulled a smile from him. "Now where would be the fun in that? You feeling better? Want to try getting into bed?"

"I think so." I let him help me up and didn't complain when he wrapped an arm around me for support during the few feet into my bedroom. There I found he'd already stripped the sheets and had another glass of water on the nightstand.

He lifted up the comforter and sheet, and I slid in, barely able to keep my eyes open. Virus plus hot shower, blow dry, and tampon explosion equaled complete exhaustion.

"Let me go to the store. When I get back, I'll sleep on the couch. If Tristan gets up, don't worry."

His hand rubbed my back, causing me to sigh with bliss. "Why are you doing this for me?"

"I like you."

I opened my eyes and saw him quickly amend his words.

"Like a friend. I meant I like you as a friend."

I couldn't keep myself from teasing him. "Oh, good. I was worried you might like, like me."

His lips twitched. "Don't worry. Only one like."

My body relaxed, enjoying the fact that he hadn't stopped his massage, moving it up to my shoulders. Maybe I could blame my sickness later, but all of a sudden it didn't feel like a single-like situation. "So maybe we can be good friends, then."

His voice sounded decidedly sexy. "I'd like that."

"Can I ask you something?"

The massage paused but then resumed as he expelled a breath. "Depends."

"Earlier, you said I was a good mom. How do you know?" It was probably the most vulnerable question I'd ever posed.

He rearranged the pillows, allowing for me to get more comfortable. Then he pulled the blankets over my body before meeting my gaze. "Because only a good mother would ever worry about being a bad one. Tristan is a lucky little boy to have someone love him as much as you do."

Damn. The man was making it impossible not to adore him on every level. "Thank you."

He kissed my forehead. "'Night, Jules. Get some sleep."

BY THE TIME I woke the next morning, I was feeling remarkably better. Not big-egg-breakfast-with-pancakes-and-syrup better, but at least I wasn't as feverish or nauseous. After ensuring I threw on some sweats, I brushed my teeth and walked out into the kitchen.

Mark was feeding Tristan in his high chair.

"Hi, Mama." Tristan smiled and showed me his spoonful of yogurt.

"Hi, baby, how are you feeling?"

"Great." It was his favorite response and made me grin.

"The real question is how are you?" Mark asked, studying my face. Before I knew it, he'd put a hand to my forehead.

"Much better. And I really can't thank you enough."

He shook his head. "We've been through this. I was happy to do it." Removing his hand from my forehead, he seemed satisfied that my temperature was back to normal.

I smirked. "You say that now, but something tells me that come tonight you might be regretting your decision. And I do want to make it up to you."

He flashed me a stern expression before relenting. "Fine. I love homemade pasta. Especially ravioli or tortellini. Is that something you make?"

Nope. Never had attempted it, but I'd certainly learn now. "Yep, definitely."

"Good, then that's how you can make it up to me. But, uh, maybe wait a couple of days."

"You're starting to feel sick already, aren't you?"

He grinned. "I'm not telling. By the way, I stocked your fridge with Gatorade and got some bagels. And don't you dare say thank you again."

Smiling, I made a motion of zipping my lips.

With humor reflected in his eyes, he reached over to tuck a strand of hair behind my ear. The gesture seemed to surprise him so much so that immediately, he dropped his hand. "See you later, Jules."

I was digging the nickname he'd given me way too much. "Sure. Later."

CHAPTER SIX

I was going to conquer these stupid high heels if it killed me. Judging by the way I was bobbling across my living room floor, this might be a real possibility. How did any woman function in shoes over three inches? And yet I'd seen Haylee wear them and manage to carry a baby on her hip at the same time. Sasha wore designer stilettos on a daily basis and even traveled in them. Maybe my feet were deformed because surely it shouldn't hurt this much. Right?

"Fuck. I mean cluck, cluck," I muttered, trying not to tip over. Nothing said sexy like cursing with every painful step. Maybe we'd be going to Disney World next summer given the rate of my swearing. Glancing toward Tristan, I saw he was playing with his stuffed animals. Thank goodness he hadn't been paying attention.

"Uh, knock knock. Your door was open." Mark's voice coming from the doorway took me off guard.

It was Monday night, and I'd wondered when I'd see him next.

"What are you doing?" he asked.

Funnily enough, instead of feeling embarrassed about being

73

caught looking silly wearing sweatpants with high heels, I merely shrugged. "Practicing." I'd already experienced far more awkward situations with the man. "And the door is open because Haylee is coming down any minute for dinner."

"Practicing for what, exactly?"

"For a party tomorrow night. Haylee had these beautiful shoes which are too small for her. Unfortunately, they're about three inches too high for me. But you know, the shoes make the outfit and all."

He seemed to contemplate my sweatpants and hoodie, with a smile tugging at his lips.

"Obviously not this outfit, but a dress. Anyhow, never mind. I think I've had enough torture for the evening." I slipped off the first shoe and let out a moan of relief.

But after both shoes were off, making me my normal height, I had to swallow hard. Mark appeared so much bigger than me. There was something about a tall man with broad shoulders which had me envisioning this one carrying me caveman style into a bedroom. Forcing myself to snap out of my little fantasy, I walked to the kitchen and picked up my beer. "Do you want one? I also made fajitas, if you're interested."

My diet was going about as well as my math class at this point.

He shook his head. "No, thanks. Nothing for me. I only was concerned because I saw your front door open."

I noticed then the Gatorade bottle in his hands and his tired eyes. "How are you feeling, by the way?" I flashed him a knowing smile. He'd no doubt caught what Tristan and I had battled.

He didn't bother to deny he'd been sick. "Better. And don't you dare start in with how sorry you are."

I shook my head. "I won't. In fact, I warned you several times. But here, I made this for you just in case." I pulled the bowl out of the refrigerator. It was homemade chicken noodle soup.

He grinned, accepting the container along with a sleeve of crackers I put on top. "You didn't have to make me soup."

"I know. Just like you didn't have to take care of Tristan while I was sick. Besides, this is merely the leftovers from the big batch I made for myself. It took a couple days for me to get back to normal food."

"Okay. Fair enough. So, uh, what type of party is it?"

"A mixer for Haylee's law school."

"Josh will be happy to know she's not going alone."

"She said much the same. But I'm free Wednesday night. Do you think your stomach will be up for cashing in your pasta dinner chip by then?" I'd looked at recipes and felt confident I could manage homemade ravioli.

He arched a brow. "I get the pasta dinner and also chicken noodle soup?"

I smiled. "The soup isn't much, so definitely."

"Wednesday is good for dinner. Who's this mixer for? Is it all law students or does it include friends of hers?"

I shrugged, finding it curious he was this interested. "I don't really know. I'm assuming it's her classmates, but I think it's Haylee's attempt to get me out and dressed up."

"So why go?"

"I guess because it's good to break out of my comfort zone. Plus, I can't be a hermit the rest of my life."

"No. But if you won't enjoy meeting new people, I don't see the point."

Something told me he spoke from experience. It occurred to me that the two of us had very dissimilar pasts that probably put us in two different situations regarding our willingness to socialize. Especially since our respective relationships had ended quite differently.

"I'm sure it'll be fine," I told him. However, I was pretty curious as to what the hell a mixer actually was.

IF I'D THOUGHT WALKING in heels was torture, a Brazilian wax pretty much said:

Here, hold my beer. You haven't seen anything yet.

It wasn't enough that hot wax brutally ripping the hair from your body hurt like the fires of hell. But having to get up on all fours for Olga, the unlucky waxer, in order to spread my cheeks had been hands-down-butt-up humiliating. And don't get me started on the level of fear instilled when she'd informed me, in a heavy Russian accent, what would happen if I let go of my butt cheeks while hot wax was between them. Visions of having my ass glued shut would not be leaving my head anytime soon.

Haylee was the one who had come up with the last-minute idea to go to the spa on Tuesday afternoon before our night out. After hearing for years from Sasha to just do it already, I'd been stupid enough to agree to my first waxing experience. Haylee assured me my assaulted girly parts would feel better by later tonight, but I'd popped Motrin and decided to ice the area, hoping it would facilitate wearing underwear to the party. Because I didn't have an icepack, I made do with a package of frozen French fries, applying it over my leggings, directly over my hoo-ha. I had the benefit of privacy since I'd already dropped Tristan off upstairs with Haylee's nanny, Natalie.

Once the coldness from the bag started to penetrate my leggings, I sighed with relief and held it there a few minutes. I figured I had at least ten more before I needed to start getting dressed for the party.

An unexpected knock at the door meant I had to get up, wincing, and then walk gingerly to answer.

But my smile was instant when I saw Mark's handsome face

through the peephole. Then I realized I was still holding a bag of French fries. After tossing them quickly onto the small entryway table, I smoothed back my hair and opened the door with a smile.

"Hey," he greeted.

"Hey, yourself."

I watched his eyes scan down the length of me as if he couldn't help himself. Oh, no. Please tell me there wasn't a wet spot from the frozen bag. Then I recalled I had black leggings on and gave thanks to the universe gods. For once, they'd spared me from humiliation. Which meant instead that he was checking me out? Huh.

"Did you want to come in?"

"Sure. I, um, brought something for Tristan. I tried to glue the old one, but it wasn't holding, so…"

My attention turned to what he held in his hands. A new red train identical to the one which had broken. What a sweet gesture. "That's very nice of you. He's upstairs with Natalie because Haylee and I are leaving in—" I stopped to check my watch. "Twenty minutes. But if you want to give it to him tomorrow, you'll be his hero for life."

"It's okay. You're welcome to give it to him whenever. I happened to be in the toy store." He put it on the table and then picked up the half-thawed bag of French fries. Yes, the very ones that had just been between my thighs, resting on my practically bald, red, somewhat-angry-with-me lady bits.

"Um, here, I'll take those," I mumbled, snatching the bag out of his hands. "Happened to be in the toy store, huh?" Nice try. Clearly, he'd gone out of his way to replace Tristan's train but didn't want to take the credit.

"Busted. Trains were also my favorite as a kid. What's with the French fry bag on the table?"

"Oh, I was icing."

"Did you pull a muscle?"

It occurred to me a moment too late that I should've taken his question as a suggestion and let him think I'd pulled something. But per usual, my words came out before a filter could be placed in front of them.

"I wish. But Haylee talked me into a Brazilian wax in prep for tonight, and it hurts like hell."

Both his eyebrows arched sky high. Once again, I'd apparently made him lose his ability for speech. You'd think he'd be used to my brand of crazy by now.

"I should've gone with muscle," I muttered, wanting to face palm.

His mouth twitched into a smile. "At least no one could ever accuse you of not always speaking the truth. Um, I might regret asking this, but is a wax customary before a mixer?"

I couldn't help teasing. "Although I'm unaware of mixer etiquette, I don't think it's required."

He laughed out loud.

"Actually, I did it because I finally gave in to Sasha. She's been pressuring me to try it for a while."

"Wh-Why?"

Now it was my turn to laugh. I'd made it sound as though Sasha was heavily invested in the grooming of my nether regions. "My guess is she wanted to hear the comedic play-by-play afterward. Or she's just really concerned I have smooth lady bits." I shrugged and watched him turn red. "And now comes the regret portion of your question. Sorry for the TMI. On another, less personal note, and switching topics, it was very thoughtful of you to buy this train for Tristan."

He rubbed a hand, the one with ridiculously sensual fingers, through his hair which made me think I needed a shrink to analyze why I was so attracted to them. And the hair he'd just mussed made him even sexier.

"It's no problem. Have fun tonight. Are we still on for dinner tomorrow?"

"Definitely. I have ravioli, salad, garlic bread, and tiramisu on the menu."

He grinned widely. "Can't wait."

———

TURNED out a mixer was basically a happy hour on campus, attended by a bunch of future attorneys. There was a cash bar on one side of the large room and about a hundred-people milling about. The ages ranged a great deal, which was surprising. There were quite a few people in their early twenties like Haylee, but there were others who'd put off law school until later in life and were older.

I donned the same black dress and heels I'd worn to Haylee's cocktail party a couple weeks ago since there was no way I'd have been able to wear Haylee's shoes and actually walk. But at least my hair wasn't in a ponytail this time. I'd left it down and managed to put some curl into it. And speaking of hair, or lack thereof, my bikini line had thankfully calmed down enough I could wear panties.

Haylee introduced me to quite a few of her fellow students. However, it was clear even she felt out of place.

"This is the first purely social event I've attended here, so I think everyone is in shock to see me," Haylee commented, sipping on her wine and looking around.

I'd already gotten that impression from the comments people had given her. 'Oh, my God, you're here' seemed to be the favorite expression.

"That's not necessarily a bad thing. It only means your priorities are studying and your family."

She nodded. "And since I applied to transfer to Columbia or NYU after the winter semester, maybe making friends here at this point is moot."

"So you're planning to transfer, after all. Good for you. Did you tell Josh yet?"

"Nope. But I intend to this weekend when we're in New York for Catherine's party. Regarding that, please tell me you're coming."

"Um. I spoke with my mom, and she said she'd be happy to watch Tristan that night. But I feel bad having her come out here and then I leave."

"I bought you a train ticket, just in case."

My eyes got wide.

She quickly explained. "Sorry. I bought one for Mark, too. Since Josh and I are on the trains all the time, we can trade them in for credit toward new tickets at a later time if you don't use them. But I wanted to be sure to get tickets in case they sell out, that being Halloween night."

"Mark doesn't want to attend?"

She sighed. "He's not much on social gatherings, but he'll go to see his friends. Of course, I haven't yet told him he has to wear a costume."

Mark in a costume might make attending the party worthwhile. But I wouldn't plan to stay the night. Hotels in New York City were too expensive. Hmm, maybe I could go to the party for a couple hours and take a late train back home. That would work out well. Also, I'd certainly love to see Catherine again. Although she was the editor-in-chief of a major fashion magazine, she'd been down-to-earth and very friendly. Her perspective on divorce had been a breath of fresh air for me, especially when she'd spoken of the importance of finding oneself again.

"All right. I'll go. But I need to find a costume, too."

"Great. I'm so happy you'll come. The people at Catherine's party will definitely be more fun than this crowd. What do you think about mingling for another half hour here and then calling it a night?"

"Sounds good." I normally had no problem meeting new

people. But here at Yale law school, I couldn't have been more out of my element. However, I refused to waste a night where I'd dressed up and hired a babysitter, so I smiled and went with Haylee to meet some other people.

As we made our last rounds, we met up with two attractive men, one of whom Haylee had class with. I forced myself to keep quiet during the ensuing conversation as it was the only way I could control the randomness in my brain and my affinity for going verbally rogue.

So when one of the guys honed in on me, I proceeded carefully.

"You're from the South?" the guy named Chad asked. He must've picked up on my Southern accent when I'd introduced myself.

I smiled, detecting a hint of his own accent. "North Carolina. How about you?"

"Alabama originally. Nice to meet another Southerner this far north." Chad was handsome, with blondish hair and brown eyes.

We chatted a little while longer while Haylee went to the ladies' room. I ensured I stuck to safe, normal topics. And when he invited me for coffee on Thursday night, I accepted. After all, if I was reinventing myself, it meant putting myself out there to meet new people and—gulp—date again.

But after he left and Haylee found me, I realized I hadn't mentioned Tristan in my conversation. Neither had I thought about who would be watching him while I went out another night. What the hell had I been thinking?

"What's wrong?" Haylee inquired as we went out to the car ten minutes later.

"I think I just accepted a date with Chad on Thursday evening—although I'm not positive coffee is a real date. But I didn't give a thought as to what I would do with Tristan. To make matters worse, I didn't even tell Chad I had a son. Or that I'm only legally separated and not fully divorced."

She frowned while getting into the car. "Well, first off, I'll watch Tristan that night. And secondly, you act as though you owe him that information. You don't. Simply go and meet him and if you two hit it off, then maybe share your son with him. If not, then why bother? You seem to think you need to put a disclaimer out there about your personal life, but you absolutely don't. It's only coffee, but if you're not comfortable, then text him and tell him you've changed your mind."

She had a point. I didn't owe anyone my entire backstory. Nope, that certainly didn't fit in with the Juliette 2.0 plan. In an attempt to put on a brave face, I said, "Okay. You're right, and it's only coffee. I know he's not in your class, but do you know him? I think he seemed nice. And he's really cute."

"I don't know him very well, unfortunately. He's a third year, and has always been polite. Take your own car, meet him at the café, and if it goes great, maybe get dinner. If it doesn't, then simply drive home."

It sounded easy enough. It wasn't as though I was looking for anything serious, especially if I was only up here short-term.

I'D JUST PUT the finishing touches on the tiramisu when Mark knocked the next evening. Making homemade ravioli had been a challenge. But I'd been excited to take it on, and I was especially glad I'd made the effort when he closed his eyes in pure bliss after taking his first bite.

"This is amazing. Seriously, the best meal I think I've ever tasted. Thank you."

"It was fun to make. Come to think of it, I might get one of those pasta makers when I get back home. Then I can do home-made fettuccine and spaghetti."

"Any thoughts about when that'll happen?"

"My attorney thinks I should remain here until the trial, but I can't imagine staying until March. As it is, I need to call Tristan's day care and un-enroll him. I can't keep paying for that service twice."

"I love your cooking and enjoy your company, so selfishly speaking, I'll be sorry to see you guys go. Haylee will, too."

"Yeah, I'll miss everyone as well."

"What DVD is on tap for tonight?"

I smiled, loving that he wanted to stay to hang out with us. "It's the movie *Frozen*. And you may end up regretting your decision after the songs get stuck in your head."

"I'll take my chances, but only if I get to pick tomorrow night and bring by some of my favorite Chinese food. You should tell me what dishes you like."

"Oh, uh, tomorrow night I actually have plans. Then Friday my mom is coming into town, and Saturday I'm going to Catherine's party in New York City. But maybe the following week? After Monday, when my mom flies back home."

His face turned red. "I'm sorry. It was rude of me to be assume you'd be free. I should've asked."

I shook my head. "No, it's fine. Normally I would be."

"Do you have another evening planned with Haylee? By the way, you never said how the mixer was last night."

"Mixer was good." All of a sudden, I felt embarrassed about revealing my Thursday plans. It was silly as Mark had made it clear he only wanted to be friends. And because I had no reason to hide it, I blurted it out. "And that's actually why I have plans tomorrow. One of Haylee's classmates asked me out for coffee. He's from the South, too, and, well, anyhow..."

The flash of disappointment in Mark's eyes hit me before his words did. "You know, just because someone offers, you don't have to go, not until you're ready."

This was a man who hadn't dated since losing his fiancé over a decade ago, so I could only imagine what he thought about me going out while I was still legally married. He had said he wasn't judging, but it sure seemed like he was. "I know, but I am in fact ready to get out there and meet people. I realize I'm not officially divorced yet, but in truth, the relationship was over years ago, and I—" Shit, I was getting defensive, trying to justify myself.

He stood up, gathering his plate and shaking his head. "I'm not judging. Not at all. Hell, maybe I'm projecting some of the pressure I've felt over the years about getting back out there onto you, and that's not fair. Who's staying with Tristan? Do you need someone to babysit?"

Right. Have the hot neighbor for whom I've worn down my vibrator's batteries fantasizing about go and watch my son while I'm out on a coffee date with another man. "Haylee is, but I appreciate the offer."

He shoved his hands in his pockets and gave me a small smile. "Sure, anytime. Who is this guy? Does Haylee know him?"

Awkward. The very last thing I wanted to do was talk about Chad with the man I'd rather go out with. "She knows of him through his friend who's in her class. But he's a year ahead. It's only coffee, and I'm planning to meet him there."

"And if it goes well, you'll probably do dinner after?"

I shrugged. "I'm not sure how these things work anymore, to be honest, but I guess so."

"Um, how about I start on these dishes while you get Tristan bathed and in his PJs? Then we can have the movie and dessert."

"Sounds good." It could only be me, but it felt like something was suddenly off between us.

CHAPTER SEVEN

*I*t was official. I sucked at dating. And I was never, ever doing it again. In fact, on the agenda for tomorrow was to go to Sam's Club or Costco and stock up on batteries. Maybe I'd even buy a different vibrator for every day of the week to keep things fresh and interesting. It couldn't be called slutty if you switched up your battery-operated boyfriends every night, right? Armed with that amusing thought, I let myself into my apartment and played over the disaster which had been the last hour of my evening.

Chad had been as attractive as I'd remembered from the mixer and smart, too. But per usual when I was intimidated or anxious, things started spewing out of my mouth at an alarmingly quick rate—sans the filter. Added to that was the fact he'd asked more questions about Haylee than about me. I couldn't shake the impression he might have a little crush on my very happily married friend.

Since it wasn't quite eight o'clock, I was happy Tristan wouldn't yet be asleep and went straight up to Haylee's apartment. I enjoyed putting him to bed, so at least in that respect I was grateful my evening was over early.

After picking up my sleepy boy, taking him downstairs, and putting him in his crib, I slipped off my skirt and donned my usual outfit of leggings and a sweatshirt. Thankfully, Haylee hadn't peppered me with questions about my date. I'd promised we could chat about it tomorrow. Not that there was much to say.

Sighing, I took a swig out of my beer bottle. At least Chad had insisted on paying for coffee and had been nice enough to walk me to my car like a gentleman. But the 'it was nice meeting you, take care' made it pretty obvious he wasn't planning to call any time soon. Just as well as I hadn't exactly enjoyed myself. And this disaster was without alcohol to blame this time around.

Intending to replace the batteries in my vibrator when I went to the store, I jotted it down in all caps on a pad of paper on the kitchen counter. Getting those was the first order of business tomorrow. Actually, milk, cheerios and pancake mix was, but perhaps I could get them all during the same shopping trip.

When the knock came at the door, I was stunned to see that it was Mark when I looked out the peephole.

Opening the door, I found him standing there with his hands in his pockets, rocking back on his heels. "Hey, I saw your car. I thought you had a date tonight?"

"I did, but it ended early."

His gaze landed on my bottle of beer, amusement evident in his expression. "I'm guessing by the drink of choice it didn't go well?"

"You'd guess right. Dating or coffee or whatever it's called these days blows. Um, did you want to come in? There's more beer. But only if you drink it out of the bottle so as not to make me feel uncivilized if you were to pour it into a proper glass."

"Sounds good to me."

He walked in, and I tried in vain not to stare at his fine ass encased in blue jeans. Snapping my eyes up to his face when he turned, I swore he could read my thoughts and blushed accordingly.

After he got himself a bottle, we both took a seat on the sofa.

We were only friends, I reminded myself, simply buddies who hung out and were not in, and would not ever have, a physical relationship. Oh, no, I shouldn't have thought about sex because now I noticed how good he smelled. And why was he looking at me funny?

"Hello. Earth to Juliette. You all right?"

"Um, yeah, sorry. I must've spaced."

"I asked you if you wanted anything more to drink. You drained your beer. You want some water?"

Looking at the now empty bottle in question, I realized he was right. Thinking about sex evidently had me chugging my alcohol these days. "Some water would probably be good."

He got up and pulled down a glass from my kitchen cabinet, clearly comfortable in my space with all the dishwashing he'd done over the last few weeks.

"Hey, is this a math book? Are you taking classes?"

My head whipped around to see him touching my books on the counter.

"Uh, it's just online courses." The last thing I'd wanted was for him—or anyone, for that matter—to find out.

He frowned as he walked over to hand me the glass of water. He then took a seat next to me. "What degree are you working toward?"

I shrugged. "It's my first two classes, so nothing yet. But I was hoping someday it'll be business administration. Um, do me a favor, though, and don't tell anyone."

"Don't tell anyone you're taking classes? Why not?"

"Because with the way math is going, I'm not sure how long I'll be doing it. Plus, it's embarrassing."

"Why would it be embarrassing?"

Because he'd gone to Yale, Brian and Josh had studied at Harvard, and Haylee had done undergrad at Stanford and was now studying law at Yale. Meanwhile, I was struggling with a math refresher course. But there was no way I wanted to voice my insecurity. It wouldn't be something he'd understand. "It just is."

He sighed but, gratefully, changed the subject. "Did you pick up Tristan?"

"Yes. At least I was home in time to put him to bed. Haylee seemed a bit disappointed, however. I think she hoped I'd get lucky, and she'd keep him overnight." I had no clue why I'd said that out loud.

He frowned. "Yeah, well, I'm glad she was disappointed. So was this guy Chad that bad?"

"I'm sure he's a good person, at least he was a gentleman, but he's just not into me. I don't know what I was thinking when I accepted the coffee invitation."

He turned his body toward me, which made sense for better conversation. But was it just me, or was he sitting really close?

Jesus, get a grip. I wasn't a teenager who'd try to measure his interest by the inches he sat away from me. I was, in fact, a grown woman who shouldn't read into something so trivial.

"What makes you think he wasn't into you?"

I gave him a look like 'come on.' Of all people to ask that question, he should find the answer obvious, especially considering the first time we'd met. My brand of cray-cray was an acquired taste.

"Don't give me a look as if there is a neon sign spelling it out for me. Tell me why on earth he wouldn't be into you?"

He was getting annoyed on my behalf, which was sweet but completely unnecessary. Maybe it was the nerve still raw from him finding my school books or perhaps it was the terrible insecurity I'd felt during the entire coffee date, but the words came out before I could stop them.

"Mark, I'm a single mom. You know what? Scratch that. I'm an about-to-be-divorced single mom who is living here only because of the amazing charity and friendship of Haylee and

Josh, and because Brian came up with the idea. I drink beer from the bottle, have a fascination with muscle cars, and buy my makeup from a drugstore. I didn't attend college, and though I'd thought maybe to start on a degree, considering the way math is sucking, I doubt it'll ever happen. And frankly, I'm happy being an office manager and don't have any aspirations of making CEO or partner. And that's only the nonphysical stuff. Don't even get me started on the other. In a nutshell, he's pretty much out of my league."

"He fucking said all of that to you?" Mark got up off the couch so abruptly that the glass of water I'd been holding partially spilled onto my lap, but I was too distracted to take notice.

In awe, I watched him pace the floor. Mild-mannered Mark turning angry was something I never thought I'd see. It was kind of hot. But when I realized he was grabbing his keys off the table, it clicked that his anger was misplaced.

"Wait, no, he didn't actually *say* those things." Standing up and grabbing his arm, I swallowed at the fact his bicep was rock hard. Good Lord. What did the man have happening under the sweatshirt he was always wearing?

"He didn't say them, but he made you feel that way?" His eyes were intent on mine.

"Not really. I mean it was all me. Come on. I'm a realist. He's a third-year Yale Law School student who comes from money and has big-time plans to become partner by age thirty-five in some prestigious firm. He's probably a nice guy, but the last thing he wants is a relationship with some girl who grew up in a trailer park, had her dad leave when she was six, and married her high school sweetheart who turned into an opiate addict. I'm a single mom with stretch marks and sagging boobs in a college town full of twenty-something-year-old coeds. Obviously, it's not a match."

I watched his mouth open and then shut as though he

couldn't find the proper words to respond. I imagine he was still stuck on the sagging boobs part. Walking into the kitchen, I grabbed a paper towel and blotted the spilled water from my leggings.

He followed me, standing on the other side of the counter. "Sorry. I didn't mean to get you wet."

My face heated while my mind went directly into the gutter. But in a rare display of restraint, I managed not to comment on it.

He'd picked up on the color of my face, however, and sought to explain. "Sorry. I meant spilling the water." He ran a hand through his hair.

I couldn't help it—I started giggling. Maybe it was the beer, or maybe it was his need to clarify. "I know you did, but I can't help having a dirty mind. I should blame all those years of working for Brian." I was unable to stop laughing and was relieved when Mark cracked a smile, too.

He smirked. "I bet. And I guess so long as this guy didn't treat you badly, I'll let it go."

I couldn't help wondering what in the heck he thought he was going to do. Charge out of here searching for some law student named Chad? But it meant a lot to know he wanted to be my platonic knight in shining armor.

"He was fine. Honestly, it felt like he might be more interested in Haylee. He kept bringing her up. But please don't share that with Josh." I knew Haylee's husband would be less than pleased to hear a student named Chad had been inquiring about her.

"That wouldn't go over well, so I won't. This Chad guy shouldn't have made you feel as though you weren't worthy of his company. If anything it should have been the other way around."

As much as I'd have loved to believe his words, there was no convincing me. I took a deep breath and decided another beer was in order, after all. Opening the refrigerator, I took one out and popped open the top.

"I'm not keeping you from a night to yourself, am I?" Mark asked.

"Nope. Not at all. By the way, do you know if there's a Sam's Club or Costco around here?"

"There's one in Milford about twenty minutes away. Why?"

Because I needed a lifetime supply of batteries for my vibrator. Luckily, my thought did not verbalize itself.

But then his gaze landed on the list with BATTERIES in all caps on my countertop, underlined and with two exclamation points after it.

I wondered if he knew. Great. Now he had me wanting him to kiss me. Deciding to put some space between us before I hopped on him like a sex-starved lunatic, I walked back toward the sofa.

"Can I ask you something?" He came into the living room, taking a seat next to me, turning his body so we were face to face, sitting even closer to me than the last time. So close our knees were touching.

"Yeah, sure."

"In our first conversation, you said you wanted sex in the dark, no foreplay, and him leaving by the morning. Why?"

I sucked in a breath and wished he hadn't been sober enough to remember everything I'd blurted out the first night we'd met. "I guess I was thinking I don't want the pressure of anything else right now."

"And the lights off are because...?"

"Because it's been two years, and I'm not ready for anyone to see my post-baby body."

"I'm confused. Tristan's father and you—I didn't think you separated until a few months ago—"

"We didn't have sex while I was pregnant because, in his words, I was enormous. Then afterwards—Let's just say there

91

was one attempted time, and it didn't go well. I guess I didn't have anything on his twenty-year-old replacement." After my admission, I busied myself with gulping more of my beverage.

"God, you are pissing me off."

My eyes went wide in astonishment. "What? Why?"

"Why are you this down on yourself? It's no wonder Chad wasn't into you. Over your coffee tonight, you probably gave him a top ten list of why he shouldn't be."

I couldn't help it. Tears welled up instantly at his nail-on-the-head assessment.

"You know what? To hell with this—"

Suddenly, he took the bottle out of my hand, plopped it on the coffee table next to his, cupped my face, and crushed his mouth to mine. Lips that were firm but soft at the same time explored mine. Heat ignited through my body at the contact. Then it was suddenly gone.

I opened my eyes to see him staring at me, as if waiting on my reaction.

"Um, was that a *you feel sorry for me* kiss or—"

I didn't have a chance to finish as he moved one hand to the back of my neck while the other cupped my chin, trailing his thumb over my lips intimately. "I've wanted to kiss you for weeks."

"But you friend zoned me."

He tucked my hair behind my ear. "I was trying to be respectful of what you have going on. Didn't want to push you into something you might not be ready for. Then tonight I sat across the hall for hours, hoping you'd be home early. Hoping I hadn't lost my chance."

Before I could register the full impact of his words or that he'd wanted to kiss me for weeks, his mouth covered mine again. This time he paused to take off his glasses and then leaned in. His tongue dipped inside and tasted me with both finesse and possession.

A low moan came from deep inside of me. Before I knew it, he'd shifted me so my knees were straddling his lap on the couch. His tongue danced with mine, dominating and consuming me more than a kiss ever had.

I found myself lost in such an unexpected pleasure. The man certainly knew how to kiss.

His strong hands angled my head, allowing him to deepen the delicious assault on my lips and exposing my neck. His mouth then traveled there until he reached behind my ear and whispered, "Do you want me to stop?"

"Not even a little bit." I hardly wanted to pause to answer his question, let alone stop kissing.

"You're sure? Because I'm about ten seconds away from taking you into your bedroom and fucking you in the dark like your plan dictates. And just so we're clear, it's not because I don't want to see every inch of you. But I want you to be comfortable before that happens. If you're not sure, then tell me you only want to be friends."

Who was this man? He was sex on an alpha stick, that's what. I nodded, at a loss for words, something which hardly ever happened.

"Yes, you want me to take you into the bedroom?"

I didn't think 'yes' was a strong enough word. But I could only manage an "uh-huh," completely stunned by how this night was turning out.

He simply stood, with my legs wrapped tightly around him, striding into my bedroom without hesitation, as if my weight was nothing. After placing me on the bed, he moved toward the window.

"Take off your clothes," he commanded, his bossy voice sending a shiver down my entire body. He drew the blinds tight, blocking the moonlight, and then closed the bedroom door, shutting out all of the living room illumination.

I scrambled out of my leggings, thankful for my torturous

Brazilian wax, after all. Moving under the covers, I licked my lips, suddenly nervous. "Thanks for understanding—" I started to say.

Suddenly, his weight was on the bed, and then he was under the covers with me, hot and, oh, so very naked. "Don't thank me. It's all I can do not to shine a spotlight on you and tell you all the ways you're beautiful. But tonight we'll do this your way."

His words made me smile while my hands skimmed down his biceps. Jesus, his arms were as cut as I'd imagined. I stroked his chest and found much the same magnificent musculature. When my fingers skimmed down his rock-hard stomach, I groaned in delight. The man was built. "You're in shape. How the hell did I not realize this?"

"Not like I have much else to occupy my time outside of work." His mouth was on mine again while his hard thigh spread my legs open. Strong hands moved to my breasts as soft lips traveled down, trailing kisses to one.

I tensed, self-conscious, especially about that part of my body.

"Relax, Jules," he demanded.

Oh, good Lord. His fingers glided down my stomach, further down, finding my wet center, as if willing me to forget about the thought of him touching any other parts of me.

He shifted his lips back to my mouth, and I met his fevered kiss with one of my own. It had been too long, and I was a woman starved. Our tongues clashed, each of us frantic for the contact. Then, when his weight shifted, I could feel the tip of his erection at my drenched entrance.

"Are you on the Pill?" he asked, clearly straining with need.

I whimpered, wanting to feel him inside of me more than anything. "I, um, yes, but sometimes I forget and then have to take two the next day. I'm clean, though. I got checked after I knew Rob was cheating, but turns out he didn't have sex with her until after he stopped having sex with me, and we had only been with one another before that."

"What?"

I'd just given him a lot of information without a real answer. "Do you have a condom, to be on the safe side?"

"No. Shit, I haven't had sex in four years."

No way. Did he say four years?

"I'm clean, too, by the way, but let me get dressed and go to the drugstore real quick."

The thought of him leaving this bed and my body made me wish I was a more responsible pill-taker. "Wait. I have a condom. I was walking Tristan through campus and some chick handed me a safe sex card that had one attached. It was annoying because she gave a judging look toward my son as if he was a mistake derailing my educational dreams." I was rambling but couldn't help it. It's what I did when I was anxious.

"Where is it?"

"Um, in the stack of paperwork on the kitchen counter. It's attached to the campus clinic's information card about safe sex and preventing STDs."

"Be right back."

The man must've sprinted because he returned in less than a minute, shutting the door. His husky voice came in the dark. "You didn't change your mind, did you?"

"Not at all."

I could hear his sharp intake of breath and sat up, but I could only see the outline of his silhouette. "Everything okay?"

"Yep, but let's just say condoms are not one size fits all."

Huh. Guess that made me a lucky girl, then. "Will you be in pain?"

The bed sank under the weight of him climbing in again. "I'd be in more if I'm not inside of you soon. But I need to get you ready for me first. I don't want to hurt you."

His hands slid down my hips, skimming straight to my heat.

Adept fingers parted my flesh dipping one inside, then another, stretching me exquisitely.

"Oh, God, I've been fantasizing about your fingers inside of me since the first time I met you."

Immediately, he stopped.

I arched my hips in protest and regretted my blurted-out internal thought. "Please don't stop."

He chuckled into my neck. "Sorry. You surprised me, but then again, there should be nothing coming from you that would shock me by now."

I wasn't sure if that was a compliment or not, but once his fingers started moving again, I honestly didn't care. Instead, I wanted to touch him. Reaching down, I could feel the extent of his hard length.

"Jesus, Mark." Evidently there was a lot I had missed while looking at the man in his suits and casual attire. He was hung like a Greek statue, the really well-endowed kind. "I think you're bigger than my vibrator." I felt him hesitate once again. "I'm sorry. My damn mouth. I didn't mean to make you self-conscious."

"Shut up, Jules," he responded tenderly, kissing me on the nose before taking my lips again.

My body started to shake when his fingers sped up and found my clit, rubbing circles around the sensitive flesh while his teeth nipped down the column of my throat. His hot breath in my ear whispered words which, along with his fingers, ignited my orgasm. "I love that you got this pussy waxed. Like it was only for me. So I could fuck you with my fingers and feel that bare skin. Now come for me, beautiful. I need to feel it."

"Holy— Oh, my God—" Words came out in a jumble. My hips bucked, tingles traveled clear down to my toes, and my eyes rolled back into my head as my climax washed over me.

Never.

Never had I experienced an orgasm such as this one. While I

was still recovering, I could feel his hips between my knees, the crown of his length at my entrance.

"We'll go slow. You're small, and I don't want to hurt you."

"I pushed out an eight-pound baby out of my vagina, so I'm pretty sure you'll fit just fine."

He froze, and I realized what I'd blurted out this time around.

"Sorry. Officially most unsexy thing ever said during pre-penetration."

He chuckled and then leaned in with his mouth to my ear. "I think it's clear that either I'm going to need to gag you, which has possibilities, or I'll need to do some more dirty talking to distract you."

Both my libido and curiosity shot off the charts. "I'm game."

He teased me with the tip of his cock, rubbing back and forth. "Do you have any idea how hard I am for you right now, how much I can't wait to feel your hot pussy clenching around me? How, when I see you in those leggings, it makes me want to bend you over something and take you deep? In fact, I don't think you'll need those batteries, but you may need more bags of frozen French fries come tomorrow morning."

Mission accomplished. He was doing it. He was turning my mind off and my speaking abilities to mush. As a result, I was growing wetter and felt him push in the first inch. Who would've ever thought the words French fries and batteries in the same sentence could be such a turn-on? Or that Mark, of all people, was a dirty talker?

"Put your hands on me. Touch me."

Didn't have to ask me twice. I skimmed my hands down to his hips and felt the strength in every patch I explored. It was almost enough to want to flick on the light so I could see every inch of him.

He slid in further, causing me to gasp at the pressure. "Let me know if it hurts."

Ahh. The sweet intrusion burned a little, but it also felt incredible.

Our tongues mated, both of us desperate for the intimacy. He pushed further inside of me, and I was almost convinced I might split in two before I could sheath him completely. Once he was deeply rooted, filling me completely, I took a deep breath at the exquisite feeling.

"You all right?" He was breathless, holding himself in place.

I nodded and then involuntarily moved my hips. My body was way ahead of my mind.

"Go easy. I don't want to hurt you."

My body felt stretched, but I forced myself to relax. "I can't help it. You feel amazing."

"You do, too. We'll go slow until you get used to me, okay?"

He pulled out slightly and then back home again.

I couldn't see his face, but I could feel the restraint in his shoulders. I thrust my hips up the next time to meet his.

"Jesus," he hissed.

The fact that he was so turned on and yet restricting himself fueled my inner animal. The one who had been starved for this for two years. Or frankly, the animal who had always been hungry for it and hadn't known what I'd been missing. I arched up and felt his muscular arm move under the small of my back. He braced me in the optimal position to hit my tender spot.

"Mark—" Just like that, a white heat rolled over me, consuming me completely with its intensity, all the way from head to toes. I barely registered his movements as the after-shocks rocked my body. I may have even blacked out a bit because the next thing I knew he'd gone from being pressed against me to pulling out slowly.

"Did you?" I questioned.

He laughed. "Uh, yeah. I don't know how you missed the whole groaning like a wild animal and grunting out my orgasm inside of you."

I laughed at his description as he curled me into his side. Both our bodies were slick with perspiration and the smell of sex was heavy in the air. "I think I may have passed out and missed it."

"Good, because I'm hoping I'll be more focused on your climax before losing all control next time. Should've given you another one first."

I was incredulous that I'd had two. "Believe me when I say I'm not complaining."

"I need to get up for a minute and dispose of the condom."

"Right. Okay."

I felt him leave the bed. When the light of the bathroom shined briefly as he went inside, I quickly covered myself.

He returned shortly after and crawled back in, gathering me close. I savored the feel of him holding me in his arms while his whispered words came in my ear. "Don't worry. I'll leave by morning, but I want to hold you for a few minutes longer."

As if I'd ever argue with that.

CHAPTER EIGHT

I woke up quite alone. Pins of light shone through my blinds, which were now partially opened. Mark's side of the bed was cold, so he must have left before dawn as he'd promised.

Moving my legs, I felt the delicious reminder of last night. We might have only had sex the one time, but it was enough to ensure I'd be walking funny today.

I threw on a robe and went into the bathroom. Catching my reflection, I was immediately grateful he hadn't seen me in the light this morning. My hair looked like a family of rats had taken up residence while my makeup was smeared where it hadn't disappeared completely. And when I opened my robe to study my once perky breasts, I had to fight my worry over what Mark had thought last night.

Given the way his body had felt, I didn't need to see it to know it was flawless. Taking a deep breath, I forced myself to relax. This type of neurosis would eventually drive both of us insane. We were no-strings, friends, buddies—although if that limitation were true and we were truly only 'hooking up,' why had it been years since either of us had had sex, four for him and two for me?

After Tristan woke up and we had breakfast, I would need to run to the pharmacy. But since nothing said mother-of-the-year like dragging your toddler to the pharmacy for condoms, I immediately talked myself out of the trip. Wouldn't they be something the guy would take care of? I wasn't sure of condom protocol, but he'd been willing to go get them last night so I assumed he still felt that responsibility. If he was coming back, that was.

Good grief. I needed a break from my own thoughts.

After checking the monitor to ensure Tristan was still sleeping, I took a quick shower and dressed. When I went out into the kitchen, I found a few things lined up on my countertop. Starting at the post-it marked with a number one and a white bag next to it, I read: "*Breakfast*"

Inside the bag were fresh croissants and muffins.

The second note had my heart beating faster: "*Put me in your nightstand*"

I dug in the bag to find a box of condoms, mega size. Clearly, the darkness and the beer hadn't made up the size illusion.

I couldn't believe he'd been so thoughtful and quickly typed out a text.

"*The bags were very thoughtful. Thank you.*"

"*I don't know about condoms being thoughtful, but you're welcome.*"

Biting my lip, I typed out the next sentence before I could overthink it.

"*Will I see you tonight?*"

"*I thought your mom was coming in from out of town?*"

Cluck. She was. And I'd totally forgot about it.

"*She is, but evidently I have sex brain and forgot.*"

"*I'll take that as a compliment.*"

I smiled at his response even though it didn't hint at when I'd see him again.

The rest of my Friday was a blur. Tristan and I went

grocery shopping and then, during nap time, I did housework in preparation for my mother's visit. There was something cathartic about the cleaning process. It cleared my mind so I only thought about last night twice a minute instead of ten times.

My mother was so excited about my invitation to New York City for Catherine's party that she tried to convince me to stay the night there on Saturday. It was tempting, but I wasn't about to shell out three hundred dollars for a hotel room I couldn't afford. And I certainly wouldn't rely on the generosity of my friends. It was bad enough Haylee had already bought my train ticket and refused reimbursement for it.

At the local trunk-or-treat, Tristan was thrilled to fill his little bucket with candy. Following that and getting him settled in with Grandma for the evening, I traveled into New York with Josh, Haylee and their daughter, Abby. I kept myself from asking where Mark was, but wondered if I would, in fact, see him at the party.

Catherine had rented out a beautiful restaurant in an area called Tribeca and hired a DJ. Everyone was dressed in costume and the drinks were flowing.

I found my gaze scanning the room for a familiar face. Finally finding my target, I smiled. Of course, he was dressed as Superman. And he looked gorgeous.

I'd donned a snow fairy costume with wings and had my long hair down in curls. It wasn't as elaborate as some of the other getups, but it was safe and easy to pull off.

I'd wondered if it would be awkward to see him again, considering the whole sex thing two nights ago, but it turned out much worse than awkward. He was avoiding me. I tried to make eye contact, stealing glances his way, but he chose to keep his distance, even excusing himself from a group once I walked up. I contemplated confronting him, but ultimately chickened out. I could take a hint, especially one spelled out in neon lights. He wasn't interested in seeking me out this evening. At least not in front of others.

If I hadn't already decided to go home early in order to kiss Tristan good night, Mark ignoring me at the party made it an even easier decision. After changing into jeans and a T-shirt, I found a cab right outside the building and headed for the train station about ten o'clock.

I didn't know what I'd anticipated, but Mark's behavior hurt. Of course, having expectations that he might treat me differently after one night of sex was unfair. But I couldn't help remembering how my ex used to be embarrassed to be seen with me. The old insecurity crept up. I shouldn't be surprised Mark wouldn't want his friends to know about the two of us. They were all sophisticated, worldly, and enjoyed a lifestyle where traveling to New York for a party was no big deal. I was just a small-town girl gawking at the lights and bustle of Times Square through the cab window.

Damn, I was doing the very thing Mark had told me I'd done with Chad. Mentally listing out the ways I wasn't worthy. Maybe it was finally time for me to stop making excuses and call for an appointment with Dr. Mac.

I climbed aboard the Amtrak train feeling more than ready to go home. The trip would take a little over two hours, but I had a book to read and would get to check on my sleeping boy before falling into bed.

Mark's name flashed up on my phone as the train pulled out of the station. I hesitated but then decided to answer.

"Hey."

"Hey. Is everything okay with Tristan? Brian said you headed up early."

Although it did something to my heart that he expressed concern, I had to wonder why he cared. "Yes, he's good. He's already in bed. I just—It's not easy for me to be away from him."

"I wish you would've told me. I could've gone with you."

"Guess I must've missed the opportunity during all the conversations we had." It was more aggressive than passive, but I couldn't help myself.

"I didn't—I mean I couldn't—"

"It's okay. I get it."

"No, you don't. Shit. I wish I would've left with you."

"Your friends probably would've noticed you missing."

"I had no clue how to act in front of them tonight. But avoiding you was shitty, and I'm sorry.

"I wasn't sure how to act, either, but you still could've said hello."

"You're right. I fucked up. And again, I apologize."

I wasn't completely over it, but I recognized some of my anger had to do with my own past issues regarding my ex. "Accepted, so long as you don't get weird again."

"Promise I won't. Is that why you left?"

"Partially. But mostly it's because I like to kiss my baby before I go to bed each night. I'm certain my neurosis is unhealthy, but it's hard for me to spend the night away from him." There was no way I wanted to mention the cost of the hotel as being a factor too.

"You're not neurotic. You're a good mom who misses her son."

Damn, the man knew how to give a compliment. So much so, I had to clear the emotion from my throat. "Thanks for saying that. Uh, I'd better go before I lose the connection."

"Yeah. Okay. I'll hopefully see you in a couple of days?"

"Sure. Maybe after my mom heads back."

"Okay. Safe travels, Jules."

MY MOM LEFT ON MONDAY. By Tuesday afternoon Mark texted

asking if he could bring by Chinese for dinner. Once I agreed, he asked for my order.

I tried to talk myself out of feeling anxious about seeing him again. But by the time he knocked, butterflies were going bonkers in my stomach.

"Hi." Sounding like I had just run five miles, I opened the door.

"Hi." He bestowed a slow, lazy smile before looking behind me. "Hey, Tristan, how are you, my man? High five."

I loved how he was so natural and was sincerely excited to spend time with my son.

"Book, book," Tristan insisted, causing Mark to laugh.

He handed me a take-out bag. "Here's the food. I'm fine reading to him if you want to dish it up."

"Uh, yeah, sure." I took the bag into the kitchen and peered out at them on the couch. Tristan was on Mark's lap while he happily read to him. We had done this countless times over the last couple weeks, so why was I about to hyperventilate about it tonight?

Because he had the power to hurt me, as demonstrated by Catherine's party. But it was much worse than that. Tristan was becoming fond of and growing attached to him. This was a level for which I was unprepared as I wasn't sure how to keep things casual. Not that I was an expert, but I was reasonably certain reading Llama Llama books to my son didn't fit the definition of no-strings-attached sex.

I turned away and put my elbows on the counter, trying to get a grip. When I felt his hands wrap around me from the back, I jumped.

"Don't overthink it. This is no different than any other time we've had dinner and spent time together. Okay?"

I turned and buried my face in his chest so he couldn't see how anxious I was.

"Deep breaths, Jules. We may have slept together, but we're

still friends. And I'm hanging out with you because I happen to like, like you, and I'm spending time with Tristan because he is the coolest little kid I know."

I smiled at his remembrance of our *double like* conversation when I'd been sick.

"You okay?"

I nodded, starting to feel better.

"And again, I'm sorry about the Halloween party. I realize it sounds lame, but I mean it sincerely. I won't ever ignore you again."

Maybe the definition of what we were doing was cloudy, but we'd started as friends. I certainly didn't want to end that nor our newfound physical relationship. "It's okay. I was probably oversensitive. And I'm a little crazy. You know that, right?"

But instead of laughing like I thought he would, he pulled back and narrowed his eyes. "I'm about to tie you to the bed and leave you there until you say something nice about yourself."

"Is it bad that turns me on?"

He quirked a brow and then laughed. "Not for me. Now, let's eat dinner and be normal until I take you into your dark bedroom and have my way with you again."

My mind went straight to the fantasy reel of what that would entail.

"Keep looking at me like that, and I'm going to fast-forward the clock to Tristan's bedtime," he whispered in my ear, giving it a nibble to drive the point home.

"How much longer until eight o'clock?" A pinch of guilt hit me even as the question left my lips. I'd never put someone before my son. But all of a sudden I was anxious to get Tristan to bed in order to have some adult time.

"We have an hour. Come on, let's eat."

The three of us sat down at the table where Tristan happily ate fried rice from his high chair, and Mark and I acted as we always did at dinner, with the exception of a lingering touch here or an innuendo there.

"How's the math class coming along?"

I frowned, not liking the reminder. "Not great. English is better."

"Math wasn't my favorite subject, either."

But I bet he'd been better at it than I was. "I'll figure it out." Or more likely I'd drop the class after my first exam next week. It wasn't looking good.

"Is it Tristan's bath night tonight?"

I was glad he changed the subject and shook my head. "Nope, we had bath time earlier. Once he's done eating, I only need to change him and read him a book."

Lucky for me, he was an easy child to put to bed. I truly enjoyed our time cuddling in the rocking chair where I read him a book and then hummed a lullaby. After kissing his forehead, I laid him down in his crib. Lastly, I covered him with his small blanket, something that would inevitably find itself wadded in the corner by morning. But it gave me some peace that he was warm enough for the moment.

Shifting my gaze toward the bedroom door, I saw Mark watching me with a tender expression on his face. My panic struck again. I was being irrational; no one wanted to take away this time I had with Tristan. Besides, this wasn't some interloper. This was my friend, my lover now, but still my friend.

As if sensing my mood, he took my hand and waited while I shut the door softly. "I didn't mean to intrude. I heard you humming and wanted to see you. You're an amazing mom, Juliette."

Once again, his compliment floored me.

"I didn't mind. It simply took me off guard, and thank you. Sometimes I wonder if it will be enough for him, just a mom and not a father. I know, I know: I'm voicing another insecurity, so I'll shut up."

He took both my hands and pulled me onto the sofa and into his lap.

"I think it's a real fear of every parent to wonder if they are doing enough. I imagine that since you're a single mom doing it all, your fear is double. For that insecurity, you get a pass. I don't think any parent out there would ever be completely confident about everything. Hell, even Josh, who isn't normally a worrier, can turn into basket case when it comes to little Abby."

"I'm glad I'm not the only one, then. So, I think he's out," I hinted, taking a glance at the monitor one last time.

Just like that, he was on me.

"Should we move to the bedroom?"

His hands found their way under my sweatshirt and were quickly unfastening my bra. "What if we turned on a light this time?"

I shook my head. "I'm just— I'm not ready. Although if you want to take off your shirt here, I wouldn't mind seeing you in the light."

He leaned back, a smirk on his face. "Tell you what. How about if you show me something, then I'll show you something? I'll take off my shirt, and you take off yours."

I contemplated. "How about your shirt for my pants?" At least my sweatshirt would cover my stomach and chest until we were in the dark.

"I'll agree, for now. But you're going to have to give it up sometime. You're too beautiful to keep hiding."

I was about to scoff but stopped, realizing he was waiting for me to do just that.

"Progress. I'm glad you didn't say out loud what you were thinking. Okay, off with your pants, woman."

I giggled while he made short work out of stripping off my leggings.

"And now it's your turn." I was eager to see him but sighed

when his undressing revealed he still had on a T-shirt under-neath. "Everything off."

He shook his head. "You still have panties on, so it's only fair."

At least the tight white T-shirt showcased his muscled biceps and strong forearms.

"Uh, you're staring."

Of course I was. He was built, with broad shoulders and defined arms. And that was with the T-shirt on. "Mark, you're really hot."

He blushed ten shades of red, but managed an adorable smile which brought out seldom-seen dimples. God, I was a sucker for dimples.

"I'm glad you like what you see. Now, let me see those delectable legs of yours."

I giggled while I was placed on the sofa.

He ran his hands up and down my calves and then onto my thighs, and then his face was in my—

"Whoa there, that wasn't part of the deal." I was half dizzy with need, almost paralyzed with lust, but fear was the over-riding emotion. I was not ready for him to be up and personal with my business in the full light.

"All right. Into the dark."

He lifted me up and took me into the bedroom, once again shutting the blinds. After that, he thoughtfully went back out for the monitor. "I'm facing this away from us, but we can still hear him. Okay?"

Insecurity instantly hit me when he climbed into the bed alongside me. "You don't think it's wrong to, you know, have you over here to have sex with him sleeping in the other room?"

"How do you think siblings are conceived? I get that it's different with me not being his father, but it's not as though you have a parade of men coming through here. Or did I miss some-thing?" He sat up, pretending to look around.

I giggled, grateful he understood enough about the guilt of single motherhood and sex to make it lighthearted. "No, you didn't. And I need to stop worrying about stuff like that."

"Yes, you do. But I think it's only natural. Now, where was I?" He traveled south once again, intent on his target.

Oh, no, I couldn't. "I can't. I just— I don't think you'll enjoy it. I mean you don't have to—" My eyes were still adjusting to the dark, but I felt the frustration rolling off him by the sudden tenseness in his muscles.

"I wouldn't do it unless I wanted to. I need to taste you, Jules."

How could I say no? But my insecurities were stronger than my lust. "It's just that, maybe some other time. I think something may be wrong with me down there where it makes it unappealing."

"Is that what your ex told you?" His voice was low, exasperation evident in his tone.

I swallowed hard, trying my best not to break down in tears. I was broken, insecure, and completely insane to have thought I was ready for a physical relationship. And I was a big ole chicken who wasn't ready to deal with these emotions in front of someone. "Maybe you should go."

He hesitated. "I'm only trying to understand, not pressure you."

"I believe you, but I think maybe this was a mistake." The words tasted bitter on my tongue.

He sighed, but then got up and walked out without another word.

Once I heard the front door close, my tears started falling, fast and furious. Next came the sobbing. It had been years since I'd let my emotions overwhelm me, but this seemed to be my breaking point. I buried my head in my pillow, stifling the noise and thinking what an idiot I was. I was letting my toxic relationship with my soon-to-be ex ruin any chance I might have with a good man. Or maybe it was self-sabotage. I was ensuring I ended something I didn't think I deserved. There I went again with the biggest turn off: self-doubt. The idea instigated another round of sobs.

I didn't notice Mark come back in until a hand stroked my hair. I sat up, startled until I saw who it was.

The light pouring in from the living room showed his tight grimace.

"I'm sorry," I managed to blubber and watched his face soften.

"Jules, baby, please don't cry or apologize. I'm the one who needs to say I'm sorry. I shouldn't have pushed."

"You weren't. You were only trying to understand. But you shouldn't have to deal with anyone who has all my issues."

"We all have issues. Now come here and stop talking." He gathered me up and snuggled me into the middle of the bed with my head propped on his hard chest until my tears subsided.

Finally, in the quiet, he spoke. "You know you can tell me anything. I want to be here for you."

I swallowed hard. "I have no idea where to start."

"How about with how you and Tristan's father met?"

I hesitated, but then realized this was a man who'd already witnessed my humiliation on numerous occasions and had never judged. "We met sophomore year in high school and dated until graduation. Got married at nineteen."

"What was it like back then? Were you happy?"

It's funny how those memories got harder to recall. "Yeah, we were. We were young, but we were becoming adults together. I started working at Singer Advertising, put Rob through college, and then afterwards he started with the police department."

"When did it change?"

"About five years into the job, when he injured his back during a training exercise. It was as though a switch flipped. Over the next year he became depressed, moody, and was taking way too many painkillers. We'd planned to start having kids, but it wasn't happening, probably because we weren't exactly having a lot of sex by then. But when he got a little drunk at a holiday party, that night I got pregnant."

Mark's hand rubbed my back, which encouraged me to keep opening up to him. "Was he happy about it?"

I didn't mince words. "Not at all. My joy about finally becoming pregnant only threw him deeper into this nasty mood. I'd hoped he'd come around after the ultrasound photo, but he didn't. Then he made up excuses not to go to any appointments. At that point, I pleaded with him to go for counseling, but he refused. He would no longer touch me. At all. I'd gained over fifty pounds with my pregnancy, which was too much—I mean, even the doctors said so. I think I turned to food while my marriage went to crap. Anyhow, he constantly made comments."

"What kind of comments?"

"Does it matter?" I felt his arms tighten around me, which eased my vulnerability.

"It does to me."

I'd never voiced my humiliation to another soul. "He would follow me around the house oinking at me. Call me fat, criticize every bit of food I put in my mouth, and say he was embarrassed to be seen with me in public."

My confession made the tension practically radiate from him.

"Don't get upset on my behalf. The truth is I put up with it longer than I should have."

"And after Tristan was born?"

"Although I lost forty of the fifty pounds, he told me that my body was stretched out and repulsive. I initiated sex one time, and he said he was no longer attracted to me. As for going down on me, he said after a baby came out of there, well, he wanted nothing to do with that particular act."

"Jesus."

"He wouldn't hold Tristan, either. He'd say a newborn was

too fragile or he was too nervous, but the truth was he didn't want to. Not even as Tristan got older. Instead, Rob was convinced I'd chosen the baby over him. He accused me of loving Tristan more than him."

"He was jealous of his own baby son?"

"All the time. After realizing it wasn't getting better, I told him I couldn't live that way anymore. Then he went out one night and didn't come home. But the next day he's all apologies. Tells me he'll start going to individual counseling. Says he's committed to working on things. That it's him and his injury, not me, blah, blah."

"What happened?"

"My guess is he met the girlfriend. At that point, he still wouldn't touch me, but he said he didn't want to lose me, either. More like he didn't want to lose my paycheck and have to pony up child support if we split."

"Did things change?"

"No. He continued to make digs, but I'd gotten so used to the 'new normal' I hardly noticed anymore. My self-esteem was in shreds. Looking back, I'm grateful we didn't sleep together if he was having sex with someone else. We were in that place for eighteen months. He'd be mean to me, I'd love him a little less, and then he'd beg me to give him another chance. It was an unhealthy cycle, getting worse by the day, but I didn't recognize it at the time. In addition to being sleep deprived, overwhelmed with a baby, and working full time, I guess I couldn't believe the man I'd fallen in love with at sixteen could change so drastically. I talked myself into believing it was the pills or the pain he was in. That it was a phase I kept hoping would end."

"He was verbally abusive to you."

I expelled a shaky breath. "I understand that now. But at the time, I truly thought if I could lose the baby weight, do more around the house, make him happy, he'd change back into the man I'd married."

"That wasn't on you. No matter what else you believe, I hope you know this was his problem. Not yours."

I nodded, getting there slowly but surely.

"What was the breaking point?"

I recalled the day with a shiver. "When I walked in on him screaming at Tristan. I was in the shower when Tristan started calling out for me. Rob was in such a rage that he'd been woken up. I knew in that moment I was done. How could I possibly stay married to a man who would flip his switch on a baby? I couldn't even trust him around our child."

I realized Mark was clenching his fists.

"Later that day, I unloaded on Brian what had happened, telling him I thought Rob was cheating on me and abusing prescription drugs. Brian encouraged me to go down and visit my sister in Florida. While I was there, he helped me hire a private investigator since I was looking for leverage to ensure I get full custody. A few weeks later, I filed for separation, and my PI turned over evidence to the police internal affairs about Rob's suspected drug use. What I hadn't guessed was that the internal affairs investigation would reveal Rob had also become a dirty cop. Here I'd thought the biggest issue was our divorce and his prescription drug habit. It turned out it was so much bigger. Much more serious."

I stayed quiet until Mark finally spoke. "Thank you for sharing all of that with me."

"Thank you for listening." Then because I couldn't help it, I added, "I'm not proud of who I became during my marriage or that I put it up with it for so long. I wouldn't blame you if you wanted to run far, far away."

He cupped my face and kissed me softly. "Not happening."

I shook my head, hardly believing that after everything I'd told him he was still here holding me. "Maybe it's you who's crazy, then."

"Who says crazy is a bad thing? We both have baggage."

"I don't know. You seem pretty close to perfect."

"I think everyone develops a way of hiding their pain. I've had a lot longer than you to get better at it."

"Sounds like it's your turn to spill it."

"Someday. But not tonight. I think we've reached our quota for the heavy stuff."

Although I was genuinely curious about his past, I knew it was very different from mine. Tragically losing someone you love when on the brink of starting a life together was nothing like putting up with a marriage turned bad. I wasn't sure how to reconcile that difference.

In an effort to change the mood to happier things, I burrowed my face in the crook of his neck. Realizing I had free license to act upon my naughty thoughts, I sucked lightly there and then kissed his delicious skin.

He breathed in sharply. "Jules, you know I'd never hurt you, right?"

I cupped his face and slipped off his glasses. The hall light pouring in gave me my first good look at him without them. In his eyes was the undeniable truth of his words.

"I want to believe you."

CHAPTER NINE

*M*ark was gone again when I woke up. He'd made love to me twice last night, proving definitively that he was a man unafraid to show his emotions through physical touch. Most importantly though, he hadn't pushed beyond my limitation of still needing the lights off.

And as after our first night together, he left mystery bags on my kitchen counter. I marveled at the fact that he'd not only gotten up early enough to leave before dawn, but had also come back to leave his thoughtful purchases. Intrigued, I moved first to the coffee cup and smiled at the Post-it: ***"Drink me. I know you're tired."***

Item number two was a brown bag with bagels and cream cheese. Also included were two containers of fresh fruit. I knew he'd gotten them mainly for Tristan, which made the gesture even sweeter. ***"Enjoy your breakfast"*** is what the note said.

Finally the third item was a rosebud and **"You're beautiful."**

Sex without strings just became a whole lot stringy-er, and I didn't mind one bit.

I lifted the flower to my nose and inhaled deeply. Maybe this was karma's way of giving me a good man this time around. The problem was the doubts which immediately followed. I wondered what in the world had him settling for a single mom with a mere high school education and stretch marks.

Taking a deep breath, I tried to shut up my inner critic. Pesky bitch was determined to bring me down. Damn, another dollar in the swear jar. Shit. Two more. Crap. Now three. Wait, internal cursing didn't count. Whew.

I texted him quickly.

"You're amazing and I don't mean just in bed."

I regretted the message the minute I sent it, overthinking my attempt at being funny, but then I shrugged. Hell, Mark had already been exposed to my madness in all its glory. If I couldn't be myself with him, of all people, then who could I be real with?

His response made me smile. *"I look forward to expanding upon that compliment tonight."*

His nerdy reply had me grinning.

———

LATER THAT NIGHT, as I stirred the chili I'd made in the Crock-pot, I waited for the knock on the door. I'd traded in my usual sweats for skinny jeans and had put on a cute top instead of a hoodie. And maybe I'd done more than merely swipe my lips with Chap Stick and put up my hair in a ponytail. I wanted to look somewhat pretty for Mark.

But instead of the knock, my phone buzzed with his number. "Hi, there. You running late?" I asked.

His audible sigh answered my question before his words did. "I wish. Instead, I'm stuck down in New York and heading with Josh to LA tomorrow morning."

"Oh." Even in the one word, I was unable to hide my disappointment.

"Sorry, Jules."

"No, don't be. I mean I am, too, but it's work, and I understand." I did. However, I was still wishing he was here. But he had an important job.

"Most likely I won't be back until late Friday. We could do something then."

"Actually, Brian called. He and Sasha will be in town for the weekend starting on Friday."

"Good grief. Don't tell me it's another party or charity event? I swear, it's something every weekend these days."

"Um, it's my thirtieth birthday, so everyone is taking me out on Saturday night. I told them they didn't have to, especially since they were up just last weekend for Catherine's party. But they were insistent."

It was true. I hadn't wanted the fuss, but Brian and Sasha wouldn't take no for an answer. Truth be told, I was happy to have a reason to celebrate. But evidently Mark wasn't so keen on these social gatherings.

In response, I heard a loud clunk on the other side of the line.

"Are you there? What was that noise?"

"That was the sound of me beating my phone against my head as I cringe. I didn't mean to be a complete asshole about your birthday celebration."

I laughed. "It's not as though you knew. And I have to admit this crowd does seem to have a lot of parties and functions going on."

"I shouldn't complain. It gets me out of the house. Is Saturday your party?"

"It's not so much a party as they're taking me out for dinner. I think Haylee mentioned she was going to ask if you wanted to come."

"Oh. Yeah. Sure."

Those three words coupled with his initial reaction didn't exactly exude excitement. "If you don't want to come, that's fine, too. Especially if it's awkward." The last thing I wanted was a repeat performance of the avoidance he'd practiced at Catherine's party.

"It won't be. Not this time. I mean, there's no reason it would be."

Was he trying to convince me or himself? "Nope. No reason except maybe that you were deep inside of me last night, and we haven't done the social thing in front of our friends yet. At least, not successfully. Are we telling them?"

"Christ," he hissed.

I hurriedly answered my question for him. "No, no of course we aren't. I wasn't suggesting we do." Even if I was slightly disappointed he wouldn't want to, I had to remind myself that it had been my decision to make this a sex-in-the-dark non-relationship.

His laughter took me off guard. "I was only cursing because you made me hard by reminding me of last night."

"Oh."

"And I wouldn't miss your birthday night. But as for the other, I think it's best to keep it between us for now. Don't you?"

"Sure. So long as you figure out a way to sneak into my bed that night. I am the birthday girl, after all."

He chuckled. "And what kind of birthday present are you after?"

My heart fluttered just thinking about him. "Tall with dark hair, sexy glasses, and a dirty mouth?"

"Call me tonight after you put Tristan to bed, and I'll give you a preview."

"Phone sex?"

"You started it. Wish I was there. And Jules?"

"Yeah."

"Make sure you have new batteries in your vibrator."

Holy crap. At this rate I wouldn't need it. His words alone made me want to combust.

BY THE TIME I finished dinner, bathed Tristan, and put him to bed, I was letting nerves get the better of me. What if I didn't know what to say? What if I blurted out all sorts of inappropriate non-sexy stuff, something I'd been known to do? I'd never attempted phone sex in my life. Although apparently I'd made him hard earlier without even trying. Perhaps, maybe, I had hope.

Mark picked up on the first ring. "Hi." His voice was husky, the one simple word full of need.

"Hi."

"Are you in bed?"

I wasn't, but moved quickly to get there. "I am now." And, embarrassingly, I was out of breath from the effort.

"Good. Are all your clothes off?"

Crap. The man was determined to have me thinking about joining the gym if we kept this up. "Uh, getting there." Note to self: call him next time after I was naked in bed.

He didn't hide his amusement. "Take your time."

Ugh. I'd already failed. "I, um... Okay, I'm now naked."

"Do you have your vibrator?"

"Fuck-a-Cluck."

Now he was full on chuckling, making my giggles well up. "You're going to owe some more money in the jar."

"Yep. If you couldn't tell, this is my first time. Sorry."

"Don't apologize. It's mine, too. And if you could see the smile on my face right now after hearing your laughter, you'd know this is the highlight of my day."

Wow. "That's really sweet. Now then, I'm in my room, naked, with a vibrator in my hand. And it does, in fact, have new batteries. Any ideas what we should do next?"

"Move your hand down and touch your pussy. Tell me if your slit is wet."

Damn. He wasn't messing around, and he sure as heck didn't sound like he was new at this. I moved my hand down, running a finger between my lips. "I am so wet."

"Good. Now, as far as your birthday night is concerned, how do you feel about your ass?"

"Pardon?"

He laughed at the fact that my voice had gone up an octave. "Are you self-conscious about it?"

"No. Probably because I can't see it, but I think it's okay."

"Baby, your ass, especially in those leggings you wear, is spectacular."

"Oh. So why are we having a conversation about it?" He couldn't possibly think he could fit there. Did he?

"Because I've had a fantasy of taking you from behind. With the lights on. If you're game."

Hm. I liked his way of thinking. A lot. "And if I show you my ass, what will you show me in return?"

His voice was laced with humor. "Birthday girl's choice."

"That's a no-brainer. And I'll expect a bow on it."

His chuckle filled my ears. "If you put it there with your mouth, I'll be happy to wear one."

"That has possibilities." And because I wasn't good at hiding my thoughts once they popped into my head, I added, "I hope this doesn't freak you out, but I miss you."

"It doesn't. Especially since I miss you, too."

"I totally killed the sex talk mood, didn't I?"

"Not possible. If anything, I only wish I was there even more now."

"Me, too. What's next with this phone sex thing? Should I Google something?"

"I don't recommend that. How about instead you put me on speakerphone, and I do the talking?"

I lay back, getting comfortable and very content to hear his sexy voice. "I do love it when you talk dirty."

"Good. Open those gorgeous legs of yours and find your clit. Imagine it's my fingers touching you."

I was back to being turned on, finding a rhythm with my fingers.

"At some point it's going to be my tongue touching you there. My beard stubble rubbing against the inside of your thighs as you come all over my face."

Oh, God. My pace increased along with my staggered breaths.

"But on your birthday night, you're going to bend over on the bed showing me your ass, letting me slide into your drenched pussy until my hips are pressed up against you. Then I'll pull out slowly and slam back into you deep."

I was almost there, on the precipice of my orgasm, until the unmistakable voice of my son broke through. "Mama. Mama."

"Is that Tristan?"

I couldn't help groaning. The timing couldn't be worse. "Um, yeah. Give it a minute. Maybe he's only dreaming." I grabbed the monitor, hoping to see him back fast asleep. Instead, he was standing in his crib, waiting.

"Maaaaaaammmmmmaaaaa"

"Um, I need to go check on him. He's standing up."

There was a smile in Mark's voice. "Make sure you put some clothes on first."

Right. Shit. I scrambled into my sweatpants, pulled a sweatshirt over my head, and paused. "Hold, please." I used my office voice, causing him to laugh.

I made a quick detour to wash my hands—because masturbation and mommy-mode did not mix—and then walked to Tristan's room. I tried not to think of the love of my life as a total cock block. Bad, bad mommy.

"What's wrong, baby?" I asked, opening his door.

He stood in the corner waiting on me. "I wet."

I felt his PJs and sighed. They were indeed soaked. "Aww, you sure are. Straight through the diaper."

Okay. I needed to get him cleaned up and then change the bed. None of which was conducive to phone sex with Mark on hold in the other room.

Picking up my son, I placed him on his changing table and stripped him of his clothes, afterward running a wipe over his skin to get him at least semi-cleanish. I then put him into a dry diaper before carrying him into my room and onto the bed. One second too late, I realized the vibrator was still sitting in the middle of everything.

Mother-of-the-year material right here.

I scooped it up quickly, put it into the drawer, and huffed out a breath. "Mark. Uh, I'm going to need a raincheck. I'm sorry. He was soaked through. Although I changed him, I still need to put clean sheets on his bed."

"Don't apologize."

"Mark, Mark." Tristan recognized his voice and grabbed for the phone.

"Hey, Tristan. How are you?"

From phone sex to talking to a toddler. I let Tristan babble on for a bit but then intervened. "Okay, baby. Say goodnight. I've gotta change your bed, and you need to go back to sleep."

"'Night 'night."

"'Night, buddy."

"Good night, Mark."

"'Night, Jules."

If I'd needed a reminder of the order of my life, this was it. First mom, then everything else.

CHAPTER TEN

oday I was officially thirty years old. Honestly, I was okay with the milestone birthday. Of course, it helped that I had amazing girlfriends who'd decided to take me shopping that morning. They insisted on a new outfit for tonight's festivities.

Now, taking a deep breath, I peered at myself in my bedroom mirror and had to blurt out, "Holy shit." I looked, well, sexy in the fitted black dress with the bottom slightly flared. The knee-high, black silk stockings had seemed silly when Haylee had suggested them, but paired with the gorgeous high-heeled ankle boots and this dress, they gave an effect that was both sexy and sophisticated. Two words I never would have associated with myself.

Sasha had done my makeup, playing up my eyes and making my lips appear full and pouty. My still-getting-used-to-being-a-brunette hair had been straightened and was silky down my back.

Sasha smiled. "Told you. You look smoking."

My gaze finally left my reflection and met hers. "I'll kill myself in these boots."

She shook her head. "Minimal walking tonight as the limo will drop us off curbside, both at the restaurant and the club."

Right. I could do that. Maybe. After all, these women did it daily. I'd always coveted their shoes but never could quite get the hang of heels. Even with my living room practice round. Still, glancing back at my image in the mirror, I couldn't wait until Mark saw me dressed like this.

Later, I gave a last kiss to Tristan and thanked Josh's mother for agreeing to babysit both kids tonight while she was in town for the weekend. Then I joined my friends downstairs to get into a limo. I wobbled a bit as I stepped toward the waiting car but recovered with the help of Sasha's arm.

"It gets easier the more you relax and drink something. The boys are already at the restaurant, by the way. So we'll meet them there."

The moment I stepped into the beautiful steakhouse, my heart started beating double time at the thought of seeing Mark. The floors were a dark wood and the lighting chic and modern. I barely noticed, though, instead scanning the room for him as we passed tables on our way toward the back of the restaurant.

His reaction was worth the wait. I watched his eyes skim over the group of us walking toward the table, only to back up and widen upon realizing I was amongst the ladies. Thankfully, the lighting was dim and no one seemed to notice the blush I knew was creeping up my face, put there by his heated gaze.

Of course, that all changed once Brian peeled his eyes away from his fiancée long enough to do a double take on me.

"Holy shit, Juliette, is that you?"

So much for not being a center of attention. Five sets of eyes focused on me. Sasha appeared proud and took my hand, twirling me around. "She looks great, right?"

Brian, the most charming man I'd ever met, didn't miss a beat. "You look beautiful. You know, for a thirty-year-old."

His sarcastic side was the reason we remained such good friends.

I scoffed. "Ha ha. Have I told you lately how much I miss your sarcasm-laced compliments?"

He laughed and gave me a hug. "Not as much as I've missed yours."

I'd wondered as the night progressed how Mark would act around me in a group setting and if he would ignore me. But I was pleasantly surprised when he was friendly without being overtly obvious that something was going on between us. I was even more pleased when I received his text at the dinner table.

"You look stunning."

I typed back, *"Thank you. I was excited to see you tonight."*

"I've been fantasizing about you all week."

He wasn't the only one who'd been fantasizing, but Haylee snapped me out of typing a response. "That's quite a smile. Who are you texting?"

"Oh, it was my mom wishing me happy birthday. She sent me a photo of myself when I was Tristan's age." I quickly flipped to her earlier text to flash the picture. My ability to recover quickly made me grateful, but I didn't dare make eye contact with Mark.

After a delicious dinner, we made our way to a club down-town. I tried not to gape, but it was surreal to walk into a trendy club through the VIP doors while a line of people snaked around the block waiting to gain entrance. This might not ever be my scene, but for one night I could certainly appreciate it.

Pulsing music hit me before I had a chance to take in the large bar which seemed to glow in the blueness of the room. My gaze was pulled in every direction and my senses overloaded. Girls danced on platforms above a checkerboard-looking glass dance floor whose squares lit different colors every few seconds. I was so awestruck that it took Sasha to get me moving again.

"Come on. We reserved a table upstairs."

The second level of the club was less noisy and separated into different seating areas. A hostess in a barely-there skirt led us to ours, which consisted of two large plush sofas and a couple of chairs surrounding a table already stocked with carafes of juices and a bottle each of Grey Goose and Patron. Clearly, Sasha and Haylee didn't mess around when it came to a night out.

Each of us ladies took seats on the leather couches and settled into small talk while the men went to the restroom. "I thought only girls went in groups to the bathroom."

Both ladies laughed, and Haylee said, "Josh is calling his mom to check on the kids. I'd roll my eyes, but honestly, I have to keep myself from doing it, too."

I held up my phone. "I already texted her from the limo. It was really nice of her to offer to watch Tristan along with Abby, and sometimes I need to assure myself he's not throwing a mega tantrum." She'd replied that he was an angel. "Unfortunately, mommy-mode doesn't turn off very easily."

Over the next hour we drank and laughed. I watched Sasha and Brian dance out on the main floor. Then, while Haylee and Josh were completely absorbed in one another on the far side of the couch, Mark slid in next to me. Drink in hand, he nonchalantly leaned in closer, as if I otherwise wouldn't be able to hear him over the noise.

"Your dress with the stockings are killing me."

Smiling, I tried to remain cool and keep my body from reacting to his words. "Oh, yeah?"

He shifted, evidently not unaffected. After glancing over at his friends, he took a deep breath. "Do you have any idea how much I want to fuck you right now?"

I uncrossed and recrossed my legs, letting my breath expel. The gesture caused just enough friction where I was throbbing to make me want more. "You should probably tell me in detail."

"I picture you going to the ladies' room, sliding off your panties."

"Lacy black thong." If he wanted a visual, he needed a good one.

"Christ."

"What would you do after I lost my thong?"

"Have you spread your legs for me, catch my first glimpse of your perfectly waxed pink pus—"

"Hey, guys, you want to stay longer or head out? I can always extend the limo's time." Brian's voice interrupted the effect of the dirty talk like splashing ice water.

I hadn't even noticed them come back to the table. But his question made me realize that the sooner we got home, the sooner Mark could finish his sentence. Trying not to appear too eager, I replied, "I'm good with leaving now."

Everyone else seemed to be in agreement.

We piled into the back of the car, stopping first at Brian and Sasha's hotel, a few blocks from my apartment building. As they got out of the limo, we agreed to meet for lunch tomorrow before they left town.

After dropping them off, Haylee spoke up. "Why don't you let Tristan stay overnight in our place? He's already sound asleep. That way you don't have to wake him."

It was a really sweet offer, but I'd never spent the entire night away from him.

"We'll call you once he wakes up in the morning. Besides, Josh's mom promised him Mickey Mouse pancakes tomorrow. She does this adorable thing with three circles to make his face."

It made sense. It was logical. Rationally, I knew he'd only be one floor away from me and staying with fantastic people. "Are you sure?"

Josh smiled. "Of course we are. My mom has already been gushing about how sweet Tristan is. And since Abby isn't old enough for Mickey Mouse pancakes, this gives her someone to impress with her breakfast-making talents."

"Okay. But if he wakes up or needs me—"

"We'll call. I promise," Haylee assured.

I bit down on the panic. I was being neurotic. It was healthy for him to be away from me one night. And I'd be right downstairs. Not unlike a house with two stories.

Once we arrived back, I said good night to Haylee and Josh and let myself into my apartment. I had to tamp down on the urge to go upstairs and get Tristan despite our recent agreement.

Mark's text came as a welcome distraction.

"Take off your lacy black thong and nothing else. Leave your door unlocked and wait for me in your bed with the lights on."

Damn. It really was the quiet ones, I mused. Upon meeting Mark Hines, I would not have guessed he was a dirty talker. Then again, I wouldn't have guessed I'd practically melt with every word, either.

When I entered my bedroom, I did as he asked, sliding the scrap of silk, already drenched, onto the floor. I'd just stepped out of it when I heard the door open.

Looking over my shoulder, I saw him standing there leaned against the frame of my bedroom door. All worries about being separated from my son evaporated.

"Hi, birthday girl."

I grinned. "Hi, yourself. Did you come bearing gifts?"

He smirked with a shrug. "I did, but I'm afraid there's no bow."

I loved his recollection of our teasing conversation from the other night. "I'm actually not much of a wrapping-paper-and-ribbons kind of girl. I like to get straight to the good stuff." I took a seat on the bed and lifted a brow, waiting.

"No arguments from me." He walked over and knelt down, removed his glasses, and leaned in for a kiss. There was no hesitancy, only the sweet luxury of finally being able to touch after waiting all evening.

My hands traveled down his arms, pulling him in closer and allowing the kiss to deepen. He was such an incredible kisser. Which almost distracted me from what I wanted most this evening.

Once Mark stood up, his waist at eye level, I set my hands to work on the task of unzipping his trousers.

"Impatient, are we?"

I nodded, watching as he helped me along with the reveal by hooking his fingers in his trousers. He pulled them down his hips, thumbs apparently grabbing his boxers at the same time because, in one swoop, there he was in all his glory. Thick, long, and protruding proudly, as if waiting for my praise.

I leaned forward, unable to keep myself from licking the pre-come that beaded on his tip.

He let out a shuddered breath. "This is your birthday, Jules."

"You're right. It is. And I want to taste you."

Suddenly he pulled back, grabbing something off the night-stand. "I, uh, need these." He grinned, slipping back on his glasses.

"Don't want to miss any details, huh?"

He shook his head and stepped forward to where I now sat up on the edge of the bed, reaching for him. I'd never been much of a giving-head kind of girl, but the thought of putting my mouth on this beautiful man was exciting. So was getting to see him in the light for the first time.

"Uh, Jules?"

I looked up and realized I'd probably been staring at it for a full minute.

His half-amused, half-aroused gaze settled on me.

"Sorry, it's just, well, it's a really great cock."

I. Did. Not. Just. Say. That.

His chuckle made me realize that yes, in fact, I had.

I slapped a hand over my mouth.

"Don't go covering your mouth now. It's only getting started."

Ha. The man had jokes. "Clearly, you've crossed into my land of the crazy. Sorry, you know I have this thing with filters or lack thereof—"

"Jules, put my cock in your mouth."

Turns out that was hard to do when you were grinning, but it didn't take long to manage because when I gripped his length and heard his gasp, all humor was replaced with unfiltered hunger.

Not wanting to wait a second longer, I leaned forward and again tasted the tip with my tongue, enjoying the rumble from low in his chest. Mouthing the crown, I sucked lightly, sliding up and down the hand which gripped him while the other hand moved to cup his balls. My lips moved down his length. I couldn't believe how velvety soft his skin was or that he was growing even larger in my hand.

Opening my mouth wider, I bobbed my head forward and took him as deep as I could. His muttered string of expletives made me revel. I might be out of practice, but he was far from complaining. Using my hand along with my mouth, I set a rhythm that took him to the back of my throat.

My eyes were starting to water from the effort, but I could feel him getting close. His fingers entwined in my hair; his gaze locked on mine. What I wouldn't give to see him completely naked.

"I'm close."

I doubled my efforts, watching him throw back his head and feeling him grasp my hair tighter while his thighs quivered.

"If you don't want me coming down your throat, I need you to stop."

As if I'd deny myself the taste of him. In an effort to show him I wasn't about to halt my efforts, I pulled him deeper, gripping his ass with both hands now. The first taste that hit my tongue was salty, but his moan had me anxious for every drop, especially since I now knew how much it turned him on.

After swallowing it down, I was shocked when he hauled me to my feet and kissed me deeply. After he pulled back, I had to ask. "I thought guys didn't kiss after, you know."

"I'm not sure about other men, but in this moment there isn't anything keeping me away from your lips."

How do you not grin when a man kisses you after a blow job because he can't help himself?

"Like that answer, do you?" He kissed down my neck, his hand making its way between my legs.

"Mm, it would be no fun to be dirty all alone."

He leaned back and chuckled. "You have no idea what you've just started. Get up onto your knees, gorgeous, in the center of the bed and show me that ass."

I moved quickly to do as I was told, my heart slamming in my chest with pure adrenaline. I refused to spare an insecure thought. My backside wasn't something I'd ever been self-conscious about. Besides, I was too unbelievably turned on to feel anxious.

I felt his weight on the bed and smelled his distinct scent of soap with aftershave. Then he touched me again. Feather light, he skimmed the exposed skin above my thigh-high stockings before one of his hands dove under my dress. There he found me wet and bare for him.

"I like to think you've been this way for me since you saw me in the restaurant. This pretty pussy waiting for me while we were eating dinner and then at the club."

"Yes," I whispered, unashamed in my desire for him.

He growled while flipping up my dress, exposing my entire backside to him.

To make it easier, I put my head down into the pillow and turned so I could still see him over my shoulder.

"This vision right here is what I've been thinking of all night. I wanted to throw you over my shoulder and bring you back here the minute I saw you in this dress."

I giggled at the thought. "That would've made quite the statement for our friends."

He inched one of his fingers inside of me slowly, as though he had all the time in the world. The gesture completely shut off any anxiety I might've felt about him seeing me in the light.

"You're so wet, but tight at the same time. Tell me how much you want me here, deep inside of you."

"I do. I want you to fuck me hard. Don't hold anything back." I could hardly believe the words had escaped my mouth.

"Jesus," he hissed, reaching for the nightstand and a condom.

I could see him frantically tearing the wrapper and putting it onto his hardened length. He'd definitely recovered from the first round.

Wasting no time once he had the condom on, he plunged into me on one stroke.

I gasped at the instant fullness.

"Shit. Are you okay? Please tell me I didn't hurt you." He was holding completely still.

"You didn't. Only took me by surprise. But in a good way." I inched forward and slammed back.

This time it was his turn to expel a harsh breath. His fingers gripped my hips before he began to move, holding nothing back in his thrusts.

I gritted my teeth, feeling on edge, and took my own hand to rub my clit, anxious for my orgasm.

"That's it. Play with yourself while I pound into you."

The sound of skin slapping filled the room along with our harsh breathing. Suddenly, he pulled out.

"Ahh, what are you doing?" I'd been so close.

His chuckle sounded in my ear as his fingers entered me, working my wetness. "Robbed you of an orgasm, did I?"

"Yes. I was almost there."

"I promise this will be worth it." Abruptly, he moved his fingers up, spreading the wetness to a place I'd never been touched.

My entire body shuddered with the anticipation.

"I want to play with your ass. Make you come harder than you ever have."

"'Kay." It was a lame response, but I could no longer talk. He'd just slid the first finger inside, gently penetrating my back hole. Then there was pressure as he pressed back inside of my pussy. He didn't let his finger stay where it was buried, but worked me in and out, the finger together with his cock.

"Oh God," I moaned, overwhelmed with the dual sensations.

"You like this? My fingers in your ass while I pump my cock in and out of you?"

"Yesss." I was close again to building.

"And do you like it when I talk dirty to you? Telling you what I'm doing to your gorgeous body?"

"Yesss." I was pushing back to meet his thrusts, biting my lip at the intensity of pleasure that threatened to overwhelm me.

"Touch yourself again. Come all over my cock. I want to feel it."

All it took was a swipe of my clit, and I was done for. Completely eviscerated from the heat overtaking my entire body. The electrical shock tingled clear down to my toes as I cried out with my climax. If it hadn't been for Mark's loud animal-like growl, I think I would've missed his orgasm completely.

"Wow," I said, feeling him pull out a minute later.

"Yeah. Wow. Give me a second."

As soon as his weight left the bed, I collapsed on my stomach, facing toward the bathroom where he'd retreated. I was too exhausted to care about the state of my remaining clothing or try to look remotely sexy when I watched him return with a washcloth in his hand.

He must've felt the same way, not caring about appearance, because the vision of him instantly had me laughing.

He stopped, giving me the adorable grin of his. "What's so funny?"

"You. You're Porky-pigging it."

"What in the world is that?" He moved onto the bed. I realized the washcloth was for me when he began intimately washing me.

"You still have your shirt on, but no pants. Like Porky the Pig. Sorry, random shit hits me at the most inappropriate times. But you know, if you want to take off your shirt, I'm game."

He smirked. "I think I need to keep something in reserve. Although if you want to show me that freshly waxed pussy of yours, we may be able to negotiate something."

He undid my boots, which until this moment I'd forgotten I was still wearing. Then he peeled down my stockings, one at a time.

"You're serious about the whole 'you show me yours and I'll show you mine.'"

His hands caressed up my legs, cupping my ass after he lay down beside me.

I flipped over onto my side, allowing me to see his face and meet his eyes.

"Absolutely. And we'll get there."

"Tonight was progress, I guess."

"It was, and it's a matter of time before I have my face buried between your thighs, completely devouring you. It'll happen, Jules."

That little voice said, 'if you don't ruin it,' but I internally told the voice to shut up. Out of habit, I turned toward the monitor on my nightstand. Too late, I remembered Tristan was upstairs. Sighing, I turned back.

"It's hard for you to let him spend the night with someone else, isn't it?"

I nodded, hating that I was once again getting emotional over it.

He leaned in, kissing me gently. "You could go get him."

"I can't. They're probably asleep by now, and Haylee was right. It was better not to wake him up. I've just never spent an entire night away from him. Stupid, I know, to get upset by it."

"I don't think it's stupid at all. Hey, I don't want to see you sad. Call them and pick him up."

I loved how supportive he was. Rob certainly wouldn't have understood. "I'll be okay. But I'd better check my phone in case they text or call me."

After jumping out of bed, I walked out into the living room and grabbed the device from my purse. I frowned at the missed calls from my attorney and held it up to listen to his voice message.

"Ms. Walker, this is Harvey. Your husband made bail today. He's been told he can't leave the state, but, uh, you may want to be extra cautious in protecting your whereabouts. I'll do my best to keep you updated if there are any further developments or if he pushes to see Tristan."

Breath left me. I didn't register Mark calling my name until he was beside me, wearing both his shirt and boxers. "What's wrong? Everything okay with Tristan?"

"Yeah. That was my attorney's voicemail from earlier this evening. Rob made bail."

Mark's jaw clenched before he reassured me. "He won't find you. Come to think of it, we'll have your PI keep track of him. Does Rob have an electronic GPS bracelet?"

"I haven't a clue. Harvey didn't mention it. I guess I can call him tomorrow and find out." As for the private investigator, I couldn't afford to have him follow Rob around day and night considering my funds were limited. Every time my attorney called me, I spent more money. Before the divorce and Rob's trial was over, I'd be in for thousands.

"You want to go up and get Tristan now, don't you?"

I nodded, trying to keep the tears from forming.

"I'm sure Haylee and Josh would understand, especially given the circumstances."

I contemplated doing that. But Rob hadn't given a shit about me or his son for years. The only reason he'd seek us out now would be because he'd heard about my part in uncovering his crimes. It had been inadvertent—I'd only wanted to prove he was cheating and using drugs—but the PI had found so much more.

Oh God. What if Rob did find out I'd contributed to his arrest? What if he was out for revenge? Nope, not going there. I couldn't. I took a deep breath and convinced myself there would be no way he could find me up here. No connection he'd be able to follow. I was thankful Mark had talked me into a new phone.

My voice was thick as my mind raced. I hated the unknown of Rob being out of jail. "I, um, I'll wait until morning. I only have a few more hours until then, anyhow."

His arms enveloped me.

I found myself sinking into him, appreciating his support.

"What can I do?"

"You're actually doing it now by just being here. Thank you."

CHAPTER ELEVEN

*M*ark held me that night while I finally drifted off to sleep in the wee hours, exhausted from letting my brain run wild with scenarios involving Rob. But, as always, when I woke up, he was gone. This shouldn't have bothered me since I'd been the one to set the boundaries. But this morning, with my emotions running high, it did.

I took a quick shower, however by six am I was already chomping at the bit to get a text from Haylee that Tristan was awake. He was normally an early riser, but chances were he'd stayed up later, and it would be at least another hour before he got up. I was trying to be patient, but my whole life revolved around a little boy whose father had been newly released from jail. It was amazing how panicked and guilty I started to feel at being away from him.

Mommy guilt. It's as though you can't leave the hospital without getting a bag of it to go with your new bundle of joy. Working mother. Go ahead and add a truckload more the first time you leave your baby for work. Of course, I'd been lucky in having my mother able to watch him over that summer until I could find a good day care, but still, I'd fretted.

Filing for divorce, leaving my husband, and moving up here may have been hands down the right things to do, but boom, on came more guilt. So that's why taking a night to myself to go to dinner, a club, and have amazing sex—Well, it tipped my balance. So much so that I promised I'd never put myself first again. Which was ridiculous, but that's what mommy guilt did to you.

Luckily, Haylee's text telling me Tristan was up came in the nick of time and saved me from any more self-lecturing.

I thought I'd be an intruder on an intimate family morning when Haylee invited me to come for the mouse pancakes, but I couldn't have been more wrong. Even Josh went out of his way to ensure I felt comfortable once I arrived, and he entertained Tristan with two stories while his mom made her famous Mickey-face pancakes.

We were having an amazing morning until I saw my attorney's number flash up on my screen. I'd been expecting his call since I'd emailed him before I'd come up. Quickly, I excused myself from the dining table.

"Hello."

"Hi, Ms. Walker. I'm sorry for the calls over the weekend."

"No, no. It's okay." Although he was probably charging me double now. "Not like it's your fault. Do you know if Rob has a monitoring bracelet?"

"He does not, unfortunately. But the good news is your PI, Andy, is watching him. Thus far, Rob's been staying at his girlfriend's place. Uh, sorry."

The thought of my ex having a girlfriend no longer bothered me. "Don't be. Wait, did you say Andy is monitoring him?" I hadn't called my PI, and I certainly didn't have the money to hire him to watch Rob twenty-four seven.

"Your boss, Brian, is picking up the tab."

"The hell he is. Tell him no."

"Uh, that's not my call. His contract is directly with Andy."

"Were you the one who told Brian about Rob being out on bail?"

"No, ma'am."

Which meant Mark had been the one to pass on the information to Brian since he was the only one to whom I'd revealed the situation.

"If you want my two cents, I suggest you let the PI do his job, especially if knowing Rob's whereabouts and activities will give you peace of mind about your safety and that of your son."

"Right. Okay. Thanks, Harvey."

I absolutely hated that part of him was right. But I was going to kill Brian when I met him and Sasha for lunch later. You know in the way which said *thank you, you're the most amazing friend ever, but you're totally a dead man.*

"YOU ARE NOT SPENDING your money for my PI to keep tabs on Rob."

I sent my text to Brian ten minutes after hanging up with my attorney. Subtle I was not. And I wasn't known for my patience, either.

"Worth the sacrifice and not up for argument, especially if you want me to treat you to lunch."

I knew he'd be stubborn, and I'd be damned if I let him pay for lunch, too.

When Tristan and I went to meet Sasha and Brian at the hotel that afternoon, my boss and friend of ten years completely disarmed me once I walked through the lobby doors. How? By stepping up and giving me a heartfelt hug and murmuring these words.

"You, Juliette Walker, mean the world to me and to Sasha. So does Tristan. Which means, for the next couple of weeks, you will let us do this. Until we have a handle on what Rob is doing, which hopefully is nothing but laying low. Because we love you. Got it?"

Shit. I stepped back and let out a shuddered breath. All of the fight immediately had left me with his words. "Oh, sure, make me cry in the hotel lobby, you jerk." There was absolutely no heat to my words, but it had the desired effect when he grinned. I smiled back.

Sasha stepped in, dabbing her own tears and giving me a hug, too. Then they did what any good friends would do, which was to make me laugh during lunch and forget about any worry over my soon-to-be-ex-husband.

I didn't see Mark until that evening when he knocked on my door. He appeared hesitant to come in when I opened it.

"Are you mad?" he asked right away.

Sighing, I appreciated that the question showed he was taking ownership of blabbing to Brian about Rob making bail. "Of course not. He would've found out by lunch anyways."

Mark didn't look relieved. "But what about the part with the PI?"

I quirked a brow but turned quickly when Tristan came running toward us.

He had eyes only for Mark. "Mark, Mark."

The object of his affection lifted him up immediately onto his hip, thus ensuring I couldn't show my annoyance regarding what he was about to tell me.

"I um, may have suggested it. And so you're aware, if Brian hadn't insisted on picking up the tab, then I would have."

Tristan chose that moment to hug him tight as if to pledge his unwavering allegiance.

"That's very generous, but wouldn't everyone have wondered why you were paying for my PI?" I'm not sure why I lobbed my question out there, but I found myself curious to hear his answer. I was disappointed when it came.

"Yeah. I suppose I didn't think of that."

"Do you want to come in? I'm about to bathe Tristan."

"Sure thing." He turned toward my son. "What kind of toys do you have? Any rubber duckies?"

And just like that, Mark became an integral part of bath time.

ON WEDNESDAY NIGHT Haylee came over for our usual dinner night. This time it was lasagna, which I showed her how to prepare. When we sat down, she took a bite and sighed with bliss.

"I'm definitely making this for Josh."

"You're definitely taking the rest of it home because you made this one."

She shook her head, but I wasn't having it.

"If you leave that pan with me, I won't eat it. I'm trying to cut down on carbs." Even in saying it, I was shoving garlic bread into my face. "You know, starting next Monday."

She laughed. "Well, he'll really enjoy it for Friday dinner, not to mention be shocked I made it."

"You could come over tomorrow after class if you want to make dessert, too."

"Thanks, but I have an appointment with Dr. Mac tomorrow."

Simply the mention of the good doctor brought on guilt since I still hadn't managed to call him.

As if reading my mind, she said, "I'm sorry if I make you feel uncomfortable by bringing him up. I promise I'm not pushing him on you."

"No, no, I know that. I think it's more about my guilt with recognizing I could probably use someone to talk to and have no excuse for not reaching out." But if I ever wanted to get past my insecurities, maybe it was time. And though Rob was doing very little, according to Andy who'd been tailing him, the fact that he was out on bail put me on edge. It was as though I was waiting for something to happen but not knowing what form it would take.

"Whether you do choose to call him or not, I hope you know I'm always here if you want to talk."

"Thank you. I appreciate that."

"Oh, by the way, I have great news to tell you. I got accepted to Columbia in New York. I'll start second semester. Josh was curbing his enthusiasm until I assured him it's truly what I want. Now he couldn't be happier. I have to say it feels as though a weight has been lifted. I swear, if I didn't have you here during the week, I'd be going crazy. So I know transferring schools was the right decision."

I was extremely happy for her while at the same time knowing I was creating an obstacle for myself by refusing to examine what was keeping me from my own personal happiness. It was time to talk with someone.

While I lay in bed later that night with my laptop, I finally got up the nerve to email Dr. Mac and requested a meeting with him at his convenience.

MARK CAME over the next evening for dinner. Over the last few nights, I'd missed him. He'd been in New York with Josh for work. And turns out I wasn't the only one to have missed him because the moment he walked through the door, Tristan immediately wanted Mark to see his new Lego set.

Later, as we lay in the dark with him holding me close, our hands entwined, I blurted out my news. "I made an appointment with Dr. Mac for tomorrow."

His hand squeezed mine, but I didn't miss the way his body tensed up first. "That's great."

It was a big step for me to have made the appointment and

also to admit it to someone. "Yeah. I'm a bit anxious, but I think it'll be good."

"Definitely. Do me a favor, though."

"What's that?"

"If you talk about us, do you mind not mentioning me by name?"

A gut punch would've felt better. "Sure. No problem." My voice was strained, but he didn't seem to pick up on it. Then I realized the only reason he wouldn't want me to mention his name. Dr. Mac knew him.

"Do you see him?"

He let out a loud exhale before answering. "I used to. That's why it would be strange to have you talking about me with him."

But if he no longer saw him, what difference would it make? "Maybe I should meet with someone else, then."

He pulled me in closer to him. "I can't speak highly enough of Dr. Mac, so please don't do that."

Right. But don't mention his name. No problem.

I CANCELLED. I couldn't help it. Because if I intended to reveal all of my insecurities, I couldn't be afraid I'd accidentally blurt out Mark's name. After all, keeping things to myself wasn't exactly my strong suit.

But if I was being honest, it was another excuse to be a big ole chicken. Cluck, cluck, cluck. So much for the Juliette 2.0 plan. If my failed diet and dropped math class were any indication, I'd be stuck on the 1.0 outdated version forever. Pity party of one here. But not for long because I couldn't stand myself that way.

On Friday night I babysat Abby while Josh and Haylee enjoyed some couple time over homemade lasagna. It was hardly an imposition. Abby, now able to smile, could sit in her chair and watch Tristan play for hours. He, of course, loved being the center of her attention.

When the knock came at the door, I opened it to a grinning Mark. He took one look at Abby and hesitated.

"Oh, hey. I see you're babysitting. Is Abby spending the night?"

"No. Haylee will probably come down in the next hour or so to get her. She's still nursing, so…"

I let my words hang and watched his face flush with the TMI.

"Okay. So how about you text me after?"

Right. Because he didn't want Haylee or Josh to know that he was hanging with us. Not even just for dinner and a movie. He certainly wouldn't want to broadcast the news he was in a sexual relationship with me.

"Sure. Will do."

He quirked a brow at my flat voice. "You okay?"

I forced a smile, not wanting to get into it in the hall and with two kids in the living room who needed their dinner. "Yeah. It's all good."

But it wasn't. Not that I blamed him, but unfortunately, he was tapping directly into the very heart of my insecurity. I wasn't good enough. He didn't want people knowing he was with me. Not even his therapist or best friends. The real problem though lie in the fact that I wasn't even angry with him over it, which only highlighted how truly low was my self-esteem.

Shrugging it off for now, I pasted a smile on my face for the kids and went about getting their food ready.

Haylee picked up Abby by nine o'clock. With Tristan already down for the night, I was tempted to text Mark, but for what? Another darkened booty call where he left by morning?

I knew I was being unfair by calling it that, but damn if it wasn't the way I felt right now. Since part of it was my own doing, I wasn't sure how to explain it to him. But it turned out Mark texted me first.

"It's getting late. Did you want me to come over?"

I read his words and finally typed out my reply. *"Sorry. I have an English paper due and am pretty tired."* And moody, and if I wasn't mistaken, about to start my period any day.

"Okay. Good luck on the paper."

"Thanks."

LUCKILY, it didn't take much to avoid Mark the next week since he had to travel overseas. I realized until I could put my insecurity over him not wanting people to know about us in a box, it was better not to see him. With my mother coming into town this weekend, I had excuses ready.

My mom must have sensed the sadness in my voice the last time we spoke because of course she'd booked a flight right away for Friday after she got off work. I swear, a hug from her made everything better.

Almost.

Because I'd found out the day before that Rob had submitted a petition for visitation with Tristan. My attorney told me it was strategic, an attempt to show he was getting his shit together in time for his trial, but that didn't matter. I was petrified. What if the petition was granted? Or worse, what if supervision wasn't instituted, and he was allowed to take Tristan on his own? What if his new druggie girlfriend was around my child, too? The fear over what could happen literally clawed at my throat, making it hard to swallow.

Although I'd thought Mark would avoid me over the weekend since I had family in town, I found a text from him on Saturday night after Tristan had gone to bed.

"Can you sneak next door for a few minutes?"

I contemplated, and evidently my delay was too long for him to wait for a response. A soft knock sounded at the door.

My mother muted the television and glanced over at me. "Expecting company?"

"Um. Maybe."

I got up and stepped outside of my door. He looked fresh from the shower and handsome as ever. I'd missed him, evidenced by the fact my body was leaning toward him without permission.

He didn't hesitate, putting strong hands at my waist. "I've missed you, Jules."

"I missed you, too." It was the truth, pure and simple. Although I might be fighting the demons of my insecurities, I craved the way he made me feel when I was with him.

"Come over?" His lips dropped behind my ear, murmuring the words.

"Give me a second." I poked my head back in.

My mom was lifting a brow. I wasn't sure what she could hear.

"Uh, I just need to help Mark find some files across the hall. I won't be long."

The brow only went up another inch, most likely not buying my flimsy excuse at all. "Okay, honey. Take your time."

When I went back into the hall, I saw his door open and him standing on the other side of the threshold. Glancing down at myself, I cringed. Too late, I realized that I was in a baggy T-shirt and even baggier sweat pants. No makeup and hair in a ponytail completed my signature weekend look.

But despite me thinking I was less than attractive, the moment I stepped foot inside his place, he was on me. A kiss so hot that it burned its way down to my toes greeted me, leaving me breathless. His hands wasted no time, splitting duties. One gripped my hair, holding me in place, while the other went under my waistband and straight to my center, finding me getting wetter by the moment.

"This is all I've thought about all week."

A moan was my response when he slipped a finger inside of me. Then a squeak left my mouth when he hauled me up, gripping my ass and allowing my legs to wrap around his waist. He strode across the apartment into the bedroom. Surprisingly, the file cabinets had been moved against one wall and now a double bed stood on the other side.

He followed me down onto the mattress, only leaving me briefly to shut the door. Now the bedroom was nothing but shadows and moonlight. His anxious fingers removed my pants and thong while his lips wreaked havoc along the column of my neck. "I need to be inside of you."

I shivered with his words. "I need that, too."

My eyes had adjusted to the dark enough to watch his silhouette shed his clothing and put the condom on. He then climbed toward me where I'd scooted back on his bed. He settled between my thighs as my fingers skimmed down his powerful shoulders.

"Tell me you missed this cock." His dirty words flamed my senses while he teased me with the crown, rubbing my clit with small circles.

"I did. I missed it so much." My back arched when he entered me one inch at a time, as if savoring the moment.

"I love how much I fill you. How tight you are around me every time."

I gasped when he rolled me over so I was on top of him.

He pulled the T-shirt over my head but left on my bra, for which I was grateful.

Arching back, I loved how he filled me completely and proceeded to ride him with abandon.

His hands gripped my hips, urging me along and setting the pace.

When his thumb centered on my clit, my moves became frantic as I chased my orgasm. He thrusted up, hitting a spot over and over, making my entire body shake with pent-up desire. "Mark."

"Give it up to me. Let me feel your cunt squeeze me when you come."

Never had that particular C-word turned me on, but the way he said it—I was done for. Completely. The icing on the cake was hearing him call out my name as if he couldn't help himself while he came on one last thrust.

I lay there on top of him for a few minutes, enjoying the feel of his hands stroking my back and not in a hurry to break the connection of him inside of me. I whispered in the dark, "You got a bed."

"Mm-hmm. Been sleeping here more often. Also, it's a good cover for when Josh sees my car here overnight."

His words were innocent enough, but once again, he'd plucked a nerve. He didn't want anyone to be aware he was with me.

"I should probably get back." I scrambled off the mattress, grateful for the shadows hiding my face. The last thing I wanted was for him to know I was upset. Unfortunately, my tone must've given me away.

"Is everything okay?"

"Sure. Why wouldn't it be?" Damn. I'd gone for light and overshot, with my voice going up two octaves. Meanwhile, I shimmied into my clothes, fumbling around for my T-shirt on the floor.

He grabbed my wrist, tugging me back down with him on the bed. "Something is wrong. Tell me."

I sighed heavily. "Nothing. If you don't want my mom wondering if finding a file is a metaphor for something else, I need to go."

My hand settled on my T-shirt, and I quickly put it over my head.

"Jules, talk to me."

I couldn't. What was there to say? That I was getting my feelings hurt by an arrangement upon which I'd put the boundaries? "It's fine. Just a lot of stress with Rob being out. Plus, he filed a petition for visitation with Tristan."

Mark cursed under his breath. "I'm sorry. Especially that I wasn't here when you found out. What does the attorney say his chances are?"

"If he can pass a couple of drug tests, they're reasonably good. It's all part of his image overhaul, though, and not because he actually misses his son. And then I'm afraid of what it would mean if he's granted unsupervised visits. Anyhow, I'll do what I've always done. Wait and see what happens and try not to wish he'd simply disappear out of our lives for good."

Whenever I had that thought, I felt guilty. After all, Rob was still Tristan's father. Sometimes being the bigger person was tough.

"Are you talking with Dr. Mac in the meantime?" Mark got up from the bed, disposed of the condom, and quickly put his clothes back on.

"No, uh, I cancelled."

"Why? Right now is when you probably need to talk to him the most. You have a lot on your shoulders."

I didn't need his judgment, especially since it was partially his fault I'd cancelled. "Yeah, well, I didn't want to accidentally bring up your name. As previously demonstrated, keeping my mouth shut when I'm nervous isn't exactly my strong suit. And since you've made it clear you'd hate for anyone to find out about our little fling, it's probably for the best."

Shit. I'd said too much. "I need to go."

"Wait." He followed me out into the living room, tugging on

my arm and meeting my eyes. His frustration was evident in them.

"It's okay. I shouldn't have said anything." I tried to let him off the hook.

"Like hell it is. Is this what you think? That this is a fling?"

"What else would you call it?"

He let go of me, his hand raking through his hair. "You know, when I told you I missed you, it wasn't just about the sex. I missed talking to you, seeing Tristan, and—hell, I don't know—being with you, whether it's to watch a Disney movie or be deep inside of you."

My lips parted, surprised by his admission and a little turned on.

"You're the one who wanted the sex in the dark, me leaving by morning. I was only trying to keep within your boundaries. You set them."

"You didn't exactly give me any indication that you wanted anything else."

He cursed under his breath again. "This—" He motioned between us. "Isn't easy for me. Okay? I don't know how to do it. And the fact that you're still married and dealing with your estranged husband while we have mutual friends does not make it any simpler."

We both stood there looking at one another. I was unsure what to say. Complication might as well be my middle name.

The loud knock at the door and my mother's voice made us both jump. "Juliette."

I opened it to find her holding out my cell phone. "Sorry to interrupt your, er, filing, but Andy called about five times in a row. I finally picked up, and he said it was urgent you return his call."

I didn't even have time to be embarrassed. Instead, I dialed his number and waited for my PI to pick up. "Hi, Andy. It's Juliette."

"Hi, ma'am. Sorry to call so late. Rob was involved in a bad car accident. He's in the hospital."

"What happened?"

"I'm not sure, but you're still his emergency contact, and the hospital needs to speak with you. His parents aren't happy about finding that out, by the way. Just to give you a head's up."

I bet. "How bad is it?"

"Bad, but they aren't saying a lot. I'll text you the number after we hang up."

"Okay." My words were automatic, hollow. I was in shock.

I hung up the phone and looked towards two expectant faces.

"Rob was in an accident."

CHAPTER TWELVE

*H*ell had nothing on the next few days.

I called the hospital immediately after hanging up the phone with my PI to learn that Rob was in critical condition and in surgery. He'd wrapped his truck around a telephone pole. His girlfriend had been a passenger and had sustained minor injuries, however he hadn't been so lucky. Terms like: internal bleeding, ruptured spleen, and severe burns were mentioned in the doctor's briefing to me. Apparently, the truck had caught on fire. By morning the word was simple.

Death.

Six days after receiving the call about the accident, I sat in the front row of chairs, graveside. The cemetery was small, situated outside of the town where Rob's parents now lived, two hours from Charlotte. Dry eyed, I concentrated on my little boy sitting on my lap. He was fidgeting because what toddler understands funeral etiquette let alone this was for his father.

Since I'd arrived, I'd been caught in a whirlwind, working with the funeral home, the hospital, and my attorney, who confirmed that, yes, I remained Rob's next of kin. His burial was modest and without police honors, in light of the charges pending against him, but I'd done my best to abide by his parents' wishes.

The most surprising fact I learned was that his death benefits and life insurance still had me listed as the beneficiary.

Although I had no interest in the money personally, I would take anything I received and put it toward Tristan's college fund. Unfortunately, once Rob's mother found out, this increased the tension.

And she wasn't the only one less than thrilled to have me here.

My eyes, shielded by dark sunglasses, slid over his twenty-one-year-old girlfriend. She sat across from me, next to Rob's parents, glaring daggers in my direction.

After his coffin was lowered in the ground, I watched his grieving mother and father each toss in a rose. His mom swallowed hard and gave me a slight nod.

I got up, holding Tristan on my hip, and gave him a flower to toss in as well. I might not have any tears at the loss of the man who'd made my life hell for over two years, but I wouldn't deny my little boy the right to say goodbye to his father. That's why, despite this being rough, I was here. For Tristan. I refused to be the mother who kept her son from attending his father's funeral.

There was a lot of sobbing from the girlfriend, who tossed her rose last and then glowered at me like I was the interloper once they started shoveling in dirt.

Goodbye, Robert, I murmured to myself, feeling sadness over the sandy-haired teenage boy I'd fallen in love with long ago. If I was going to grieve, it would be for the man I used to know, not for the prescription-drug-addicted, dirty cop who'd turned into a person I didn't recognize.

Brian's arm went around my shoulders, and I leaned into the strength of him. Along with Sasha, he'd insisted on being here for me today. My mother and stepfather were present, too. I was grateful to have all the support. With one last glance, we walked silently to where the car was waiting.

As we opened the doors, I cringed as I heard Rob's mother's voice calling out.

"Juliette," she huffed. She was a larger woman and had obviously rushed over to address me.

It was unfortunate that over these last tension-filled days they hadn't said one kind word and had opted instead to act hostile. I'd chosen the high road, but it wasn't easy. Especially when Rob's mother wholeheartedly believed her son had been framed for drug use and was innocent of all charges.

Not even the toxicology report showing he'd been using when he'd veered off the road into the pole had swayed them. But it wasn't my business or, frankly, my job to convince them otherwise. Let them think what they wanted about their son. And about me. None of it mattered.

I stood by the car, waiting for her to catch up while I held Tristan on my hip. He was already rubbing his eyes. It was late for nap time, and he was tired.

"You should come by the house with Tristan. Or better yet, I could take him with us. We don't have a car seat, but it's not too far of a drive to the house, and we'll drive slowly."

Uh, no, definitely not happening. But she'd just buried her youngest son so I felt some measure of compassion even if the woman had taken some horrible potshots at me this week.

"I appreciate the offer, Betty, but it's Tristan's nap time. Besides, I wouldn't feel comfortable going when Delilah intends to be there." It was obvious that his parents had formed some sort of bond with Rob's girlfriend, most likely because she'd been with him during the accident. For my part, I wouldn't expose my son to her glares and hostility.

Betty's eyes flashed with a temper reminiscent of the one I'd seen often enough in her son. "Tristan is Rob's son and all we have left of him. It would be nice of you to put aside your petty differences and let him be with his daddy's parents on the day we had to bury our son."

"I'd be happy to bring him by tomorrow to visit. We'll be staying overnight to ensure we can do that." Although I was in a hurry to go home, I wasn't completely heartless. I wanted them to spend some time with Tristan. Suspicious, however, that over the last week I'd been in town, today was the first time they'd stopped taking potshots at me and had simply asked for Tristan to visit. I tamped down on the thought that it might be because today they wanted people to see him there. It seemed they weren't actually interested in spending time with their grandson but more in the show of it.

"That's not good enough."

No. It never was.

"I'm sorry." I was trying to be reasonable, but there was no way I was letting my baby go home with people he didn't know and who had Rob's druggie girlfriend staying with them.

"You're sorry. You should be sorry. You drove Rob to this. And then, when he needed you the most, you disappeared. His death is on you. I always knew he could do better than trailer trash—"

Her verbal assault took me off guard. She'd been passive-aggressive—emphasis on aggressive—and resentful of my presence, but this was so much more. This was an all-out attack.

Brian didn't let her finish. "Enough. Juliette, why don't you get in the car on the other side with Tristan?"

Sasha stood like a guard dog, taking my arm and leading me around.

I quickly slid in and put my half-asleep baby boy in his car seat, thankful he wasn't old enough to understand the hate that his grandmother had just spewed toward me. My mom and stepdad were already in their car behind us, most likely wondering what was happening. Luckily, they weren't witnessing the drama. I kept the door open so I could hear Brian.

"Ms. Walker, I realize today is very upsetting, but please respect the fact that these are not easy circumstances for anyone," Brian cajoled in his soothing voice. The only evidence of his temper was the tic in his jaw.

"They sure as hell seem more convenient for her. She doesn't have to fight for custody, and she thinks she's receiving Rob's life insurance check. That's not going to happen—"

Yeah, because I was all about the money. Indescribable exhaustion set in and suddenly I couldn't get out of here fast enough.

I could hear Brian say, "Mrs. Walker, this isn't the time or the place. If you have anything more you want to say to Juliette, then I'll provide the name of her attorney. Good day to you."

Both his and Sasha's doors opened and closed while I was happy to finally shut mine as well. Brian wasted no time putting the car in gear and pulling away, leaving a stunned Mrs. Walker behind.

As we left the whole nightmare, I lay my head back and murmured a thanks to him. Tristan and I were both out cold by the time we hit the main road.

I SHOULD'VE STOOD up for myself better. I said as much to Brian a short time later as he and Sasha bid me goodbye. My family would stay for one more night before returning to Charlotte, but Sasha and Brian needed to get back there for work.

He shook his head. "You're far too close to the situation. They'd just lost their son, and in their eyes, there wasn't a thing you could've said correctly. So it was better for me to be the bad guy instead."

I hugged him again, appreciating that he'd taken on that role. One last embrace for Sasha, and we waved goodbye in the hotel parking lot. My mom took my sleeping toddler and insisted I go to my room and take a nap.

"Honey, you go take a long bath and an even longer nap. We'll let him sleep, then order room service later once he wakes up. You do the same."

I hesitated but then recognized that the very best thing for me now was to cry it all out and spend some time to myself. I kissed Tristan's head and gave my mother a watery smile. I appreciated her allowing me this time to decompress. "Thanks, Mom."

After a long bath, I lay on my bed, but I was unable to sleep. My appetite wasn't faring much better, but my growling stomach had me ordering room service anyhow. I hadn't eaten all day.

Loneliness crawled over me like a heavy blanket. I was sorely tempted to go pick up Tristan, but it wasn't fair to put this flood of emotions on him. The last thing he needed was to see his mommy cry. And right now, I'd be a mess.

Crap. The tears started falling fast and furious as my mind went through the memories, focusing on the good and casting out the bad. Prom, graduation, our first house, and our wedding all came to mind. I sobbed for the loss of the man I'd once loved. But most importantly, I made peace with the man he'd become.

It hadn't been my fault. My self-esteem might be at an all-time low, but I refused to take the blame for Rob's death. We all had choices, and he'd made his. I refused to beat myself up for it. Or feel guilty because his death had, in fact, resolved my fear involving custody. Or because I'd confessed out loud that my life would be easier without Rob in it. Ugh. It wasn't like I'd asked for this.

Wiping my face and taking a deep breath, I greeted the server who knocked on the door. Gladly, I took the room service tray from her. She smiled in sympathy, most likely because my eyes were puffy and swollen.

I ate my grilled cheese sandwich without tasting it. As I ate, I realized how much I'd missed Mark over this last week. He'd texted me a few times, letting me know he was thinking of me and telling me to let him know if I needed anything. But I hadn't heard from him today. He hadn't brought up our fight—if you could even call it that—and I had no clue where this left us. To be honest, aside from returning to the apartment to get my things, I wasn't sure I'd be spending much more time in Connecticut. The thought of ending something which had only begun made me sadder than I could've imagined.

But before making any decisions on moving, I'd have to speak with my attorney. I wasn't sure, despite Rob's death, if it was safe to return yet. If his parents intended to come after the life insurance, the last thing I wanted was to make it easy for them to find me. Better to let them go through the courts. The thought of having to fight over Tristan's rightful inheritance had me setting down the sandwich, losing what little I had of an appetite.

The knock at the door made me hopeful Tristan had woken up and wanted me, so I opened it without looking. Mark stood on the other side. I didn't hesitate to pull him into the room and allow his arms to come around me tightly.

He held me like that forever, not saying a word, simply allowing his strength to envelop me. As we stood there, it occurred to me how much I'd needed him to be here.

"I couldn't stay away," he murmured in my ear.

"I'm glad." I pulled back and cupped his face. "I was thinking how much I missed you, and then you were here." I couldn't believe it.

"It took everything in me not to come to the funeral and sit beside you to hold your hand. But that would've been inappropriate."

It was ironic he would be respectful that way because Rob's girlfriend, the one he'd cheated on me with and done drugs with, had had no qualms about sitting with his parents. "It means a lot you'd want to. And that you're here now."

"I hated the way we left things."

I sighed and then let him lead me to the bed and pull me down into his lap. "Me, too. And I'm sorry. I was the one who originally said I wanted in the dark, no strings—"

He interrupted. "You have nothing to apologize for, except for maybe not telling me when you wanted more. Because so did I."

When I turned, our faces were inches from one another. "You did? But you said you didn't know how to do this."

He winced. "I'm sorry. I'm still trying to figure it out, but that's all in my head. The one thing I do know is I want to do it with you. I didn't mean to make it seem like you were too complicated. Hell, I'm complicated, too. But the way you make me feel when we're together—How easy it is to be with you—I don't want to lose this thing between us. And I'm especially sorry for making you feel as though you couldn't talk to Dr. Mac. I never should've suggested you don't mention me by name. It was misplaced guilt that I hadn't seen him in quite a while."

His apology meant a lot, and his reasoning made me under-stand his motivation better. "Apology accepted and returned for not communicating my feelings." Swallowing hard, I leaned forward and met his lips. The kiss was soft at first and then turned deeper before he pulled away and put his forehead to mine.

"Where's Tristan?"

"With my mom and stepdad down the hall. I needed some time to, uh—"

He leaned back, studying my face. "Cry."

I nodded slowly. "It's so stupid. The man I once loved has been gone for years, but today was just—it was still hard."

His hand caressed my face in an intimate gesture. "Sounds like your whole week was rough. I spoke with Brian. He told me about Rob's mother's threats and how awful they've been toward you."

"They blame me."

His jaw clenched. "I don't see how on earth they could, but I hope you don't blame yourself. You didn't have anything to do with his choices."

I smiled sadly. "After a good cry, I've come to the same conclusion. I'll reach out to his parents one last time tomorrow morning to see if they want to see Tristan. But if I'm being honest, I hope the answer is no. I'm well aware that makes me selfish, but I can't help it."

"There's absolutely nothing selfish about you. But maybe I'm a bit self-centered because I want to know when you're coming back up to New Haven."

"Um. Probably in a couple of days. I need to meet with my attorney to deal with the life insurance stuff and figure out how I can get my house on the market. Unless, of course, I can simply take a match to it. Because at this point I wouldn't mind watching it all go up in flames."

He smirked. "That's arson."

I smiled for the first time all day. "You're so lawyerly and proper."

He kissed me on the nose. "Not always so proper."

No, he wasn't. And I loved it. "I need to find out when I can move home."

He let out a heavy exhale. "We went into this knowing our time was limited, but I don't like to think of it that way."

"Me, either."

He kissed me again, this time moving his mouth down my neck and behind my ear. "What if I'm not ready to let you go? What if I want more?"

My wide eyes pulled back to meet his. "More?"

"A lot more. No more boundaries. No more dark. With lots of strings."

My heart was beating quickly, my mouth dry over his words. "When you're ready."

"I want to be ready. I really do."

He kissed me softly. "Tell me your worst fear in letting me see all of you?"

I swallowed past the lump in my throat and admitted it out loud. "That I'll turn you off, and that'll be it. It seemed like overnight it happened with my ex. I know you're not him. Believe me, I do. But I'm not sure what I'd do if I was no longer sexy to you in the light of day. I think it would break whatever fragile self-esteem I have left."

He cupped my face. "Do you trust me?"

I nodded, needing his reassurance more than I'd ever admit to. Once his lips met mine, I sank into him.

"Come on, I have an idea." He took me by the hand and pulled me up to stand in front of the mirrored closet doors. As he stood behind me, his strong, tanned hands were quite the contrast across my pink, buttoned-up, cotton shirt.

"Keep your gaze on me, okay?"

My eyes burned, and my legs shook, but I did as he requested. If we were to ever move forward, I needed to get past this fear of rejection. Trusting this man to help get me there, however, was one of the hardest things I'd ever done.

His blue eyes bored into mine in the reflection, heavy with desire. His expression made some of my self-confidence flicker to life.

"Do you know what I see when I look at you?"

I shook my head, biting my lip to keep from crying.

"First, your beautiful face." His fingers stroked my cheek. "When those big, honey-brown eyes of yours landed on me at the party, I knew I was a goner."

I couldn't have been more surprised. "Even after my verbal vomit?"

He chuckled. "Especially after that. I kept thinking I should try harder to get you to stop talking when I realized you thought I was Dr. Mac. But at the same time, I was absolutely intrigued by every word."

To hear his perspective on what I'd considered the most humiliating experience of my life was completely flooring.

"And your hair. I thought you were beautiful as a blonde, but this brunette brought out your eyes and made me have fantasies of pulling on this ponytail while you were on your knees, your mouth wrapped around my cock."

Goose bumps appeared on my arms, the kind from getting turned on.

"Sorry, too crude?"

I shook my head, smiling. "Nothing out of your mouth ever is. Instead, it takes me out of my head when you talk dirty to me."

He kissed the back of my neck. "Thank God. And speaking of mouths. You have the very best one, from your sweet Southern accent to the way you can give the greatest blow jobs on the planet."

I chuckled, beaming on the inside from the compliment.

"Now, moving onto your body. How about we first take off your pants? You have amazing legs, so I want you to show me those first."

His fingers hooked into my sweats and pulled them down slowly, exposing my legs to my gaze in the reflection. I exhaled a shaky breath, thinking at least that part of my body didn't look too bad. I stepped out of the sweats and watched him throw them to the side.

His hot breath tickled my ear. "Your legs are unbelievably strong and toned. I picture how many times they've been wrapped around me and fantasize kissing down the insides of your thighs up to your hot center waiting for my tongue."

Oh, good Lord. He was going to make me climax before he even touched me.

Next, he slid my panties down, moving my legs slightly wider. I shuddered when he cupped me fully with one palm, shielding my center from both our views and putting my fears to rest one at a time.

"Obviously, I'm biased when I say your pussy is one of my favorite places to spend time. You're so wet and the perfect fit for me."

Moving his fingers slowly, he massaged me but made no attempt to rub my clit or put his fingers inside of me.

I pushed my ass back into the impressive erection contained in his jeans. I wanted—no, needed—more.

He shook his head, smiling. "Not yet, beautiful. Although I certainly crave you that way always, this moment isn't about sex. This is about showing you how very sexy you are."

I noticed my body had started to relax under the influence of his hypnotic, erotic voice. But I sucked in a large breath once he started unbuttoning my shirt. My mind hyper-focused on the stretch marks evident on my stomach and exposed to his gaze once he was finished. Closing my eyes, I felt my body tense until his fingers caressed me softly.

"Open your eyes and look at mine."

I did so hesitantly, feeling myself start to tremble.

"Look at how sensual you are in the mirror, Jules, with my hands on your beautiful skin."

I tried, I truly did, to see what he did, but he must've detected the disbelief in my expression.

"You're focusing on flaws, aren't you?"

I nodded, a tear leaking out in spite of my best efforts. Nothing said provocative like crying in front of the man undressing you. Good one, Juliette.

"Do you know what I see?"

Shaking my head, I braced myself for whatever he would have to say.

"I see a petite body that carried a big, healthy baby boy. It took some stretching to hold him in there for nine months. I see strength. A badge of honor, if you will, that says 'you're a mother.' You should be proud to wear those marks."

He was doing it. I was completely distracted from the fact he was viewing my stomach in the mirror. Instead, I relaxed into him and his beautiful words.

His gaze traveled down my body while his fingers ghosted over my skin, from my stomach down to my clit. "You're absolutely beautiful, Jules. These slight imperfections that you see make you even more perfect because of the reasons you have them. Witnessing the way you mother your amazing son only cemented for me how very special you are."

Next he unclasped my bra. Both his hands came around to cup the weight of my breasts, which didn't sit as perky as they used to.

"When I look at your breasts, I think of how you must have looked while rocking your baby and feeding him at night. How beautiful it must've been to know you were sustaining a life with your body."

How? How could there be someone this perfect on the planet who wanted me? His moving, heartfelt words had tears tracking down my face.

He spun me in a half circle and knelt down in front of me, kissing those marks that I'd been so embarrassed about and had concealed for years. "No more hiding. You're exquisite. The moment you have any doubt, I want you to remember right now, me in front of you wanting nothing more than to worship your gorgeous body."

My breath caught. In that moment I knew I was undeniably in love with this amazing man. He was making me feel like I was the most incredible thing in the world. "Thank you," I whispered, the tears falling freely now.

He kissed my stomach and then stood so he could travel his

mouth up to my breasts, my neck, and finally capture my lips. "Don't cry, beautiful."

"They're happy tears, I promise."

He smiled tenderly, wiping my cheeks with his thumbs. "Let me hold you on the bed?"

Calming my nerves, I took a deep breath. This. This was what trust and intimacy were all about, and I wanted all of it. That meant I needed to let go of my insecurities and believe the words he'd told me. "I want you to make love to me. In the light."

He hesitated. "Are you sure?"

I framed his face with my hands. "I've never been surer about anything or anyone in my entire life."

He met my lips, pouring so much emotion into the kiss that it left no doubt how much this meant to him. Backing me up to the mattress, he lay me down gently. I watched him pull his shirt off first, followed by his pants, boxers, and socks. My eyes immediately tracked to the small S tattooed above his heart on his chest. It was the first time I'd seen him in the light, as well.

S had to be for his fiancée's name. I wasn't prepared for the emotion that hit me upon seeing it. He was clearly devoted to the memory of the woman with whom he was supposed to have spent the rest of his life.

"I can put the shirt back on if you want." He was watching me, honing in on my fixation with his tattoo.

"No. It's part of you. And I don't want anything more between us."

His tender smile almost caused me to tear up all over again. Then he covered my body with his. Skin on skin, he rolled me slightly onto my side. In this position, I wasn't supporting his full weight, and he could put his thigh between mine, entwining us together naked.

The kiss he gave me could've melted steel. It was hot and sensuous, leaving no doubt how very turned on he was. Nuzzling my neck, he whispered, "You know this is more to me than sex, don't you?"

I murmured, "It is for me, too."

"I want to be part of your life and that of Tristan's. And I realize the timing—Jesus—I shouldn't be saying these things to you on the day of your husband's funeral. I'm sorry."

I leaned back, so we could be eye to eye. "Today made me sad because someday I'll have to tell Tristan that his father chose drugs over him, over us. And that he ultimately died because of it. You knew I'd need you here, and you came. Please don't apologize."

"I want—No, I need you in my life. Both of you."

His expression was so intense that I swallowed hard. "What are you saying?"

"I'm saying I want a future with you." He muttered a curse, running his hand through his hair. "And again, today isn't the day I should dump all of this on you."

"No, no, don't stop. I want to hear it all."

He took a deep breath. "When you left, I felt lost. Instantly. I never argued with you against the idea I should leave the morning after sex in the dark because I didn't want to scare you off. Especially when I realized I wanted more."

"I want more too."

He peppered my face and throat with kisses.

It was strange. It seemed I'd said yes to something undefined and completely arbitrary, and yet I couldn't remember a time I'd been happier.

We rolled around on the bed, teasing one another with touches and kisses before Mark uttered a request.

"Will you sit on the edge of the mattress and show me your pussy?"

I gulped, thinking this man's dirty mouth and unexpected alpha side would be the death of me. Moving on shaky legs, I got into position, spreading my legs and baring myself for him.

He moved a bench, which had been across the room, in front of me. Much to my confusion, he took a seat there.

"Spread your legs wider."

I did as he asked, watching his expression darken while he shifted in his seat and palmed his erection. I licked my lips at the sight. He was so sexy. Watching him grip himself notched up my level of arousal.

"Now touch yourself. Show me how wet you are."

I moved my fingers down, separating my lips and then running them through my wetness. All reservations were gone. The only sounds in the room were our heavy breathing and the slick sound of my exploration.

"Put your fingers inside your pussy."

My hips arched involuntarily when I complied, a small moan leaving my lips.

He wasted no time in moving closer, this time getting on his knees in front of me with a hand on each of my legs, burning hot on my skin. "Will you let me taste you? Put my tongue inside of you. Have you come in my mouth?"

My heartbeat kicked into overtime with his delicious words, and I did my best to keep my anxiety from rearing its ugly head.

"I can smell your arousal, and it has me unbelievably turned on. I can barely keep myself from diving into you." He removed his glasses before skimming his hands up my trembling thighs, his eyes searching mine for permission.

Fueled by pure lust and a great deal of hope, I gave him a slight nod, trusting him and his words.

He wasted no time putting his mouth on me. "Fucking incredible." His murmured praise was barely audible as he swiped his tongue over my clit. Softly at first, until his hands gripped my hips, pulling me into his face like a man starved.

A gasp escaped my throat with the intimate contact of his lips. Teeth, tongue, and, oh, now his fingers completely overwhelmed me. When his mouth fastened on my clit, my hands tangled in his dark hair, pulling him in closer.

"You taste amazing. I could never get enough," he murmured against my thigh, trailing kisses while he worked my wetness in and out of my entrance. "Lie down, beautiful."

The back of my head hit the soft bed, my hands finding purchase by gripping the sheets. Gone was any residual insecurity, replaced by sheer desire.

In this new position, he shifted, pulling me closer to the edge and putting both of my legs over his shoulders. Then he lifted my ass off the bed and buried his face back between my legs.

"Mark—" My moan was cut off with the climax that slammed through me. Its force completely annihilated my senses. I was barely aware that he remained between my legs, licking, biting, and sucking and evidently going for a gold medal in oral sex as he went for another orgasm.

"I can't," I pleaded, knowing I didn't really mean it. Instead, curiosity took over. Was it possible? Sixty seconds later, I discovered it was. I had to bite my lip to keep from screaming when the second wave washed over me, my internal muscles gripping him while I came around his mouth and fingers. When I finally found the ability to open my eyes, I saw Mark's handsome face hovered above mine.

"You've been quiet for more than a minute. Should I call the paramedics?"

I giggled. "In addition to your super-talented tongue, you've got jokes."

He smirked, and I pushed up and kissed him. His surprise was evident when he pulled back. "You don't mind?"

I shook my head. "Call it research. Does that make me dirty?"

"Only in the very best way. Now then, time to expand upon the talented tongue compliment."

Yes, please.

CHAPTER THIRTEEN

J woke the next morning in my hotel room bed to find Mark wrapped around me. Judging by the hard length poking the small of my back, he was wide awake.

"I like mornings with you," I murmured, stretching my limbs. I hadn't had such a good night's sleep in months. Must have been the heady combination of multiple orgasms and the human heater behind me.

"Good, because I intend to do it more often."

I entwined my fingers with his and relished the feel of his hard body behind me. "No arguments from me."

"I don't suppose you've gotten more consistent about taking the Pill?"

He shifted, notching his cock between the cheeks of my ass. It would be so easy for him to slip into my heat at this angle, which would also allow him to move his hands to my breasts.

"I was, but then I up and forgot them in the craziness of traveling down here. Sorry. What I should do is get the shot, then we won't need to rely on me remembering to take the Pill."

"Nothing to apologize for. Luckily, I have another condom."

He kissed the top of my head regretfully before getting out of the bed and searching his wallet.

Turning, I saw him hold up a foil square. Rather than the packet, I focused on his gorgeous body. Strong shoulders topped a firm chest with a smattering of dark hair that went down, down. Good Lord, his happy trail was turning me on now that I had a clear vision of its endpoint.

"Last one, so we better make it good."

I wanted to ask if his warning meant he was leaving today, or if it only meant he'd have to go to the store later. But I kept quiet as I didn't want to ruin this rare morning to ourselves by trying to define our relationship, especially when so many things were up in the air.

He hopped back into the bed. Once he'd assumed the same position as before, he pulled my hair to the side and kissed where my neck met my shoulder. "Miss me?"

I giggled, absolutely enjoying this playful side of him. "I counted the seconds until —ahhhh." I lost my thought and words as he pushed inside of me, splaying one hand across my stomach and pulling me onto him, going deeper.

"I'm a fan of this position."

"Me, too."

The sex was unhurried, languid, and felt decadent in the morning light. Once his fingers trailed down to find my clit, I was completely done for, coming in spectacular fashion.

Just as I was about to doze off in post-coital bliss, the hotel phone rang.

Picking up, I heard a woman who sounded like she was from the front desk. "Ms. Walker, there is a woman from Child Protective Services here with a police officer. We can't give out your room number without your permission so—"

"WHAT?"

"Do you want me to send them up?"

"No, no. I'll come down."

"Okay. I will let them know."

I hung up and immediately dialed my mom, trying to explain to Mark in the interim what was happening. "Child Services is here with a police officer. Why would they be here?"

My mother picked up on the first ring.

"Mom, is everything okay this morning with Tristan?" I'd gone by their room last night to kiss him goodnight and he'd been very content to spend the night with his grandparents.

"Yeah, honey. He woke up about ten minutes ago. I was about to text you. We planned to take him downstairs to breakfast."

I let out a breath. "Unfortunately, there is someone from CPS downstairs to speak with me. With a police officer. I, um, I don't know what to do. Part of me wants you to take him and run."

Mark shook his head. "As hard as this is, they may need to see him to check on his welfare. Rob's parents are probably behind this."

I couldn't believe it. I'd realized his parents were upset, but this was a whole new level of evil. Turning my attention back to my mom on the phone, I spoke. "Keep him in the room. I'll update you soon."

I hung up, fighting the angry tears that threatened. "Why? Why would they do this?"

Mark pulled me into a hug. "I'm sorry, Jules."

After taking a deep breath, I knew I needed to pull it together and wiped my eyes. "I have to get dressed and brush my teeth."

He let me go and finished dressing himself. "I'll go to my room and then join you down there."

I stopped mid-shimmy into my jeans. "I don't know if that's a good idea." Hypocrite much? But when it came to Tristan, I didn't need any additional possible judgment against me. Such as one about my sleeping with a new man during the same week my estranged husband was buried. Not now. Not with CPS involved.

"Tell them you called your attorney, and I'll come in from

the parking lot instead of from inside the hotel. You can say I'm in town to assist you since Rob's mother threatened to go after Tristan's inheritance."

"Okay. That might be good. Thank you."

He stepped closer and lifted my chin. "We will get through this."

We. It sure felt good to hear.

———

MY LEVEL of anxiety rose with each floor that dinged in the elevator ride down to the lobby. Once the doors opened, I immediately spotted the police officer in uniform. Alongside him stood an older woman dressed in a suit, clipboard in hand.

Swallowing hard, I squared my shoulders and approached them.

"Hello, I'm Juliette Walker."

The officer let the CPS representative take the lead. "Ms. Walker, I'm Tamra Fields. This is Officer Duncan. I apologize for the early morning visit, but our office received a call yesterday alleging child abuse."

My eyes flicked from her to the officer. "I'm assuming it was from my deceased husband's mother?"

He gave a curt nod. "Yes, ma'am. She's alleging that after the funeral she saw you shake your son hard."

I had to swallow the urge to shout out what a load of shit this was. "I can assure you that never happened. In truth, my son was half asleep by the time the service was over and we reached our car. My former mother-in-law followed me there in order to spew terrible things. I'm sorry you were called. She's displeased that my son is getting his father's inheritance. That's what this is. Revenge. And I have witnesses to back up my story."

She didn't look surprised. I wasn't sure if that was a good or bad thing.

"I'll need the names of others who were there. And I apologize for the trouble if that is true. But unfortunately, we'll need to see the child. Where is he now?"

"With my mother and stepfather. I'll call and tell them we need to come up." This went against every fiber of my being. Instead, I wanted to take him and run. I tamped down on the urge, reminding myself I'd done nothing wrong. When I saw Mark come in from the front door in a suit and tie, I realized I hadn't mentioned him.

"My attorney friend has arrived. I called him immediately when I found out you were here."

Mark introduced himself, checked their identification, and had them recap the allegations. As I watched him in action, I was grateful for his presence.

After calling my mother, we went up to their room for privacy.

My baby immediately lit up upon seeing me and reached for me to pick him up. I did so, trying to fight the tears.

Ms. Fields gave him a friendly smile. "Hi, honey. How are you?"

"Great," he said with a smile, hugging me close.

"Can I see his arms?"

I tensed but appreciated that she had a job to do. I put Tristan on his feet and knelt down. "Let's take your shirt off, baby."

After helping with the shirt, I had to stand there with a mixture of rage and indignation while the woman from CPS inspected him. The police officer simply stood by the door without any expression on his face. He, too, was here with a job to do.

I had to keep myself from screaming.

Thankfully, Mark was the voice of reason. "As you can see, the child is in excellent health, with no bruising or hesitation toward his mother. These allegations are bogus. I've written down the names of the witnesses you can call in order to corroborate her story. Unfortunately, you have not only wasted your time, but you've also put more stress on Ms. Walker during an already difficult time."

Ms. Fields, obviously used to this type of thing, gave him a nod and took the slip of paper from him with the names. "The child does appear in excellent health Mr. Hines, but please understand that this is our job. The only thing left for us to do here is take some pictures showing that for the file. After that, I'll follow up with the witnesses and hopefully close the case."

I gritted my teeth while she took several snaps of Tristan's torso and then made more notes. Mark ensured she had my contact information and provided his, as well, in case she had need of a follow-up.

I didn't let out a breath until the door shut and they left us alone. Sitting on the bed, I cradled my head. My entire body was shaking with rage. "The money isn't worth this."

Mark's voice came quiet and steady. "That's what they're hoping you'll say. If you're okay with it, I'll call your attorney Harvey and we'll strategize. In the meantime, you should all go back to Charlotte."

I took a deep breath while thinking I couldn't get out of here fast enough. "Good idea."

A COUPLE HOURS after we arrived at my mother's house in Charlotte, I was in her car driving downtown. Fury fueled my adrenaline. I was in no mood to sit around waiting. Mark had been considerate in offering to meet with my attorney for me, but I absolutely wanted to be a part of this meeting. This was my life, my son. I wasn't okay with sitting at home waiting for others to come up with suggestions. I needed to be part of the decision-making; otherwise, I'd go crazy.

When I arrived at the law office, the receptionist only lifted a brow at my presence. Perhaps she'd been warned I might show up. "Right this way, Ms. Walker. Mr. Hines arrived about fifteen minutes ago."

Smiling tightly, I murmured a "thank you" and followed her inside the conference room. I recalled the first day I'd come here. I'd been impressed with the beautiful marble floors, rich wood, and leather chairs—not to mention the view from the fourteenth floor. But today, I was all business.

"Ah. Ms. Walker, I was just telling Mark here that I wouldn't be at all surprised if you decided to show up."

I glanced between both men and relaxed some. Apparently, I wouldn't be considered an intrusion. Absurd, but I'd started to get worked up in the car about the possibility of being left out of a meeting of which I was the subject. "Yes, well, I want to be a part of any decision or strategy."

Mark blushed slightly. "I didn't mean to exclude you."

I pulled out a seat and exhaled my residual agitation. "I know, and I appreciate you offering to be here, too. Okay, gentlemen, what are your thoughts?"

Both exchanged an uneasy look, cuing a foreboding feeling. "What?"

"Rob's parents are challenging Tristan's paternity. They are demanding a DNA test to prove he was their son's child."

I should've expected it, but I hadn't. I should've been prepared to reach a new level of rage, but I wasn't. "I see." The two words came out between clenched teeth.

"We can fight it since Rob is on Tristan's birth certificate and—"

I held up my hand. "I have test results."

Both men were caught off guard.

I had to steel myself against the shame ready to descend upon me. "Rob. He, uh, he wanted proof when we first separated. He was trying to get out of paying child support and, in the process, took a swipe at me by claiming Tristan might not be his."

Harvey cleared his throat. "Well, that makes things simpler, then."

Yes, I suppose it should. And yet I felt my humiliation on display. My husband, the only man I'd ever slept with up to that time, had demanded a paternity test when I'd filed for divorce. Funny how he'd been the one to cheat, but I was the one in the relationship treated like a whore.

"I'll, um, get you a copy of the results, but what I really need you to tell me is if Rob's parents have a shot in hell at custody?"

Harvey shook his head. "Not unless they can prove you unfit. Even then, they'd have to battle as I'm sure your mother would step in. Since she's been more in his life than they have— Anyhow, long story short is I don't see that happening. They made a knee-jerk attempt at it this morning with false allegations. That's not something the state will forget."

"Okay. What do you think their next move will be?"

Mark spoke first. "They may ask for a settlement. A portion of the life insurance."

Their own grandson's rightful inheritance. I had to swallow down the acid rising up in my throat from the thought.

"Or they could throw some more charges at you. Probably would be better if you went back up to Connecticut as soon as possible."

"I'll, um, see what I can do about getting tickets to leave tomorrow." They'd be expensive, but the sooner I got out of here, the sooner his parents would be at a disadvantage, not knowing where we were.

"Josh has offered the use of his plane. It can be ready by this evening if you'd like," Mark spoke up.

I released a breath. "That would be great."

I BARELY SAID three words to Mark after leaving my attorney's office and walking to our cars. Not because I was upset with him, but rather because I didn't know how to get beyond this latest mortification. I'd never told anyone that Rob had insisted on a DNA test to prove Tristan was his. Now it was in the open. And this was after a visit from CPS calling into question my fitness as a mother.

Once we were on the private jet later that evening with Tristan about to return to Connecticut, I finally breathed a sigh of relief. Only a few weeks ago I had been filled with dread at leaving my home, but today I couldn't wait to put it in my rearview mirror. At least for now.

"You okay?" Mark handed me a diet Coke and took the seat across from Tristan and me.

"It's been a day, but I'm better now."

He smiled kindly and took my hand. "It started out great but definitely went downhill from there."

I returned the smile, enjoying the memory of how he'd woken me up this morning. "Thanks for being there today."

"I hope you believe I wasn't trying to cut you out of the meeting with Harvey. I was only trying to be helpful."

"I do believe that. Time was of the essence, and you were giving me the option to avoid dealing with one more thing. But I needed to be part of it. Otherwise, I'd have felt helpless and inadequate in dealing with my own life."

I hadn't always made the best choices. For example, I'd stayed in my marriage for too long. So, participating in the meeting with my attorney was a way of gaining confidence about making good choices going forward.

"I understand. And I'm glad you showed up. I'm just sorry for the other."

"Nothing for you to apologize for."

"It's not that kind of 'I'm sorry.' More like I wish there was more I could do. You don't deserve this."

For the first time, I was starting to believe the same. "No, I don't. Neither does Tristan. But we'll get through it."

"I want to be there for you through this, too, Jules."

"Why?" The question hung, heavier than the single syllable implied.

"Because, if you haven't noticed, I'm absolutely crazy about you. You're the second chance at happiness I didn't ever think I'd get. I want to be yours."

My heart beat double time with his words. I was absolutely head-over-heels for him, too, but I couldn't keep from voicing the obvious. "I know you have lived in New Haven for years, but I love my job in Charlotte. Plus, my mom is there. Although Tristan and I are coming back up to Connecticut now, I don't know for how long—"

He cut me off. "I like Charlotte. In fact, I wouldn't mind living there."

"Oh."

He grinned. "Yeah. Oh. And if any of this is freaking you out, tell me, and I'll dial it back a notch."

I shook my head, grinning. "Nope. No notch take backs."

IT WASN'T until I lay in his arms later that night in my New Haven apartment that I realized Mark's admission he'd be willing to relocate to Charlotte had left me with additional questions.

"What about your job if you moved?"

His fingertips skimmed down my arms. "I can work from anywhere. Funny enough, Josh is hoping to ask Haylee if she wants to move down there after she's done with law school. If he relocates his office down to Charlotte, it will make it even easier for me to move."

"Will you miss New Haven?" Obviously, he had a connection to this place, including his history with his fiancée.

"Maybe the snow. Has Tristan ever seen it?"

"No, he hasn't, but maybe we'll get the chance before we move." I chewed my lip, but then went for it. "I feel as though you know everything about me, both good and bad, but I hardly have any of your history."

He tensed. "Some of mine isn't easy to talk about."

His fiancée. "Maybe talk about the stuff that is?" I was greedy for information and thankful when he relaxed and started talking.

He spoke about his childhood with an older sister, who now lived in London with her husband. His parents had moved to a retirement community in Florida. He saw them twice a year as they were constantly traveling all over the globe. His memories went to freshman year at Harvard, where he'd met both Brian and Josh. We both laughed at stories involving my boss in his youth.

"Who was the woman from four years ago?" It had been on my mind to ask ever since our first time, when he'd admitted how long he'd been without sex. I'd wondered if he'd had another girlfriend in between me and his fiancée.

He stayed quiet for so long that I peered up to see if he'd fallen asleep. Finally, he sighed and spoke. "I hadn't been with anyone since— Anyhow, I was in Vegas with Colby, and there were some women. It had been years, and I was lonely. But it was an empty, one-time thing."

I interrupted. "You don't owe me any explanations. I was only wondering if you'd had another girlfriend or something."

"Not even close. I mean, you're the first one since."

I pushed up on his chest and scooted so I could kiss him. "Are you saying I'm your girlfriend?"

"A guy can hope, but with the timing, I'd understand if you want to hold off on the title."

Right. I'd buried my husband yesterday. But he hadn't been my husband in years. Didn't I deserve to be happy? I wished I could definitively say yes.

I tried to shut off the internal voice threatening to undermine the moment. "Not a chance. And as my boyfriend, I think you should know something."

"What's that?" He was grinning.

"I have developed an affinity for dirty talk."

THE NEXT DAY, Mark had to leave early for a train to New York since he was trying to get a couple days of work in there before Thanksgiving next week.

I forced myself out of bed to start the day. It had occurred to me suddenly that I had no idea how much Rob's life insurance was actually worth. In all the chaos, I hadn't asked.

Since it was still too early to call my attorney, I sent a quick email and then went about my day, getting Tristan up and ready.

It was late afternoon when Harvey returned my email with the estimated amount. The number was staggering. Combining Rob's life insurance and accidental death policies, there was over a million dollars on the line. Holy crap. I knew he had signed up for everything available through the police department, but I hadn't counted on them actually paying out. After all, he'd been suspended from the force. But evidently, one didn't depend on the other. For that, I was grateful. And now I understood why his parents were pursuing the money. They didn't have much of their own.

Taking a deep breath, I made a decision and replied to my attorney. Rob would've wanted his mother and father to have something to make their lives more comfortable. Although I absolutely loathed how they'd treated me, settling with them would alleviate a long, drawn-out battle. Most important, it would put them permanently in the past. And now that I had a wonderful future with Mark within grasp, I needed to shut that door.

But Harvey brought up a good point in his reply, advising me to wait to receive the insurance check before making an offer. The insurance company might appeal because of Rob's autopsy results. After all, he had been high on drugs at the time of the accident. I didn't know if there were any clauses to preclude payout for that reason, but we'd wait and see.

———

By Friday I was excited at the prospect of seeing Mark after our separation of two days. We'd exchanged text messages and one phone call, but that was nothing compared to being wrapped in his arms at night. Thankfully, he was on his way home, arriving later.

But as all good days seemed to be ruined with a phone call lately, this one was no exception. My attorney's number flashed on my phone after I'd put Tristan down for bed. "Hi, Harvey. How are you?"

"Good. Sorry for calling you this late, but uh, Rob's mother contacted me this evening."

I braced myself. "What did she have to say?"

"Since she didn't know how to get a hold of you, she wanted me to pass on a message. I have to say I'm confused by it. I thought you were waiting until you received the insurance money to settle."

He wasn't the only one confused. I had no idea what he was talking about. "What's the message?"

"She said she wanted to apologize. That she appreciated the settlement and wanted you to know how very sorry she was for her behavior. For calling CPS and insisting on the DNA test."

"What settlement?"

"That was my question for you. I didn't ask her since I couldn't be sure whether or not she was fishing. So you didn't offer her money? Because if you did, I would highly recommend you have an attorney to draw something up ensuring she signed away all rights that might allow her to go after more."

"I didn't give her anything. And you didn't tell Brian about this, right?"

"Of course not. I take attorney-client privilege very seriously."

"I'm sorry. I'm just trying to figure out—" Because I hadn't told Brian anything yet, either. Even if I had, I couldn't imagine him doing something like this without asking me if it was all right. And then, boom, it hit me.

Mark.

No, he wouldn't. He wouldn't go behind my back. Not after I'd told him how it made me feel inadequate if I didn't participate in the decisions. At the very least, he'd discuss it with me first and value my opinion and input. And yet, who else would it be?

As if by design, the knock came at the door. I told Harvey I'd call him back and walked over to open it. Upon seeing Mark's handsome face, I felt betrayal wash over me.

"You weren't really in New York, were you?"

CHAPTER FOURTEEN

*T*he immediate guilt shown by the color staining his cheeks said it all.

He came in and shut the door, following me into the kitchen and setting down his bag. "Shit, you weren't supposed to find out yet."

I stopped and turned, feeling my temper snap. "That's what you have to say to me? You regret that I already found out?"

Thankful that Tristan was already in bed, I took a twenty out of my purse and stuffed it in the swear jar above the refrigerator.

Mark's eyes went wide. Yeah, it was about to get real. "I'm sorry. I had every intention of telling you."

"You had no right. No fucking right at all. This was my fight. And you know how important it is to me to be the one making decisions. Hell, you know how much it bothered me when Brian overstepped and paid for my PI to keep track of Rob. So, how did you think this would go over? How can you say you're crazy about me and then go behind my back this way?"

His face blanched. "Jules, I only wanted to make it better. I didn't want you to suffer during the next few months, waiting on the money and, worse, trying to anticipate what new awful thing they'd come up with. I had them sign away their rights to go after anything more, including custody. I was only attempting to help."

"You would've helped more if you'd discussed it with me. I'd already decided to settle. I was only waiting to see if I received all of the insurance money first. That was my attorney's advice. Advice I was following until you intervened. Then you go and lie to me by telling me you were traveling to New York when instead you were in North Carolina."

"I did go to New York. I flew to North Carolina this morning."

"Semantics. You still fucking lied to me."

"I know, and I'm sorry. I didn't realize how it would all look to you. How it would make you feel. I was only trying to close this door for you, honey, once and for all."

I pointed to myself. "Did it ever occur to you that I needed to close this door for myself? That this entire thing—from moving up here, taking favors left, right and center from friends and family—has battered my pride? But more importantly, I needed to close this chapter. I needed to do this for my son and for myself to prove I could."

"You have to trust I had the best intentions." His expression was as sincere as his voice. There was no doubt Mark was a good man. He'd only wanted to make life easier on me. But his actions still made me feel as though he hadn't thought I could do it without his help.

I blew out a breath, adrenaline waning. "I believe you, but it doesn't make me any less upset with you right now."

He sighed, taking my hand. "I know. I should've discussed it with you first. I really am sorry."

"How much?"

"What?"

"How much did you pay them?"

"Uh, it doesn't—"

"Don't you dare tell me it doesn't matter. One, it very much does. Two, I'm paying you back once I receive the settlement or sell the house."

"You don't need to. I have absolutely nothing else to spend my money on."

"How much?"

"Jules—"

I dropped his hand and put mine on my hip. "Dammit, Mark, don't you 'Jules' me. Now tell me how much and show me the agreement they signed before I call Harvey and have him nullify the whole thing. You did not have permission to act on my behalf."

"One hundred thousand."

My breath left me at the amount. "Holy shit." I paced, finding it hard to believe he had the money to be able to write a check for that amount. Truth be told, I'd been thinking of giving Rob's parents the same amount. But the problem was I had no guarantee I would receive all of the insurance money, and I would be lucky to make that amount from the sale of my home since we hadn't built much equity.

"The money doesn't matter to me. Only you and Tristan do."

I stopped and stared at him. "I can appreciate that. I really can, but it doesn't change how it made me feel to discover you did this without consulting me."

He stepped closer but, at my warning glare, didn't touch me. The last thing I needed was to have him think he could pacify me with a hug.

"I know, but please don't make me go."

I lifted a brow. "I'm hardly in the mood to slip into bed with you right now. I need to think. Need to figure out how to get past this. And don't fight me on paying you back. This wasn't your debt. It's mine."

His jaw ticked, but he nodded. "I won't. And I realize it's a lot to ask, but let me hold you tonight. I won't talk, won't try anything. Just hold you."

I was indecisive.

He must've seen it on my face. "Be mad. You're certainly entitled. But please don't make me go. I can't stand it. Please."

Something vulnerable reflected in his eyes, and I wondered if I was seeing shadows from his past here. It gave me pause about telling him to go home. Besides, as upset as I was, I wasn't willing to throw away what we had over it. "Okay. You can stay."

As I crawled into bed and his arms went around me a short time later, I understood the irony that I wanted comfort from the man who'd caused the pain to begin with. It wasn't long before I felt the familiar hardness pressed up against my stomach.

"Ignore the erection. My cock doesn't understand that when you're mad at me, it includes him, too. But he'll get the message eventually."

Despite my best efforts, I giggled. Then I sighed. It was difficult to stay angry at him, but I needed for him to understand why I was so upset by his actions.

"I feel like you didn't think I was capable of dealing with this on my own. That I wouldn't be smart enough and needed rescuing."

His arms squeezed me tight. "I absolutely didn't think that. You're the most capable woman I know. As a single mom, you've made the hard decisions despite how rough it was on you. Through it all, you've never played the victim. You brush yourself off and keep on going. You're unbelievably strong. That's why, for once, I wanted to take the burden off your shoulders. And maybe part of it was self-serving in that I wanted to show how I can contribute."

"I don't want you for your money."

"I'd never think that. I didn't mean a monetary contribution. I only meant I don't know what would you need me for. You

187

have it together, you and Tristan, so I suppose I was looking for a way to show that I could help. And in my mind, I'd thought to surprise you with no longer having to worry about it. It's not because I thought you needed rescuing. I guess I wanted to be the hero in putting this whole mess behind you. It was selfish, but I did it because I can't wait for us to start our lives together."

"You can and have been my hero in so many other ways, but I have to be able to trust you in order for us to work. I have to believe you value my opinion and thoughts. I don't need you to solve all of my problems. I need to do some of it for myself."

"I don't want to solve all your problems. I simply want to be there for you, so you aren't facing them alone."

His reply brought a flood of emotions over me.

He rolled toward me, stroking my face. "I'll never lie to you again."

I leaned up on him with a smirk, never one to be able to hold a grudge, especially when the intention had been good even if the action wasn't. "What if I ask you if certain jeans make my ass look fat?"

"I would tell you. Maybe from a hundred feet away, but I would tell you. Scout's honor."

I lifted a brow, fighting the smile. "Were you ever a scout?"

"Eagle Scout, actually. Nerdy, I know."

That didn't surprise me. "Nerdy Mark is a big turn-on, to be honest."

"Oh, yeah? At the risk of sharing too much information and keeping you mad at me, you should know feisty Juliette is a big turn-on, too."

"Seriously?"

His warm lips trailed down my neck. "When you put your twenty in the jar, it made me part fearful, part turned on. Although I don't like fighting with you, I do love that you stood up for yourself. I clearly didn't see things from your perspective and how it would make you feel. I'm sorry."

"You're kind of hard to stay mad at with your heartfelt apologies, so it's accepted. You know, I don't think I used most of that twenty."

"In that case, feel free to ask me to fuck you, fuck you harder, and never fucking stop."

His words instantly shifted the vibe in the bed. "Are you angling for make-up sex?"

His hands had already moved down to the elastic of my panties. "I sure as hell hope so. You don't mind if I use some of your credits with my cursing?"

I moaned when his fingers found my clit. "I'd be disappointed if you didn't."

"Where do you keep your vibrator?"

"Uh, in the nightstand. Why?"

One of his fingers entered me. "I was thinking of something a bit more naughty. Matter of fact, I'll be right back."

He was out of the bed and bringing his bag into the bedroom in a flash, wearing only his boxers and a T-shirt. That left me to grab my vibrator. By the time I'd shed my clothes, he stood there watching me. Since our time together in North Carolina, I no longer felt anxiety at being naked with him.

He grinned at me in the moonlight. "You're so sexy. So beautiful."

"You make me feel that way. Uh, what do you have in your hand?" He had a pouch of some sort.

"Toys I bought for you. Unless you'd rather wait. I suppose it's rather presumptuous to think a butt plug has a place in make-up sex."

I burst out laughing. "Oh, I don't know. It might really make me feel good sliding it home in your ass."

He froze, a look of panic on his features. "It's not for me. It's —" He grinned. "You were totally messing with me, weren't you? Hopefully."

My body was so wracked with laughter I could barely speak.

His fingers tickling my sides as he moved to hover above me didn't help. "Oh, my God. Your face."

Laughter turned to a gasp, however, when he stopped tickling and pressed my vibrator up against my center. Throwing my head back, I let my legs fall to the sides as his hands gently pushed them.

"I deserved that. Now, hold the vibrator on your clit."

I took the device from his hands and moved it in circles, watching with curiosity while he stripped, then opened his bag of goodies. He took out what looked to be the plug as well as a small bottle of lube. "When did you get these things?"

He blushed slightly. "They came in the mail while I was gone. If there's anything you don't like, tell me."

"You go from all alpha to considerate in a hurry."

"Which one do you prefer?"

"I don't want to choose as I like them both."

He smirked. "Good. Get up on your knees and keep that vibrator pressed to your pussy while I play with your ass."

Damn. He was taking the dirty talk up a notch. I moved the pillows so I could put my head and shoulders into them and position my backside in the air. With my one arm under my body, I positioned the vibrator as he asked.

"Gorgeous."

I'd been prepared for his hands, so I wasn't expecting his mouth to feast on me from this angle. "Oh, God."

"I missed the taste of you. Sweet and sassy, just like you." His fingers joined the assault, and my climax rushed over me without warning.

As I was coming down from my high, I was aware of the sound of lubrication and then his finger circling my tight bud, working itself inside. Then there were two fingers stretching me before the hard object was inserted. Breath rushed out of my lungs at the foreign sensation.

"How does it feel?" He leaned forward, kissing the small of

my back before I heard the familiar sound of him opening a foil packet.

"Strange, but good."

"I'm going to slide inside of your tight pussy now. Fuck you so hard you'll have to bury your face in your pillow to muffle the sounds of your orgasm."

He filled me then on one stroke.

The pleasure from the fullness took my breath away. I could feel his hips pounding against me, thrust after thrust. When his fingers started moving the plug in the same rhythm, working my tight hole, I had to bite down on the soft cotton pillow to keep from crying out. When my climax rolled over me, it took no mercy and left no coherent thoughts in my brain. I saw white light and felt every nerve ending explode with ecstasy.

He had slowed his pace of moving in and out of me and removed the plug. "Fuck, that's sexy. Did you like it?" His fingers quickly replaced the object.

"Yes. And I don't care if it makes me dirty, but now I want you there."

He stilled.

"Mark?"

"I'm here. But I think my neurons fried with that statement. Are you sure? I may not fit."

"We could try it. I mean I never have."

"Me, neither."

The thought of doing something so intimate and new for the both of us fueled my desire for him. "It felt good, before, so…"

Evidently, I didn't have to convince him. He pulled out of me and replaced his fingers with the head of his cock. But since that wasn't enough for him, he grabbed my vibrator and put it inside of my pussy. "I've fantasized about filling you both ways. About giving you so much pleasure that you come harder than you ever have. But if this hurts, you have to tell me."

He slid forward an inch, and I let out a shaky breath.

There'd been a sting of pain, but it wasn't intolerable. The pressure was already mounting from his hand working the device inside of my pussy. I pushed my hips back to take him deeper.

His gasp was my reward. "You're tight. I don't think I'll go all the way in, honey, but this, this feels amazing."

He moved with controlled thrusts then, his breathing labored, his one hand gripping my hip, the other moving the dildo in and out.

I wasn't sure my body would survive this latest assault, but I was certainly willing to find out.

When his groan filled the space and he folded over me, smothering the sound on my back, my orgasm followed, slamming into me as if the other two hadn't just happened. It left me completely and totally spent. My knees buckled, no longer able to hold my weight once he pulled out.

He left for a couple minutes to go to the bathroom but then returned to get back in the bed and pull me close.

"I should probably put my vibrator away," I murmured, barely able to stay awake.

"I'll take care of it."

I smiled, snuggling into him. "My hero."

A HOT MOUTH fastened on my breast woke me up. My eyes snapped opened to see a dark head of hair hovered over my nipple and lips teasing it to a stiff peak.

"Good morning."

I stretched, running my hands through his thick hair. "'Morning. What time—?"

"A little after five. And before I started my exploration, I ensured Tristan was still sleeping."

I was grateful he understood my priorities.

"I missed doing this last night, and when I saw your gorgeous body in the morning light, I couldn't help myself."

"Mm, I'm glad." Talk about a boost to my self-confidence.

His lips moved up onto my collarbone and from there onto my shoulder. That's when I noticed the smell of his minty breath and covered my mouth.

"No fair. I'm brushing my teeth."

He laughed but let me up for the fastest teeth brushing in history.

Soon I bounced back into bed with him. My hands rubbed down the planes of his chest, exploring, before I scooted down to flick my tongue over one of his nipples. With his sharp intake of breath, I knew I'd found his sweet spot.

"At some point, I'm exploring your body inch by inch."

He smiled, kissing me on the lips. "I won't argue a bit. But for now—" He rolled me onto my back, pinning me down with his body.

I sighed in bliss.

"Open your eyes." His voice cajoled as he eased inside of me.

His forearms were on either side of my head, his hips pressing into mine as he possessed me fully. Lips met mine as he robbed me of breath and then gave it back to me.

Then he suddenly stopped. "Shit. I forgot a condom. No wonder it felt so different."

"Better different?"

He tried to back out, but I locked my ankles around him, pulling him deeper.

"Yes. Fuck. And if you keep doing that, I won't last long."

"Sorry." I let him go with regret.

"Unless…" He'd pulled out but was still at my entrance.

"Unless what?"

"What if we took the chance?" He eased back inside.

"What are you saying?"

"I'm saying you told me you want more kids someday. And I, I hope I'd be a great father."

Even as I gasped in pleasure, my mind was working overtime. "You realize there's only room for one crazy person in this relationship, and that spot is already taken. I mean, that's a big step."

He pulled out and grabbed a condom from the dresser. "It is, and I'm sorry. Decisions such as this shouldn't be made in the heat of passion."

He reentered me, taking us both to orgasm and not leaving a lot of room to discuss the subject further.

MARK'S ARMS came around me from the back while I was making pancakes. Tristan was in his high chair, happily starting breakfast with fruit.

"I'm sorry for bringing up a baby the way I did this morning. I didn't mean to rush you into anything."

I took the golden cakes off, sliding them onto a plate on the counter, and then flicked off the stove. I turned, wrapping my arms around him. "You aren't. I definitely do want more kids, and I think you'd make a fantastic father. But have you thought about the rest?"

He leaned back and smiled. "If you knew how much, you'd probably be alarmed."

I studied the seriousness in his expression and swallowed hard. "Like what?"

He hesitated but then leaned in, whispering in my ear. "Like marrying you. Building a house with you. Waking up with you every morning. Making more babies with you. And eventually, once Tristan gets old enough to decide and if you're okay with it, adopting him as my own."

Wow. So, yeah, he'd definitely thought about it. When he

moved back and cupped my face, I took a shaky breath. "I don't know what to say."

He kissed me softly. "Don't say anything. Not until you're ready. I don't mean to push. It's just that—"

"Just what?"

He sighed. "Life is short, cruelly sometimes. And I know what I want. A future with you and Tristan. Whether it's tomorrow or a year from now. I'm not going anywhere."

"I want that, too. But—"

"When you're ready. Okay?"

I nodded. How did I voice my doubts? He'd never said he loved me. We still hadn't told anyone about us.

Tristan's voice broke through the moment. "Pancakes, pease."

"You got it, buddy." Mark grabbed one, testing the heat, and then cut it up like a pro. He set the pieces on Tristan's tray.

The conversation was tabled for now.

ON MONDAY HAYLEE came over for lunch after her classes. I'd told her bits and pieces about the last few days, including the funeral and the behavior of Rob's parents. I'd omitted the part about Mark paying them off or the DNA test.

"Wow. You've been through hell. With Rob's death and the settlement with his parents, do you think you'll move back soon?"

"I think maybe in a couple of weeks."

Funny. I'd had the same conversation with both my PI and my attorney this morning. Both agreed that I would need to sell the house, which was on record belonging to Rob. They'd also agreed I ought to move to another suburb where the people wouldn't know me as the dirty cop's wife. Since that had been my intention all along, it wasn't a hardship.

Then both had suggested I change back to my maiden name. But if I did that, did I change Tristan's last name, too? I didn't want to have a different name from him.

Thanksgiving was coming up on Thursday. Haylee and Josh were staying in town since she had a big paper due the following week. They'd invited me to have dinner with them. I was happy to join them since Mark was traveling to Florida to be with his parents on a trip he'd planned months ago and my mom was spending the holiday with my sister.

"I find myself already missing our girl's time."

Haylee smiled. "Me, too, but Josh bought property down in Charlotte. And Brian purchased the lot next door. I swear I overheard them on the phone the other night discussing plans for a treehouse on the property line."

I laughed, thinking the childhood friends were probably giddy with excitement over living next door to one another again. "Mark mentioned you might be moving down there at some point. That Josh was relocating headquarters from New York?"

"Yep. The best part is that Nigel, his assistant, wants to make the move, too. He and his partner, David, are looking for a quieter life, which makes me happy. Everyone else who works directly for Josh will simply move into the other building in New York to consolidate the two offices. They're also being offered relocation to North Carolina if they want."

"That's great. Where is the property located? How many acres?"

"Fifteen acres, but we'll only build on three. Just like with this building, Josh wants to control how close the neighbors can get. The place is south of the city, but I'm not sure exactly where. The land still needs to be cleared. It's exciting to build a house from scratch, and it'll probably take the next two years to get everything done."

"I can't wait to have you both down there."

"Me, too. So you've been talking to Mark, huh?"

"Sure. We're friends." Although I could use someone to confide in about my feelings, the wife of Mark's best friend was not the right person.

"That's good. I bet he'll miss you guys. He raves about your cooking, and I think you and Tristan have had him spending more time in this building than he ever used to."

Speaking of which. "Have you ever been to his house?"

She shook her head. "No. Josh doesn't go over there, either, as far as I know."

Well, at least I wasn't the only one.

"I MISSED YOU." Mark slid into bed with me in the middle of the night. It was the Monday after Thanksgiving, and he'd just returned from his trip to Florida and his parents' house. It was hard to believe we were already heading into December.

"Mm. I missed you, too."

His hands froze when they made contact with my naked skin. "This is a nice surprise."

"I wore it for you." I might not have sexy lingerie, but this appeared to get directly to the point.

"Officially my favorite outfit," he chuckled.

I met his eager lips, sliding my tongue in his mouth and enjoying his intake of breath at my aggressiveness. His reaction fueled my confidence, especially when I pushed him onto his back and straddled his lap. It was a vulnerable position for me since I'd be on display for him.

But Mark's eyes were simmering with lust as he filled his hands with my breasts. "I love seeing you like this. Will you ride me?"

I nodded and enthusiastically enclosed my hands around his hardening length. It made me smirk that I wasn't the only one who'd come to bed naked. "It's funny we wore the same outfit to bed tonight."

"I'd suggest we go to bed together every night this way, but I suppose when Tristan gets a big-boy bed, we might have a visitor sometimes and should wear clothes."

My eyes went wide with the vision. Suddenly, I had a picture of our future so clearly that it knocked the breath from me.

"Shit, Jules. Sorry. I got carried away with my thoughts. I didn't mean to spook you. And here I said we could go slow and I wouldn't push you. Then I up and say that."

I held a finger to his lips. Oh, how times had changed. He was the one rambling while I was the one shocked into few words. "I want that future. I want you."

I might not be sure of everything, but the one thing I did believe was that I absolutely wanted a life with this amazing man who was now under me.

Hovering over him, I aligned his thick length with my entrance. Then I sank down onto every glorious inch. We were skin on skin, and the intimacy could not have been greater.

He took a shuddered breath and pulled me down for a passionate kiss that left me completely drunk on the taste of him. But he didn't stop there. He rolled me over so he was on top of me, spreading my legs wider and then moving with long, measured strokes. "I love the thought of coming deep inside of you. You have no idea how much it turns me on to be with you like this. Nothing between us. I promise I'll never stop making you happy."

My hands stroked his face and then down over his chest before he lifted my hips up and found the spot which made my toes curl.

After we'd both come together in a frenzy, we lay there connected for the longest time. This was so much better than him getting out of bed to dispose of a condom.

"I realize this sounds primitive, but I hope I knocked you up tonight."

I smiled in the dark, waiting for the panic to hit me, but none came. Mark wasn't the type of man to make promises he didn't intend to keep. And he wasn't the type to let himself feel again after the death of his fiancée if it wasn't real.

"I have to actually stop the Pill I just started taking again and even then it may not be right away. Sometimes it takes a while."

He kissed my nose. "Oh, ye of little faith in my sperm. I give it a month, two tops, with all the trying I have in mind."

I wouldn't argue with that plan. "I want to move back down to Charlotte before Christmas. I was thinking next week, if possible."

"Into your house?"

I shook my head. "I don't ever want to live there again. In fact, I want to have a massive garage sale and sell everything except for Tristan's things and my clothes. Um, what about your house? Will you sell it?"

"Either that or rent it out."

"Do I get to see it?" Although the words were light, the intention behind them wasn't. He was keeping some of his past from me. Although I understood that he didn't want to relive the pain, I needed some reassurance that he was ready to move on. Chalk it up to my insecurity, but I wanted to put my mind at ease.

He pulled out, tucking me into the curve of his body. "I'd rather you didn't, at least not until I can clean it up. When it comes to crap everywhere, the place makes my office look like child's play. I need to get rid of a lot of stuff."

It wasn't a no. And considering how embarrassed he'd been with the state of his office, his feelings about his home made sense. "Okay. And what about telling everyone about us?"

It occurred to me that I should've asked these questions

before we'd had unprotected sex. But now they were flowing out as if I'd opened the floodgates.

His words were measured. "I'd prefer to tell both Josh and Brian in person. They're my best friends. More than that, though, I'm afraid Brian might be weird about it. I presume, given your friendship with him, you'd want to be there, too?"

"Yeah. I suppose I would. But why would he be weird about it?" Brian thought the world of Mark, and I would hope he'd want me to be happy.

"There are three women in Brian's life who he's always respected more than anything. Sasha, of course; his little sister, Kenzie; and you. Given his reaction to finding out Josh's younger brother Colby was dating Kenzie, well, I'd like to ensure we tell him before we tell anyone else."

I laughed. "Don't tell me you think Brian is going to punch you? He only did that to Colby because there was a misunderstanding. Brian thought Colby had gone from sleeping with a stripper straight to Kenzie's bed. Plus, if you want the truth, he still feels terrible about it. It's not as though he's a violent kind of guy, usually."

"No, but he's going to want to ensure you're happy. That I didn't take advantage of you in a rebound phase or something."

I frowned. "I'm a big girl, and I'm definitely not rebounding."

He chuckled. "No, you're not. It's only because he loves you like a sister that I bring this up. How about once we get to Charlotte and get settled for a while, we'll take Brian and Sasha out to dinner and tell them? After he knows, we can tell Josh and Haylee."

That would be weeks away, but at least he was thinking about how and when he wanted to tell people. "Okay."

"Do you have an idea of where you want to move?"

"I'm not sure. I was thinking of renting while I wait for the house to sell. At least in the short term. Are we, uh, I mean I don't want to assume, but are we moving in together?"

"Eventually, I would hope so. But until we tell everyone, probably best for me to stay in a hotel. I'll probably have to travel back and forth quite a bit in the beginning anyhow. Although that'll be torture as I can't stand the thought of a night away from you."

I chewed on my lip, trying to think of the logic in his statement. At this point, what were a few weeks? I'd be so busy with the move and selling the house, I'm sure the time would fly by. "Okay."

"I realize your mom does pickups for Tristan at day care, but I have flexibility because I work from home, so I could help out. At least I'd like to."

If anyone would've asked me three months ago if I could imagine a man like Mark coming along in my life, a guy who I would trust with my son and with whom I'd look forward to spending the rest of my life, I would've said they were crazy. And yet now we were planning a future together. "We're really doing this, aren't we?"

"I sure as hell hope so. Does it scare you?"

I tamped down on any residual anxiety. "A little, but mostly it makes me happy."

And it absolutely did. So maybe what had me feeling uneasy was trying to believe I actually deserved it.

CHAPTER FIFTEEN

*A*lthough Mark had given me no tangible reason to feel this way, I couldn't shake the sensation that something was off the next day. Which was ridiculous. We'd made a plan, and he'd answered all of my questions logically about his house and telling our friends about our relationship.

Which meant the problem had to be me. That I hadn't fully accepted I deserved this second chance and worried Mark would wake up one morning realizing he'd made a mistake. It was this unexplainable insecurity which had me knocking on Dr. Mac's door for a long overdue appointment.

The older gentleman with kind eyes and a graying beard answered the door and then ushered me into his beautiful home. "Hi, Juliette. I was happy to get your phone call this morning."

"Yes. Well, thank you for seeing me on such short notice."

"Of course. Right this way into my office. Can I get you coffee, tea, water?"

"Oh, no, nothing for me, or I'll have to pee, probably at the most enlightening moment ever." Ugh. Nerves were already getting the best of me as I was completely over-sharing.

He chuckled. "I understand and can only hope for such a

moment. Now, then, take a seat. Tell me what brings you here today."

I took a deep breath. "I think I can't let myself be happy. Almost as though I don't think I deserve it. And I'm worried I'll end up sabotaging this new relationship with a man who is so very good to me. Who wants a future with me and my son. Who makes me feel like—Gah, I can't even describe it. I think my past keeps making me wonder if I'm good enough. Keeps me questioning when it's going to turn. It's as if something is off, but I can't put my finger on it, which probably means it's me and my neurosis."

He blinked at me before adjusting his glasses. "All of that is good information. But how about you start at the beginning? Take your time and tell me about yourself and this past you referenced."

So I did. For the next thirty minutes in a continuous upchuck of information.

During it all, Dr. Mac simply made some notes and posed a few questions. Once it was all laid out for him, he set his pen down and met my eyes.

"Hearing about your history helps me get the entire picture and understand you better. If you don't take anything else from this session, what I want you to hear is how very proud of yourself you should be for getting out of your marriage when you did. For making that decision for your son and leaving."

A single tear tracked down my face. "But why did I stay so long? How did I get so low that I put up with it? That wasn't me. At least not the me I pictured myself to be."

"The short answer would be because you'd been with him since you were sixteen. The man he started to become was so very shocking that you were stunned in place. Another theory could be because your own father left your mother to raise you and your sister alone, and you didn't want Tristan to grow up the same way."

Wow. This psychoanalysis stuff went deep and way back. "I never considered my childhood might be coming into play."

"You can spend hours, days, months trying to figure out what led to your decisions, thought processes, and reactions, but is it worth doing that? Because if I'm hearing you correctly, despite everything you've been through, it got you to this place which you're saying is pretty good."

"It is, but then why can't I shake this feeling that something will go wrong?"

"Because fear is a powerful thing. You have something you don't want to lose. Once you've been through heartache, the stakes are always higher for the next relationship. I don't want you dwelling on what you could've or should've done differently in your marriage. What I do want to encourage is for you to learn to forgive yourself. I think there is a part of you that is still questioning what you could've done differently that would have made the marriage work."

He'd hit the nail on the head. "What if it was partially my fault, though? What if I made him so unhappy he turned to drugs to cope? Or drove him to become this other person?" This question came from a dark place that until now, I hadn't been able to vocalize.

"This is where you have to remember when he started using the pain killers. After he sustained an injury. You didn't cause the injury. If you continue along with this logic, you'll see he left behind everything he loved for the drugs. You, his son, and even the police force. He became an addict in the truest sense. Nothing mattered but his next hit. Not his family, not his career, not the law and, ultimately, not his life."

"You're right. And the logical part of my brain believes that."

"Then you need to focus on those thoughts. Walk yourself through the logic whenever you start to go down the other road. Understand that from this experience you are stronger, wiser and, most importantly, will never settle again. From the sounds of it, you've found someone who builds you up."

"He does, but he's also damn near perfect." Don't say Mark's name, don't say Mark's name.

"Ah. Is he? Are you saying he doesn't ever make mistakes?"

I thought of how many times Mark had apologized for not getting things right and smiled. "No, he has. It's been a long time since he's been in a relationship, and we, uh, fumbled at first. I suppose we'll keep on fumbling to a certain degree."

"Do you think if you got your degree, cursed less, or lost those ten pounds you mentioned as being part of your Juliette 2.0 plan, he'd want you more?"

I thought about it a second but ended up sure in my answer. "No. I don't think he cares about any of that except for supporting me in what makes me happy. But I do want to get my degree, regardless. Although I need to take a simpler math class next time."

"Then you should do that. But for yourself. For your goals, not because you think it'll make you more worthy of someone's love or affection. You've been through a lot, Juliette, but it doesn't define you. It shapes you, and therein lies the difference."

I nodded, agreeing with what he was saying.

"You took a big step by talking to me today. A step toward letting the past go and focusing on your future. If you like, I'd be happy to see you again tomorrow. We'll work on some techniques for turning off your negative voice and continue to build your self-confidence."

I smiled for the first time, relieved that the hard part of laying it all out there was done. "Good. Let's set it up, then."

OVER THE NEXT WEEK, I met with Dr. Mac a few more times,

trying to cram the sessions in before we moved. I was becoming more comfortable with each visit and making progress against my insecurities. Although I'd gone in with the intention of ensuring I didn't sabotage my relationship, what I'd gotten out of our sessions was so much more. I could feel myself growing more confident and more forgiving of myself regarding the past. I was ready to focus on our future. Together.

That future was also on Mark's mind, judging by the mission he'd undertaken to knock me up. Not that I was complaining considering the man could hardly keep his hands to himself. I found myself looking forward to this new chapter of my life. A life with Mark, Tristan and, with any luck, a new baby. I wondered how Tristan would take to being a big brother.

Intending to leave town in the next couple days, I spent the entire morning on Wednesday packing and cleaning the apartment. By afternoon, I felt restless. I picked up Tristan from upstairs, bundled him up, and put him in his stroller. We could take one last walk across the Yale campus.

Winter was settling in, with the air crisp and fresh. I walked with a pep in my step, admiring the Christmas decorations starting to crop up around the town.

The plan for the move was that Mark would drive down with me. I'd stay with my mother for a week while he did some business-related travel and prepared to relocate his job down to Charlotte. I'd lined up a couple of rentals we'd be viewing this weekend. With some luck, I could move in plenty of time to put up a tree for Christmas and make it festive. Then Mark would hopefully be moving in after the new year.

I listened to Tristan jabber while I pushed him and shifted my thoughts to the dinner I was planning to make tonight for Haylee. It would be our last girls' night, but at least I got to look forward to her moving to North Carolina in the next couple of years.

Imagine my astonishment when, amongst the dozens of students milling around in the quad, I spotted Mark coming out of one of the buildings. He was walking toward us. Since he was still affiliated with the law school, it didn't strike me as strange that he was here. But it wasn't until I was less than five feet away from him, about to say hello, that I realized he wasn't alone. Walking with him was a pretty blonde with a fuzzy beret and a long down coat cinched at the waist. She was smiling up at him while he said something to her.

I saw the moment Mark's gaze focused on us. Telling my inner doubts to shut the hell up, I swallowed down my unease. She was probably a student or a colleague. "Hey, Mark."

"Mark, Mark," Tristan said excitedly.

"Hey, guys." His voice sounded weird, strained.

The blonde stopped, looking at us curiously and then back at him. Since it was clear he had no intention of doing so, she made the introductions. "Hi, I'm Lauren."

I smiled, as she appeared warm and friendly. Definitely not catty or the least bit territorial. "I'm Juliette, and this is my son, Tristan."

She gave him a little wave and then glanced between us and Mark. "Uh, how do you guys know one another?"

The moment suddenly suspended, seemingly slowing down while I awaited his answer. I was unprepared for how much his next words hurt.

"Uh, they're my neighbors. They moved in a couple months ago."

I could feel my face heating with a combination of humiliation and anger.

"Oh, in the Tinkermans' house? I've always loved that place."

"Uh, no, I meant at the building with my office."

She knew where he lived? Knew the Tinkermans lived next door? "And how do you, um, know each other?" I was impressed with how calm my voice sounded despite the dread settling in my stomach.

"Gosh, I guess we're sort of like family. He was engaged to my sister." Checking her watch, Lauren gave me an apologetic smile. "Sorry. If we want to make dinner on time, we'd better go, but it was nice meeting you, Juliette. And you, too, Tristan."

I forced myself to smile in return as she'd been nothing but kind. Though Mark wasn't meeting my eyes, I didn't want to make a scene. "You, too. Take care." I turned on my heel before Mark had the chance to say something even more hurtful, like "see you around, neighbor."

ONE OF THE things I'd become scarily adept at doing toward the end of my marriage was completely internalizing the hurt and shutting off the pain. It was a coping mechanism that came in handy as I made dinner for Haylee that evening and listened to her chat on. I refused to think about the knock that didn't come, the explanation which wasn't given, and that Mark was at dinner with Lauren and her family tonight.

Haylee and Abby provided a welcome distraction through the meal.

"Everything okay with you?" Haylee looked at me curiously after we'd stuffed ourselves on chicken parmesan.

"Yeah. Sorry. Just stressed, I suppose, about moving back."

She smiled. "I bet. And please don't worry about cleaning the apartment before you go. One less thing."

As if. "Thank you. I don't only mean for that. I mean for everything. I, um—" Damn, I was getting emotional. If I didn't rein it in, I would be a blubbering mess. "Offering Tristan and me a place to live and being so very generous with everything. I really can't thank you enough."

Haylee teared up, giving me a hug. "Aww. We're going to miss you a lot. And I love that we became even closer friends."

"Me, too."

After Haylee had left, I put Tristan to bed and was working on the dishes when I heard the knock on the door. I called out that it was open. As Mark came in, I felt the emotions start to overwhelm me.

He shed his coat and walked to the kitchen, eyes on me. "Talk to me, Jules."

I dried a pan and put it in the cabinet. I was grateful that at least he wasn't pretending everything was normal. "What would you like me to say?"

He sighed loudly. "I realize you're upset, but it was my fiancée's birthday today—or would've been. All I did was have dinner with Lauren and her family."

Not former fiancée. His fiancée, as if she'd always be that to him. I stopped what I was doing and faced him. "What was her name? Your fiancée? I only know it started with an S."

He hesitated, then softly said, "Sarah."

It was the first time he'd spoken her name to me. I thought how sad it was that, in this entire time, he'd never mentioned her and I'd never asked until now. "You could've told me where you were going. What today was."

My voice was sympathetic. I refused to shout or fight. I simply wanted answers.

"I didn't know how. But I'm sorry."

I swallowed hard. "You called me and Tristan your neighbors."

"I know, but I couldn't tell Lauren the truth—not on her sister's birthday."

"Then when? Maybe the same time you'd get around to telling anyone else about us." Because, suddenly, I didn't believe him when he said he wanted to tell Brian in person and Josh afterward. I saw it for what it was: a delay tactic.

"It's not like that."

I walked into the living room, needing space. "What's it like, then?"

He answered my question with one of his own, deflecting and looking increasingly uncomfortable. "Where is this coming from? We agreed to wait."

I fought the nausea that threatened. "No, you convinced me to wait. But today you completely dismissed not only me, but also my son. The two people you professed to want as a part of your future." My voice was down to a whisper with the last word.

"Jules—" He took a step toward me.

I knew if I allowed him to touch me, all of my resolve would be gone. So I held up my hand to keep him from coming any closer. "Please don't make this any harder."

His gaze searched mine. "Why does it need to be hard? I don't understand. I thought we were on the same page."

"And what is that page?"

"Planning a future together. I didn't mean to make you feel dismissed, and I'm sorry."

"Do you love me?"

His eyes flashed in panic at my question. "You know how I feel about you."

I shook my head, feeling an absolute fool for not under-standing his limitations sooner. That he might not be as ready to move on as I'd assumed. I had attributed my doubts to my own insecurities and hadn't asked him the hard questions for fear of the real answers. "Actually, I don't know."

"I wouldn't be planning a future with you—which includes having a baby—if I wasn't serious about us."

"But that's not what I asked. I asked if you loved me."

He raked a hand through his hair, frustration rolling off him in waves. "I just—I'm the sort of person who has a hard time saying it, that's all."

"Did you say it to Sarah?" I kept my voice quiet.

Now that the door was open, I was jumping in head first. Whether I was doing this in pursuit of the truth or to punish myself for not realizing all of this sooner, I wasn't sure. But saying her name out loud for the first time caused chills down my body.

His jaw clenched in response. "Don't."

The tears started to well up as insecurity overwhelmed me. "Don't what? Ask questions? Say her name? Why? Am I not worthy, Mark?"

His fists clenched. "You know that isn't it. But this is between us. It has nothing to do with her."

I smiled sadly. "It seems to have a lot to do with her, actually."

"A relationship is more than those three words between people. I want my future with you as my wife. Tristan and more kids with us as a family. Don't actions count for something?"

I could taste the salt from a few escaped tears on my lips as I willed myself to go further towards the point of no return. "You're right. They do. Then let's go get married. Before I'm pregnant. We could go down to the courthouse tomorrow morning."

The alarm on his face told me everything I needed to know. "You don't want a courthouse wedding. At the very least, we'd want your mother there."

I was pushing, even while recognizing that in doing so our relationship would never be the same. But I hadn't been brave enough in my marriage and it had cost me years of settling, which had eventually turned into a ball of resentment. I wasn't about to ignore my gut feeling on this. Not this time. "Then we'll set a date for a month from now and tell our friends and family tomorrow. Call them in the morning with the news."

"I don't have a ring."

"I don't need one." It was interesting he hadn't bought one yet if he was so set on our future together. Once again, this high-lighted my naiveté.

"Yes, you do. I don't want to announce an engagement without a ring on your finger."

"Fine, then we'll go get one tomorrow and tell everyone after."

He paced the room, obviously out of excuses. "Why are you pushing this?"

"Why? Jesus, Mark. We're trying to make a baby together, but you can't tell me you love me. You can't tell people about me as though I'm your dirty little secret. And it seems like you won't propose or marry me unless I get knocked up first."

The reality of what I'd just said out loud slammed into me. "You're hoping I get pregnant so you're then obligated to marry me, aren't you? That way you don't have to feel guilty for wanting to."

"That's ridiculous."

"Is it? Apparently, I can't have anything you had with Sarah. Not a real date, not your love, and not even a ring on my finger before the two pink lines."

"This, between us, along with Tristan—this is all I need."

"But it's not all I need." My voice broke with emotion. "I know you care about me, and I believe you do want a family, but it's not enough."

Exasperation was etched on his handsome face. "I'm giving you all I can."

"I know." God, did I. "But for the first time in my life, I can't settle for that."

"Now I'm like him? I'm like the asshole you were married to?" His temper was evident with the flash of his eyes and clipped tone.

The tears started falling freely now as I was resigned in my answer. "No. You're nothing like him. You're the man who helped me realize I deserve more. But it's as you said: you're giving me all you can."

"Why isn't that enough? You've been married. You're thirty

years old with a son. There's a lot more to think about than going on pointless dates and contrived romance. What we have is real."

I sucked in my breath. I knew he was hurting, but that didn't excuse his implication. "So, because I'm a single mom who had a shitty first marriage, I'm supposed to—what? Be thankful for anything that's thrown my way?"

"That's not what I meant, and you know it. It came out wrong."

His condescending voice instantly pissed me off. "No, but it's what you said. You make it sound as though I should be grateful for whatever I can get."

"I would never even think that. But you're caught up in the trappings of convention. What did it do for you the last time around, huh? You had the courtship, the engagement, the wedding. This is more."

"Then tell me you love me. Tell the world about us as a couple without me getting pregnant first," I challenged.

"Jules, don't do this."

My heart didn't just break in two, it shattered. He was unable to want me for only me. Every insecurity I'd been conquering over the last few weeks slammed back with a vengeance. "You'll have to be more specific about what you don't want me to do: want more? Love you? Want you to love me?"

He stepped closer, looking exhausted. I felt a measure of guilt about bringing all of this up on Sarah's birthday.

"I want to give you the world."

But not his heart. That still belonged in the past.

"If that's true, then why can't our friends and families know about us? Do you realize how it makes me feel that you want to keep us a secret? It's as though you're embarrassed to be seen with me."

"That's not true."

"But it feels true." In my gut, I knew that any woman in my

situation would have had the same reaction to what had happened on campus. It didn't matter that it hit my trigger points.

"I didn't mean to make you feel that way."

"I know you didn't." I did believe him in my heart and my head, but his lack of intention to hurt me only proved the point. He wasn't ready to move on. He might not mean to make me feel this way, but he couldn't help himself, either.

He ran his fingers through his hair in frustration. "Can we please table this until tomorrow? I'm approaching capacity for today. This on top of it is a lot."

In that moment, I grasped that whatever he was struggling with went deep. "I know it is."

"I would like to go home, get some sleep, and start over tomorrow. Can we do that? Please?"

I nodded, trying not to resent the fact that I'd yet to see the home where he would be sleeping tonight. "Sure. Of course."

Relief immediately came over his expression. He came over to give me a kiss on the cheek. "We'll talk more tomorrow."

He left, going out my door without a glance back, seemingly in a hurry to get away.

I lasted the time it took to hear his retreating footsteps down the hall before I collapsed in silent sobs onto the floor.

AFTER A FULL HOUR OF CRYING, I picked myself off the floor and thought one thing: I needed to leave.

Right now. Because I didn't trust myself to stay. Tomorrow, Mark would come over. Did I really think he'd be ready to love me then? He'd said everything by not saying enough. Although it was tempting to wait, hoping he'd change his mind, I knew myself too well. Hoping for that change would end up becoming a rabbit hole I wouldn't be able to pull myself out of it. I'd stayed once, waiting for someone to love me the way I deserved. I couldn't do it again. I couldn't stay.

Hope was for optimists, and I was a realist. My reality was that I needed to plan for my future with my son. I refused to wallow in misery. I didn't have the luxury. Instead, I had a little person relying on me to keep my shit together. Step one was going home.

Knowing Mark would be by tomorrow, I took the chicken way out and started packing up my SUV tonight.

It took two hours and a dozen trips to load everything up, then another hour to finish cleaning the apartment from top to bottom. The last thing I wanted was to skip out leaving a dirty apartment behind. That would hardly show my appreciation.

Finally, I penned a note to Haylee and another one to Mark. I left them both in envelopes, thinking I would slip them under their doors in the morning. Settling onto the couch, I planned to get on the road at the crack of dawn.

AFTER EIGHT HOURS OF DRIVING, two of them stuck in commuter traffic, we finally stopped at a Marriott I'd reserved online. We were ten miles south of Washington DC off of I-95. This would split the trip in two parts and ensure I didn't take risks with a long drive straight through. I counted my blessings that the drive had been uneventful thus far. Tristan had slept for more than half the time, and we'd only stopped once for gas and his lunch. I made two trips, toddler in hand, to get our suitcases into the hotel room. God willing, nothing would get stolen from my car while it sat overnight in the hotel parking lot.

Thankful I'd packed snacks, I went about getting Tristan bathed and into pajamas, ready for bed despite the fact it was only late afternoon. Doing so now made one less thing to do before falling into bed tonight. As it was, I was ready for sleep now.

We'd settled down for television, and I'd ordered room service when Mark's number flashed up.

"Hello."

"Where are you?"

"Did you get my note?"

"Yes, but I don't understand. On a whim, you decided to pack up and move? I thought we were tabling this until today to talk some more."

"We're talking now." My voice was flat, resigned.

"I wanted face to face. And I was supposed to drive down with you. Why did you leave?"

I closed my eyes, finding my strength. "Because I knew you still wouldn't be able to tell me you loved me today and I couldn't bear to be there when that happened."

"Jules, since I've met you, this void has been filled. I don't want to be without you. I care so much."

But he didn't love me.

My tears ran down my face as I said the toughest words I'd ever uttered. "I deserve to be more than a filler of a void for you."

After a long pause, during which all I could hear was his breathing, he finally said, "Yes. You do." His voice was thick with emotion. "I'm sorry, Jules."

"I know." I couldn't even be angry with him. It wasn't as though he was doing this to hurt me on purpose. The situation was so unbelievably sad.

"Where are you?"

"Outside of DC. We'll leave in the morning and get home tomorrow afternoon."

"Are you in a good hotel. It's safe?"

Leave it to him to worry about such things. "Yes. It's a

Courtyard. I lugged in all of our stuff, and Tristan is watching cartoons."

"I wish I could be there helping you."

What I wouldn't give for a partner in it all. Someone with whom I could be a team. Something I'd had a glimpse of with Mark before it had disappeared.

"I'm fine. We're fine."

"What happens if you're pregnant?"

Shamefully, a part of me hoped I was. Wished it would be fate's way of forever tying me to this beautiful man who'd showed me what it was to love and trust again. But on the other hand, I knew it would be better if I wasn't. "If I am, I'll let you know right away."

"Then what?"

"I think we need to cross that bridge when/if we come to it."

"So this is really it?"

"I think it has to be."

Again with the long pause. "What about Tristan? I want to be in his life."

"I won't keep you from seeing him if you want to visit. He needs good, strong men to look up to who care about him."

"You mean that?"

My voice softened. "Of course."

"Will you call me and let me know you made it in tomorrow?"

"Sure. I will." Although it would most likely be a text.

"And your period is due in two weeks?"

He knew my cycle better than I did. "Yes. I'll tell you when I get it."

"Or if you don't."

"Yes."

"I hate this."

"I do, too." But I'd hate myself more if I continued in this relationship with a hope he'd change. A hope that someday he'd love me the way he loved Sarah.

"I— God, Jules." His voice cracked and then, on a long sigh, he said, "Call me later?"

"Okay. Bye, Mark."

"Bye."

Hanging up the phone, I wiped the tears and glanced over at my precious son watching cartoons. I prayed I was doing the right thing by deciding to leave, not only for me but also for him.

CHAPTER SIXTEEN

*I*t felt strange to be back in Charlotte in my office at work on a Monday. But as soon as Brian came in and gave me an exuberant hug, I knew I was where I needed to be.

"I can't tell you how happy I am that you're back. Sasha is traveling until Wednesday, but we thought we'd take you out for a celebratory dinner on Friday if you're free?"

"Yeah, dinner sounds great."

"What's happening with your house?"

"It went on the market and it sounds like a family is putting in an offer this week. Also I found a two-bedroom that I can rent. Moving in mid-January." Although my mom and stepfather were more than generous in letting us stay with them, I was anxious to have my own space again.

"Great. We'll help you move."

He was always so generous that way. "Thanks, but I'm sure that with your wedding coming up you have a ton to do."

He shrugged. Then he shut the door and took the lone chair across from my small desk. "I'll still make the time. How are you doing?"

The old Juliette would've smiled big and convinced him

everything was great. But I didn't have the energy to fake it. "Okay. It's gonna take some time to adjust to all of the changes in my personal life, but it helps to be here in the office. Keeping busy with work. Also, um, I wanted to talk to you about taking classes after the first of the year. Probably twice a week. I know the company has a tuition reimbursement program, so I was hoping maybe—"

"Done. Approved."

"I don't want it as a favor for a friend. I want to make certain I qualify as an employee."

He frowned. "Why wouldn't you? You've been here over ten years. There's a clause which says you have to stay for a certain amount of time, but I don't think that would be a problem."

"I just didn't know if it would make sense for the company to invest in the education of an office manager." Clearly I wasn't over all of my insecurities.

"Juliette, you're the most important person here. You make this place run. Ask anyone how much you were missed these last couple of months. Hell, if it's about your title, then I'll make you the Vice President of Office Operations."

I laughed for the first time in days. "I'm okay with Office Manager, but thanks for the reassurance. I needed it."

He cocked his head to one side. "Everyone does from time to time. In fact, I need you to tell me how amazing I am as a boss because the temp they had in here did not appreciate my sense of humor. I mean, how does anyone resist my charm?"

I'd heard stories about how the older woman hadn't cracked a smile with anyone. I appreciated that Brian was shifting my insecurity to humor. "I have no idea. Because everyone else I meet falls in love with you instantly."

He smirked. "I know, right? Now, then, on another subject, I need your help desperately. I have no idea what to get Sasha as a wedding gift."

I was grateful for the distraction, which took my mind off

how much I missed Mark. Throwing off my sadness, I started brainstorming gift ideas with him.

No matter how busy I kept myself over the next few days, I couldn't help checking my phone ten times every hour. Hoping for a text. A call. Something. But I hadn't heard from Mark since I'd sent him the message that I'd arrived safely at home. He'd responded that he was glad I'd let him know. But there'd been no more contact after that.

My heartache was especially rough when I lay in bed at night. It was as if all the thoughts about him I'd put off during the day would come to a head. A flood of memories would overwhelm me. And guilt. Because maybe if I'd been honest with him about my insecurities and doubts, it wouldn't have blown up the way it had.

"Who are you hoping to hear from?"

I snapped out of my thoughts to see Sasha framing the open doorway of my office. "Um, what do you mean?"

She walked in, shutting the door and taking the chair in front of my desk. Then she nodded toward my phone. "Since you returned, you look at that thing incessantly. And before you give me a line about checking on Tristan, I wouldn't believe you."

I wanted so badly to have someone to confide in. She must've recognized my internal war.

"If you aren't comfortable talking to me, then speak with Brian. I won't take offense. I hope you realize we're both worried about you."

I shook my head, thinking he would be even worse to talk to since Brian was Mark's best friend. "The problem is Brian can't know. And if I tell you, then you're in an awkward position."

She grinned. "Been there, done that when his sister had a huge crush on Colby. I kept that confidence. And look how it turned out. Bottom line is that although I would never lie to Brian, I certainly don't need to be the one to tell him information he wouldn't ask about."

"Okay. Here goes." I took a deep breath and blurted it out: "I'm in love with Mark." And because admitting those words out loud triggered such emotion, I instantly teared up.

A smile spread across Sasha's face. "I knew it. I mean I didn't know it, but I noticed you talking to him the night of the party. And then the evening we came over for dinner, he kept stealing glances at you. I wondered if it might be the beginning of something."

I smiled despite the way it hurt to think back. "I was completely clueless he might be interested in more than friends until he came over after my disaster of a date with this law school guy."

"You went out on a date? And you didn't tell me?"

I shrugged. "Nothing to tell. I was home early, and then Mark came over and— Anyhow, it doesn't matter. The relationship, or whatever you'd call it, is over now."

"Because you moved back to Charlotte?"

I shook my head. "Long story short is he isn't yet over his fiancée or ready to love again. Maybe I wasn't ready yet, either. Because I didn't see his issues even when my gut was trying to warn me. I'm not saying I won't ever date again, but maybe I need some time to figure out how to love myself before expecting someone else to do it." Plus, it wasn't like Mark was an easy guy to get over, either.

She gave a sad sigh. "You're going to see him at the wedding. What do you think will happen?"

I smiled, having pictured that scenario more than once. My visions ranged from him ignoring me, as he had at Catherine's party, to him pulling me onto the dance floor and not caring who in the world knew about us. The latter was the fantasy I most wished for.

"It'll be fine. Honestly, it makes me happy to have an excuse to see him again. Don't worry; neither of us is the type to cause a scene. I mostly tend to embarrass myself in small, selective groups."

She laughed. "Yeah, well if I start to have a panic attack at the reception with all those people, I'm counting on you to come up with a very public scene to distract everyone."

I held up my hand as if I was taking an oath. "I, Juliette Walker, do solemnly swear to make a complete and utter fool of myself in front of a lot of people if you give me the sign. Which will be...?"

She pretended to contemplate. "I will say the code words: *Help me, Juliette.*"

I burst out laughing. "That's the worst code ever, but it'll work."

She was giggling, too. "I'm pretty uncreative when it comes to that kind of stuff." Then she got serious. "You know what I wish?"

I shook my head. "No, what?"

"I wish I could take all the love everyone has for you in this office, with Brian and me at the top of the list, and put it in a bottle so you could have it whenever you need it. Because moments like these make me realize how terribly I missed you over the last couple of months."

I fought the tears. This only proved I'd made the correct decision in coming back. This was where I could steadily gain my confidence and feel it daily with people who lifted me up.

THE NEXT DAY I decided to employ a tactic that Dr. Mac had suggested in one of our sessions. Although it had sounded silly at the time, at this point, what did I have to lose? So I started my day with thinking something positive about myself. A daily affirmation if you will. It could be something little, such as I was happy I'd picked the pink nail polish, or something bigger, such as patting myself on the back for a good-mom moment.

But in addition to that, I needed to start believing the compliments others would give me. No longer scoffing when someone said something nice about my appearance or about the holiday party I'd put on for the office, I made myself soak the comments in and agree I was worthy of the praise.

Easier said than done. But after a couple of weeks, I noticed it was getting easier to find something good about myself. At least until the Tuesday morning I got out of bed and realized I'd started my period. I sobbed for ten full minutes with a mix of relief and sadness at this evidence that I wasn't pregnant. In the end, I knew it was for the best. But the funny thing about emotions is they don't always want to listen to logic.

I waited until I arrived in the office to get up the nerve to text Mark.

"I got my period this morning."

Watching while those ominous little dots appeared on my phone, I waited for what he might say. I'd be lying if I didn't admit to hoping that over the last couple weeks Mark might have recognized his feelings were deeper than he'd realized. That somehow my leaving would've triggered something more for him. But his response slammed the door shut on any hope I might've had left.

"Thanks for letting me know."

OVER THE NEXT couple of days, I kept plenty busy with both my job and trying to get everything done with the house before it was officially sold. Although I acknowledged the hurt from Mark's text, I also refused to dwell on it. After work, I'd go straight to my old house for at least an hour each evening and set things into three categories: donate, save, and sell. Although I didn't have a lot of money to spend on new furniture, I'd rather sit on the floor than be reminded of Rob's favorite place on the sofa or where we used to have our family dinners. This meant most of our things were going. I'd already boxed up all of his clothing and personal belongings for his parents, only holding onto a few things I wanted to give Tristan someday.

I made sure to be back at my mom's house before bath and bedtime each night. Afterward, I would fall into bed exhausted. The packing certainly did wonders for helping me feel proactive about closing a chapter. It also helped to keep my mind off of Mark. Every time I was tempted to call him, I realized I couldn't afford the risk of having him break my fragile self-esteem again. Not when I was just gaining it back.

Three days before Christmas while I was sorting through the mail, Sheila, our receptionist, came running into my office. "Juliette, I have Mr. Singer on line four. He says it's urgent he find Brian. Do you know where he is?"

He was in a client meeting and couldn't be disturbed. "I'll take it, Sheila."

"Mr. Singer, this is Juliette." Although I might be friends with his wife, old habits were hard to break. Josh Singer was the owner of the company. "Brian is in the Shadow Sports Arena contract negotiation at the moment. I expect him out of the conference room in about twenty minutes or so."

"Hi, Juliette. Um, okay. Can you have him call me the moment he steps out? I tried his cell phone, but most likely it's off. It's quite urgent."

I couldn't help myself; I had to ask. "Is everything okay with Haylee and Abby?"

His voice softened. "Yes, yes. They're fine."

"Sorry, I didn't mean to pry. I'll have him call you when he returns."

"Thanks."

Hanging up the phone, I sat there for a minute, unable to quell my curious nature nor the uneasy sensation that Josh's call could have something to do with Mark. It was a silly idea, however. The likelihood was his call was business related and had nothing to do with anything personal.

———————

THE MINUTE BRIAN walked out of his meeting in the large conference room, I intercepted him. After years of working together, he knew the look I was giving him and followed me into his office.

"What's wrong?"

"Josh called saying it was urgent you get in touch with him."

"Everything okay with Haylee and the baby?"

"I asked, and he said yes. I'm hoping it's only a professional crisis."

He nodded and picked up the phone to dial. I hesitated but then asked. "Will you let me know, so I don't worry after your call what it is?"

"Sure."

I paced the small space which made up my office, watching the light on my phone that indicated Brian's phone line and waiting for it to go off. The moment it did, I had to keep myself from charging into his office.

Luckily, I didn't have long to wait for Brian. He soon came out of his door, shrugging into his coat and clearly on his way out. "I have to head up to Connecticut. I'll call Sasha from the car. Josh has a private plane waiting."

"For what?"

"Uh, Mark needs some help with something. Do you mind rescheduling my three o'clock?"

"What does he need help with?"

His eyes met mine. The indecision reflected in them told me he wasn't comfortable in giving me all the information.

"Please tell me."

He finally sighed, giving me a bit. "My guess is that the holidays coming up are taking a toll on him."

"Josh didn't say why?"

Brian must've sensed something from my worried questions. "Is there something I'm missing here? Why are you so curious about Mark?"

I swallowed hard. "Just tell me if this is something about his fiancée and happens every year."

"It hasn't happened in eleven years, since losing her, but Josh said Mark checked out four days ago."

That was the day I'd told him I wasn't pregnant. I knew in my gut the timing wasn't a coincidence. But what did I do? I'd spent years trying to help someone I loved work through his issues and had failed miserably, losing myself along the way. What if I went up there and Mark shut me down?

But Mark wasn't Rob. And I wasn't the same person, either. "I want to come with you."

He lifted a brow. "Because?"

"Because he and I became close while I was living in New Haven. I don't know if I can help, but I want to try."

"How close, exactly?"

"The kind that is none of your business." I was a grown woman and not about to spill my personal life to him. "I care about him a lot, okay?"

He relented. "All right. What will you do about Tristan?"

"I'll call my mom. And then cancel your three o'clock."

CHAPTER SEVENTEEN

*O*nce we each made phone calls to inform people where we were going, we traveled in silence, both of us worried and involved in our own thoughts. I tried to keep my nerves from getting the best of me.

What if Mark didn't want me there? What if this was all about Sarah and the holidays and nothing about me? Furthermore, I'd only just begun the attempt to move on without him in my life. What if this set me back? But then I thought of how much he'd been there for me, and it was a no-brainer that I had to at least try to give him something.

When Brian pulled the rental car into the driveway of the bungalow-style home in a quiet residential neighborhood, I swallowed hard. Mark's house was quaint and cute, with a nice yard in front. It was also a painful reminder of the part of his life into which he hadn't allowed me.

The engine of the rental car quieted, and Brian turned toward me. "I don't know what happened between the two of you, but if this is too much…"

I gave him a small smile, putting on my brave face. "Only one way to find out. Come on."

Brian knocked on the door.

It wasn't a surprise that Josh answered. But what was shocking was how out of sorts he looked.

"That bad?" Brian asked.

Josh let us in, obviously having expected the both of us. "Not great. He's been in the whiskey."

Brian heaved a sigh which cued me in that they'd been down this road before.

"And he's been calling for Jules." His gaze focused on me. "I'm assuming that's you?"

I nodded.

"Then you should know he's mixing up his past and present. Calling for you, then Sarah. Then he's incoherent. Unfortunately, Dr. Mac is out of town until morning. If you'd rather wait to see him until after that, it might be easier."

I took a deep breath. "I didn't come all this way just to wait. Is he awake?"

"In and out. I keep hoping he'll pass out and then sober up by morning."

"Okay. Well, I'll go in and see if I can help."

Brian led the way to what I assumed was Mark's bedroom. On the way there, walking down the hall and through the large living room, I realized I might be in over my head. Everywhere I turned, I saw pictures.

Photos of Sarah. Sarah and Mark. In a frame on the corner table, on the wall. Some appeared to be their engagement photos. Along with the photos were feminine touches, making it look as though she'd just stepped out to go to the store instead of having been dead eleven years. Even her shoes were by the front door. I suspected her coats still hung in the closet.

"You okay?" Brian followed my gaze.

I shouldn't have been surprised by the contents of the house considering he hadn't ever invited me over, but the realization hit me now.

I'd never stood a chance.

Unbeknownst to me, I'd been competing with a memory, one he clearly wasn't ready to let go of.

"Yeah." I swallowed past the lump in my throat, willing myself not to meet the gaze of either man. If I saw the sympathy reflected in their eyes, I'd lose it.

His bedroom was as cluttered as his office had once looked. The image put a smile on my face. My adorable, dirty-talking dream guy was a slob of absolutely epic proportions. My amusement was quickly erased, however, when I took in his form huddled on the far side of his king-sized bed.

I closed the door, giving us privacy before I slipped off my shoes and crawled over the empty side of the mattress toward him. Wrapping my arms around his waist, I breathed in his scent. Despite the odor of whiskey and stale clothes, he still smelled like my Mark. The scent evoked such nostalgia and longing that it nearly made me weep. I'd missed him badly.

"Hey, you," I whispered.

"Jules...?" He shifted suddenly, almost squishing me with his weight when he flipped over.

"Yeah, I'm here."

I was suddenly wrapped up in his embrace. "Am I dreaming?"

"No. I'm really here."

He nuzzled my neck and then softly sighed against my skin. "I've missed you, Sarah."

His somewhat slurred speech and Josh's warning were the only things that kept me from freaking out. "I know."

"I'm sorry."

I rubbed my hand up and down his back, keeping my voice soothing. I sensed he needed to talk but didn't have a clue who he was talking to: me or Sarah. "For what?"

"It wasn't cold feet. You told me it was, but I was only trying to be rational when I said I wanted to postpone the wedding. Then I didn't have a chance to make it up to you."

My motions ceased as the implication of what he was saying sunk in. No wonder he had such guilt. He'd been trying to postpone the wedding right before she'd died.

His hot tears could be felt on my neck, and my heart broke for him. "You would've. We both know that." I was here to comfort him even if it meant I was her voice for the moment.

"I loved you so much."

"I know." My own tears trickled down to join his.

"And I swore I'd never meet anyone else, but I did."

I stopped breathing in that moment, waiting for him to say more.

"You two couldn't be any more different."

"I bet." Those were the only words I could manage. I wasn't prepared for him to continue.

"Jules is like a tornado, coming into my life when I least expected it."

I wasn't sure being compared to a natural disaster was a compliment, but I stayed quiet.

"It's the first time I've been truly happy since you."

It would be so easy about now to say something like: "then you should go and be happy." My conscience wrestled with it, but in the end, I couldn't offer the blessing he desperately sought from her. He needed to come to the conclusion on his own that he could move on in life. Instead, I held him as he bawled in my arms while saying, "I'm sorry" over and over again.

His soft snore finally came once he'd exhausted himself.

Extricating myself gently was no small feat as he had me completely tangled up in him. Once I was off the bed, I let out a breath before tiptoeing over to his side to cover him with a blanket.

My poor, tortured, beautiful man. At the heart of it, I didn't know how to fix this for him. Didn't know how to absolve him of this guilt which had been eating him up for years, let alone the newfound guilt about being with me.

Walking out into the living room, I found Brian and Josh talking in low tones on the sofa. Both looked up when they saw me.

"He's asleep."

Relief washed over both of them. "Dr. Mac will be here about nine o'clock tomorrow morning," Josh provided.

I took a seat in the recliner, curling my feet underneath me. "What happened? How did you find him like this?"

Josh spoke up. "Whenever I talked with him over the last couple weeks he sounded off kilter. I didn't put it together that his behavior dated from the time you left. Then four days ago he sent me a text saying he was sick. I was in New York, so it wasn't until today that I swung by to check on him, finding him in the bottle."

"What happened four days ago, Juliette? If you don't mind telling us," Brian asked.

I was careful with my response, not wanting to reveal the intimate details. "We sort of ended things. I never meant— I thought it was me who was the most torn up over it. As much as I think he wants to move on, he can't. And I couldn't—" I held up my arms, indicating all of the pictures of Sarah surrounding us. "I couldn't wait around hoping he'd eventually get there. I needed to get home with Tristan and get him back into a routine close to my family."

Brian held up a hand. "You don't owe us an explanation of why you left, honey. There's no one to blame in this situation."

I dabbed at my eyes, not wanting to cry. "No, there's not. That's what makes it even harder. Mark is probably the best man I've ever met, but I don't know how to help him. It goes beyond me."

"It goes beyond all of us. All we can do is be supportive. He may not be ready to move on, but clearly your leaving triggered something, so obviously he has feelings," Brian offered.

Unable to contain my interest, I uncurled my feet and stood up in order to walk over to a wall with a number of photographs of Sarah. She'd been beautiful. Blue eyes; classic, straight, shoulder-length blond hair; slim and tall, with high cheekbones and effortless class. She couldn't be more the opposite of me. I ran my fingertips over what appeared to be an engagement photo of the two of them together and smiled. He looked so young in the picture.

Although it would be easy to slip into insecurity through comparison, I found myself more curious than anything else. Maybe I'd conquered some of my demons, after all. "What was Sarah like?"

I glanced over my shoulder. Judging by their expressions, the question appeared to make both men feel awkward, so I mitigated. "Guys, he just thought I was her for the last twenty minutes. Give me something here."

Brian cleared his voice. "Sarah was quiet and shy at first, but once you got to know her, she was more fun. She was always kind. They had a lot in common: law school, love of art, and tennis."

I had to bite my cheek because I hadn't known Mark loved art or ever played tennis. "How did she die?"

Josh sighed. "She was driving home from her parents' place when she had a brain aneurism and went off the road. It took a few hours before they could locate the car in a ditch. By then, it was too late. She'd died."

Brian came over to stand next to me, gazing at the photographs. "Mark was a mess. Blames himself for not being with her in the car."

I noticed neither man mentioned cold feet. It occurred to me they might not be aware of that part of the situation. "When did he buy the house?"

"About six months before. They moved in together and planned to settle here in New Haven."

"And, of course, he thought they had plenty of time." I took a shuddered breath, thinking it tragic. "Thank you for telling me. I'm going to stay with him in case he wakes up again."

"Are you sure?" Concern reflected in Brian's expression.

I squeezed his hand with reassurance. "I love him. Whatever comfort I can give him, even if he thinks I'm her, I'm going to offer, at least until he can get help in the morning. If you like, I can call you once he wakes up."

Brian shook his head. "I think Josh should head home, but I'll stay in the guest room in case you need help."

"I'm only five miles away if you need me." Josh got up, probably anxious to get home to his wife and baby. "Juliette, you've been like family to Brian and Sasha for years, and with your stay up here, you and Tristan have become that for Haylee and me, too. I say this because I want you to understand how much you've come to mean to all of us. Your willingness to stay with him is admirable, but not even Mark would want you to do it at the expense of your well-being."

"I appreciate your concern. We all know he may not be happy about me being here come morning, but I'll see it through until then. Tomorrow afternoon, though, I need to leave in order to be home in time to put Tristan to bed."

What I didn't say was that I needed to put a time limit on this. I was here to help Mark, but I was also restricting how far I went in doing so. I didn't want to lose myself in his problems. I couldn't become consumed by them to the point I lost the progress I'd made in rebuilding my self-esteem. Nor would I allow Mark's problems to take any more time away from my son.

"I'll have my plane ready to take you home tomorrow afternoon. Call me, whatever time it is, if you need anything. Otherwise, I'll see you in the morning." Josh looked between us, and we both promised to do so.

After seeing Josh out and getting Brian settled in the guest room, I tiptoed back into Mark's room. He was still fast asleep. Thankfully, I'd had my little hygiene kit at the office and had brought it along. I thought I'd take a quick shower, brush my teeth, and slip into bed.

About to open the door to his master bath, I prepared myself for what might be on the other side. What if Sarah's things remained in there? Her toothbrush and toiletries sitting there after all these years? When I stepped inside, I let out a breath, grateful to find my fear unfounded. Only his things were visible.

After showering, I put on one of his clean T-shirts and slid into bed. In doing so, I noticed Sarah's picture on the nightstand. Maybe it had been a mistake to come. I found myself wishing for the time to go by fast, so I could get back on a plane, away from the painful reality that Mark was far from moving on.

I AWOKE REALLY hot and with a heavy weight on part of me. Mark's legs were intertwined with mine. I tried to shift, but he only snuggled me closer, burying his face into my neck.

"I missed you, Jules," he said on a sigh.

At least he knew who I was this morning. "I missed you, too."

The next time I woke, I saw light peeking in through the partly shut blinds. The clock revealed it was already pushing nine o'clock. After extricating myself from Mark's warm body, I quickly made myself presentable, dressing quietly.

I left some Advil I'd found in the bathroom on the nightstand before walking out to the kitchen in search of a glass of water. I also put on a pot of coffee, knowing he would need it.

Brian walked into the kitchen from the hall. "How is he?"

"Still asleep, but I'm sure will wake up with quite a headache."

"I bet. You okay?"

"Yeah. At least he called me by my name this morning."

"Dr. Mac and Josh should be here soon. How about, while they get Mark up and talking, I take you for breakfast?"

"Deal. Let me set this on his nightstand and check on him one last time."

Tiptoeing back into the master bedroom, I put the water next to the Advil and took a moment to appreciate Mark sleeping. Despite looking like hell and most likely about to wake up with an epic hangover, he was still so very handsome.

Hearing conversation coming from the living room, I gave him one final glance and stepped out. I wondered how Mark would feel about waking up to see his friends had brought in his therapist. Given his history, however, this was probably the best thing for him.

"Ah, Juliette, it's nice to see you," Dr. Mac said by way of hello.

"Nice to see you again, too." The way he was studying me was a bit unnerving. He was probably putting two and two together and figuring out that Mark was the man I'd been talking about during my sessions.

"Do you want to have a chat about last night and what happened with Mark before we wake him up?"

My eyes darted between all three men. "Actually, no."

Everyone appeared taken aback by my answer, but I had a good reason. "I'd rather talk about things in front of him. He'd feel some disloyalty from me if I gave his longtime therapist my version of what happened. Just know that I love him, and I'm willing to speak with you later if he won't and if you think talking to me will help him."

Dr. Mac's expression softened. "I understand and respect your choice."

I was thankful when Brian came to the rescue. "We're going to breakfast. Why don't you keep us up to date once he's awake?"

Josh nodded and squeezed my hand. "Thanks for staying."

ONCE WE WERE SEATED at a diner a few miles away, I checked in with my mom to be sure Tristan was doing okay this morning. I was already anxious to return to him, feeling guilty that I'd spent the night away from him and was putting Mark first right now.

"Tristan good?" Brian asked from across the booth.

"Yep. He's fine." I put my phone away and put my elbows on the table. "Do you think I should've spoken with Dr. Mac about Mark?"

"No. I think what you did was respectful. Makes his job harder if Mark doesn't want to talk about his problems, but Dr. Mac's a smart man, and Josh already filled him in on the minimum."

I ordered an omelet and sipped the coffee the waitress brought. "Distract me with wedding plans. I mean, is it just me, or does it feel like it's taken forever to get here?"

He chuckled. "It has taken forever. But what can you do when your wife-to-be wants a winter wedding on the beach in North Carolina? February can't get here fast enough."

The ceremony would be intimate with only close friends and family invited. Afterwards, there would be a larger reception indoors at a local country club. Since Sasha had grown up in a small town where her father had been the sheriff for many years, there'd be plenty of people attending the latter. Given Sasha's anxiety, I knew Brian was worried she'd push herself into a panic.

"Why is she putting herself through having a big reception when crowds of people aren't her thing?"

"I know, right? But she wants to prove she can."

It didn't surprise me. Sasha was stubborn. But I also knew my friend would accomplish anything she set her mind to. The ceremony was for her, but the reception she'd put on for her family.

Over the next hour, Brian and I chatted about his upcoming nuptials. We also discussed possible leads for houses for sale once I was ready to buy again. When Brian's phone buzzed, I waited expectantly. The tic of his jaw told me that whatever he'd read had irritated him. Could I read my boss or what?

"Everything okay with the text?"

"Yeah," he lied.

My raised brow was all he needed to relent.

"I hate it when you do that."

"What? Look at you like a liar, liar, pants on fire?"

His lips twitched, fighting a smile. "Josh says it may be best if we don't come back. Things aren't going terrific back at the house."

"Me or we?"

He blushed slightly. "Juliette, Mark's embarrassed. And pissed at Josh and me for involving you and bringing you up here."

"So, I should turn around and go home? That's it?" Part of me wanted to. At the heart of Mark's reaction was simple rejection. And it hurt. "Too bad. I'm not doing that."

Brian expelled a breath and grabbed the check before I could, only pissing me off further.

I threw down a twenty, but per usual, he shoved it back at me, refusing to let me pay.

"Will you drive me back to his house, or do I need to call a taxi?" I wanted to know.

He watched me push the twenty toward him again and sighed. "Uber."

"What?"

"People don't call taxis anymore. They get Uber or Lyft rides."

I knew he was only trying to distract me, Brian style, but it wasn't working. "Thanks for the tip. Now, are you driving me back there or not?"

"I don't want to see you get hurt."

Me, neither, but I'd already left Mark once without being honest about my feelings. I wasn't doing it again. This time I'd ensure he knew where I stood, and hopefully, we'd both put it all out there. "I'm tougher than my size." This time it wasn't an act; I was actually starting to believe it.

"Which is why I'm taking this twenty instead of arguing. What will you do if he refuses to see you?"

After leaving my son and dropping everything to get up here, I certainly wasn't turning around now. I'd gone in without any expectations, but at this point, it pissed me off to be dismissed.

"I don't know, but in my current mood, he's certainly going to hear me, at the very least."

CHAPTER EIGHTEEN

*A*fter pulling up in Mark's driveway, Josh met us at the door, giving a pointed look toward Brian, clearly not expecting me to have returned with him.

"Would you believe I left my purse here?" I quipped.

Josh's gaze focused on the one currently sitting on my shoulder, and his lips twitched. "He's in the living room."

I let out a breath, happy Josh hadn't shut the door in my face.

Steeling myself against the possibility of Mark's rejection, I nevertheless drank in the sight of him on the couch, awake and speaking in low tones with Dr. Mac.

His head turned, and his eyes met mine; I witnessed his physical reaction and felt his words like a dagger to my heart. "What are you doing here?"

He stood up, unsteady on his feet, but his features were firm in the declaration despite a blush staining his cheeks.

"I came in last night to see you. And didn't want to leave without talking to you."

"Now isn't a good time. It may be better if you left."

Being shut out hurt like hell, but I hoped it was only his

embarrassment talking. "If that's what you truly want, then I will. I left my son at home and dropped everything because I wanted to be here for you. No matter what happens, I do care about you."

"But if you never want to see me again, never want to talk to me, and absolutely don't want me in your life, then I'll walk away right now. Because I refuse to try to help someone who doesn't want it or appreciate it." Again. My voice was down to a whisper as I hoped I wasn't pushing him into just that. I prayed I hadn't read this situation all wrong. It was damn hard to make myself completely vulnerable this way.

"However, if there's any chance that's not true, then don't make me walk out your door. Because I won't ever come back."

Time stood still. Although there were three other people in the room, it felt as if it was only Mark and I, incredible emotion flowing between us. Finally, as I turned on my heel, his voice broke through.

"Wait, Jules. Please."

Three words had never sounded better. Air filled my lungs again. I wasted no time in closing the distance between us and putting my arms around him. I felt thankful when he did the same, squeezing me tight.

"I'm sorry," he murmured into my neck. "It was the humiliation talking. I can't believe you came." He let out a shaky breath.

"Of course I did. I can't believe you didn't tell me you were upset about me leaving. I thought when I didn't hear from you that you weren't as affected. That maybe you'd moved on."

He leaned back, glancing around the room and gesturing with his arm. "If you haven't noticed, that's not exactly my strong suit."

I couldn't keep myself from grinning. Especially since he was now smiling, too. When I glanced at the others in the room, I saw his comment had given everyone the levity they'd needed.

At least he wasn't afraid to address the elephant in the room. "No, I don't suppose it is."

"Mark, would you feel comfortable having Juliette join us in our talk?" Dr. Mac asked.

"Yes, but not here. Maybe at the apartment or your office."

He must've seen my involuntary flinch and understood I felt he was shutting me out of his house again. "It's not you, Jules. I just think it might be easier for me to talk some place neutral, without everything from the past around me. I shudder to think of how my house looks through your eyes."

It looked like the home of a man who'd once been deeply in love with his fiancée. The question was whether the image matched the way he still felt. "Who am I to judge you hanging onto everything? My own preference would be to take a match to the house I shared with my ex. My attorney friend informed me that's arson, though, so my options are limited to selling and giving everything away."

He smiled in response. "Sorry I'm such a stickler for wanting to keep you out of prison. I'm going to take a quick shower, talk with Brian and Josh for a few minutes, and then meet you and Dr. Mac at the apartment building. Is that okay?"

I nodded and accepted the office key he handed me.

DR. MAC WAITED until we were in his car to start talking. "You doing all right, Juliette?"

I figured he could probably see my hands shaking. "Better now, since he didn't kick me out."

Dr. Mac pulled out onto the street and started driving the short distance to the apartment building. "The confrontation couldn't have been easy for you, I'm sure."

"It wasn't. But I have to remind myself Mark isn't Rob. Nor

am I the same person I was back then, either. If I'd just turned around and gone home, I know I would've regretted it."

"Do you feel stronger?"

"I do. And less scared if it doesn't work out. If that makes sense."

I wasn't scared because I wasn't going to give another human being the responsibility for my happiness. Only I was in control of that. Bottom line was that I had no idea where Mark was in his head with this. With us. I still wanted a relationship with him, but I had to be okay if it didn't work out. Not only for me, but also for my son.

"It does. You've been through hell and came out on the other side. Now that you know you can, you can go into this wiser."

"Although I feel bad about it, I do need to leave in another hour or so. Tomorrow is Christmas Eve. Besides, one night away from my son is enough."

"Even if it wasn't Christmas, I'd suggest you go home. You need to put some boundaries on what you can be for Mark. Let him deal with the things only he can do for himself."

I managed a nod and then posed the question I knew was probably unfair, but I had to ask. "Given how much he loved Sarah, do you think it's possible for him to move on? To love someone else?"

"I wish I could tell you what you're hoping to hear, but I don't know for certain. I will say I've seen plenty of people move on from losing their significant other and find love again. But recognize that if he can't, it's not on you."

"Maybe instead of carpool karaoke, they should totally start a segment called carpool therapy."

He grinned and pulled into the parking lot. Turning off the engine, he turned toward me. "This session may not be easy for you. If you need to leave at any time, I'd certainly understand and I think so would Mark."

Right, because at the end of it, Mark and I could be no better off than when I'd left the first time. But I was genuinely curious to hear what he had to say.

MARK SHOWED up looking newly shaved and out of the shower. Other than his red, bloodshot eyes, he didn't seem too much the worse for wear. His gaze landed on mine and then flicked toward Dr. Mac. "Do you mind giving us a few minutes?"

He smiled at us both. "Not at all. How about I come back in five? I forgot my notebook in the car, anyhow."

I wasn't sure what to expect, but when the door shut, I hadn't counted on Mark stepping close and putting his arms around me. I instantly melted against him, absorbing the emotion pouring from such an all-consuming hug.

"I'm sorry for earlier. I should've been thanking you for coming instead of trying to get you to leave. I'm glad you're here."

"Me, too. But why didn't you tell me you were this upset?"

He stepped back, cupping my face. "Same reason you didn't tell me the same thing, I suppose. I thought you were moving on. Besides, I couldn't give you what you deserved."

No, he couldn't. But could he now?

Five minutes later, Mark and I sat on the couch, close to each other but not touching, while Dr. Mac took the single chair.

As I recounted what Mark had said to me last night in his drunken confusion, I watched his jaw clench when I got to the part about Sarah's accusation he'd had cold feet.

Mark's mouth opened and shut. Then he sighed and revealed the whole story. "Two days before Sarah died, I asked if we could postpone the wedding. She called it cold feet. I thought I was only being practical, considering we had law school to finish and the bar exam to study for. As far as I was concerned, we had plenty of time. She was upset and went to stay with her parents. She called me the night it happened and told me she had some things she wanted to talk to me about. She said she was on her way home. Then she never showed up."

My heart broke for him as I listened to him recount that tragic night. I couldn't help speaking what was on my mind. "Mark, I didn't know Sarah, but I know you. I believe you both would've worked things out."

"But we didn't, because she died. Because I'd upset her enough she went to go stay with her parents, and so she was on the road at the time of her aneurism. For all I know, she could've been coming over to break things off permanently."

Dr. Mac put in his opinion. "Considering she didn't tell her parents about any of it, I'd say that was never her intention."

Mark sighed, taking my hand. "It's the first time I've ever admitted this to anyone other than Dr. Mac. Her parents thought I was out of town and that's why she'd gone to stay with them. I didn't even confide in Brian or Josh about our fight."

"I'm glad you could tell me." Because his last argument with Sarah had a lot to do with why he had a hard time moving on.

"I'm sorry if it's hard to hear me speak about her."

"It's not a competition. I want you to feel comfortable talking to me. I know you loved her, and I certainly never wanted you to have to hide it. Although the circumstances are completely different, I have regrets and guilt about Rob, too. Wondering if I should've seen the signs sooner of his drug use. Gotten him help." As I admitted it out loud, I saw Dr. Mac's encouraging smile.

"We all wish hindsight would've afforded us opportunities which we couldn't possibly have seen at the time," he remarked.

We both sat there absorbing his words until Dr. Mac asked the next burning question. "Did you feel guilty being happy with Juliette and planning a future with her?"

Mark hesitated. "I wish I hadn't."

Therein lay a big problem. His guilt. Unless he could get past it and stop blaming himself, we didn't stand a chance.

Dr. Mac adjusted his glasses before asking, "Do you think Sarah wouldn't want you to be happy?"

"I know she would've, but how do I reconcile having told her that she was the love of my life to finding that someone else could be the same?"

His admission might've caused me pain if I hadn't thought I'd married the supposed love of my life, too. The big difference, however, was that Rob had systematically destroyed our future. Sarah's had been tragically cut short.

"Juliette, I'd like to hear what you're thinking at this point." Dr. Mac turned toward me.

I knew I needed to own up to my part in undermining the relationship. "I think..." I hesitated. "I think I should've been more honest with Mark about how I was feeling."

"How's that?" Mark's gaze completely focused on me, and he looked surprised by my admission.

"I didn't tell him how much it hurt me to be a secret to everyone. How it affected my self-esteem profoundly. I should've told him how much it was upsetting me. How it brought up a lot of insecurity because of my past."

"Why do you think you kept it from him?"

I swallowed hard. "Because I was afraid it was all me. So I discounted my feelings and thought that if I ignored them I'd be able to skip past anything that could potentially ruin things."

Mark squeezed my hand. "You weren't the only one. I didn't set out with the intention of hiding you or us, but I was struggling with how to tell our friends. I felt so damn guilty for moving on. And I'm so fucking sorry for not realizing that what I was doing was hurting you."

"And I'm sorry for letting it get to the point where it all came to a head. I should've told you how I felt sooner."

The question was where did this leave us? While we were both regretful, did that give us a future? Or was this closure on a relationship that never truly had a chance?

I listened for another thirty minutes while Dr. Mac spoke about the importance of being honest in our communication and about our pasts. Then I found myself glancing at my phone. Despite wanting to stay with Mark, I needed to get back to Tristan.

"You need to get home, don't you?"

I afforded Mark an apologetic smile. "I do. What will you do for Christmas?" I halfway hoped he'd want to come down to Charlotte to spend the holiday with me, but I knew that step was premature.

"I normally spend it with Sarah's family."

Right. I should've expected that.

"As long as you're not alone." I meant it. Even if he wasn't with me.

I stood up, and Mark did the same, holding onto one of my hands.

"Can I call you?"

"I'd be disappointed if you didn't."

Maybe we were simply meant to be friends. Put in one another's lives to help us work through our painful pasts. Regardless, I knew I'd made the right choice in coming up here.

———

BRIAN PICKED me up and drove us both to the airport since he was going home, too.

"How are you?"

I'd been asked that a lot today, but considering the emotional gauntlet of the last twenty-four hours, it was a fair question. I took stock of my feelings. "Better than I was the last time I left. I wish I could make this better for him. Know what the future held and even if there will be an us. That's the toughest part."

"I realize the circumstances are different, but I know how it is to love someone who has some issues to work out for themselves."

I bet he did. He'd once learned Sasha had an anxiety disorder she'd hidden from him. "What do you do?"

"Love and support them. Most importantly, be patient with them. The hardest part for me is to watch when she struggles and not try to fix it for her. One, she would resent it, and two, I can't. But I don't want her hiding it from me. If she thinks every time I'll jump in to try to fix it, then she'd start to conceal her feelings. Of course, it's different for you. Hearing about Mark's past with Sarah has to be tough."

It was, but probably not any tougher than for Mark to listen to me talk about Rob. "Thank you. Not only for sharing, but also for not making a fuss about Mark and me being together. I think he was kind of worried you'd punch him."

He frowned. "Jeez, you punch one guy because you find out he's sleeping with your sister and bam, you have a reputation. For the record, I still feel awful about the punch, although don't you dare tell Colby that. I've gotta keep the threat alive in case he doesn't treat my sister right."

I scoffed. "You and I both know Colby adores Kenzie. And we know that you're a softie despite how your greatest jump-to-conclusions moment made you a temporary asshole."

He grinned, amusement dancing in his brown eyes. "It has served me well not to do the same ever again. It was kind of a shock at first to find out about you and Mark, but once I saw the way he held you today at the house, I knew you two were made for one another. Let's just say I always hoped he'd find someone again, and since you're both some of my favorite people in the world, I can't be anything but supportive. Oddly, Sasha didn't seem very surprised when I told her over the phone."

He clearly guessed I'd already told her. "No?" Guess the cat was officially out of the bag. I'd already received a text from Haylee about it, too. I wondered if it bothered Mark that everyone knew now. Then I realized if it did bother him, we were not in a place where things could ever work out.

MARK'S PHONE number flashed up at nine o'clock on Christmas Eve. Tristan had long been in bed. Earlier, we'd set out cookies and milk for Santa. Then, once he was in his crib, my mother had helped me set up gifts from Santa, including a new, bright red tricycle.

"Hi."

"Hi. I hope when you said you didn't mind me calling, this wasn't too soon."

"It definitely isn't."

"Do you have time to talk?"

I went into the small bathroom off of the guest room we were using so I wouldn't wake Tristan. "Yeah. Everyone else is in bed."

"I bet it'll be fun in the morning when Tristan wakes up."

"It will. I got him a tricycle. I mean Santa did. Has a bell and everything on it."

"Sounds amazing. I wish I was there."

I didn't know what to say to this, especially if he was with Sarah's family, so I stayed quiet.

Mark spoke up again, sounding nervous even through the phone. "I realize the last two days couldn't have been easy for you, and I guess— Well, I guess I needed to know if you're anxious to get far, far away from me."

"They weren't easy for you, either, but you opening up in front of me with Dr. Mac meant a lot to me. And I'm not that far. Only in Charlotte."

"I met with Dr. Mac again today, and something he said really resonated."

"What's that?"

"If Rob hadn't turned to drugs or Sarah hadn't died, things would've been much different for both of us. But those things did happen, and now here we are. Nothing we can do or ever hope for will ever change the past."

No. It wouldn't.

"Jules, I still want my future to be with you and Tristan. I want to give you the sort of love you deserve. I've been miserable since you left. It's as though you took all the sunshine with you."

I sucked in a breath, not knowing what to say. I loved this man so very much. Now wasn't the time to tell him, but I could feel it in every fiber of my being. "I want that, too, but where do we go from here?"

"Take it slow. Not skip over our feelings and be honest with one another."

Okay, but with me in Charlotte and him up in Connecticut, how did that happen?

"What do you think about me coming to spend Christmas Day with you and Tristan and your family? I'd get a hotel room or something and wouldn't stay long, but I have a gift for him. And for you."

I was shocked. "But that's tomorrow. And I thought you were spending Christmas with Sarah's family?"

"I went over there tonight. That was enough. If you're okay with me coming over in the afternoon, I wouldn't stay long."

I forced myself to focus on what he was asking. I didn't want to get my hopes up about what it meant that he was leaving Sarah's family in order to spend the holiday with us. "Um, yeah, we'd love to have you. You could stay as long as you want. Dinner is around three, but if you can't get here in time, then come whenever."

Jesus, I sounded like a freaking-out teenager who was about to introduce a boy to her parents for the first time.

"I'll be there by three. Can I bring anything? Maybe beer?"

I smiled. "Beer would be most welcome." Actually, I could use one now.

"Okay. See you at three."

CHAPTER NINETEEN

*O*n Christmas Day, the options for buying a gift were limited to 7-Eleven and Walgreens. I found myself at the latter of the two, trying to think of something to get Mark. I settled on a completely ridiculous item, hoping to get him a real gift at a later point.

I still couldn't believe he was coming. After stifling a yawn from an early wake-up, I grabbed my purchase and raced home in order to help my mom finish cooking the big meal. Tristan had woken up at six o'clock this morning. Thankfully, he was down for a nap now during this span of time before dinner. I'd loved the expression on his face when he'd come downstairs to see his new trike. After that, he'd torn through the presents like a maniac, having come to an understanding of what Christmas morning was all about.

I'd held off on telling him Mark was coming just in case he'd changed his mind. But at three o'clock when the doorbell rang, I let Tristan go answer the door.

"Mark, Mark." His excited voice carried down the hall.

The man I loved hastily set the things in his hands on the floor so that he could pick up the boy I loved and swing him up onto his hip. "Gosh, did I miss you. Did you get bigger? Was Santa good to you?"

"Yep. I got bike. Wanna see?" Tristan wiggled until Mark put him down and then took his hand, intending to drag him through the house to see his new toy.

"Hold on a sec, buddy." He closed the door and focused on me, picking up the items from the floor and handing over flowers. "Um, these are for you."

"Oh. Thanks." After taking the bouquet from his hands, followed by a six-pack of beer he then snagged from his feet, I awkwardly accepted his kiss on the cheek. Neither of us seemed to know what to do.

"I'm gonna go see his tricycle if that's okay."

I smiled at an anxious Tristan. "Of course. You can even ride it again outside if we get your coat on. We have a little bit of time before dinner."

Tristan whooped and rushed to get his coat and shoes on.

A few minutes later we were outside in the cul-de-sac where my mother lived, watching Tristan pedal his way around. Mark stood next to me but kept a careful eye and helped him get turned around when he got stuck.

"Merry Christmas."

"Yeah, Merry Christmas. Thanks for letting me come."

"You don't have to thank me. I— God when did this get so awkward?"

He smiled. "I was thinking the same."

"Where are you staying?"

"At Josh's house. He and the family are up in Virginia, so he offered his Charlotte house to me while I'm here."

"How long are you down for?"

"That depends on you."

"Me?"

"If you're up for it, I was hoping I could take you to dinner tomorrow night. That is, if your mom can babysit."

"Like a date?"

He blushed slightly, reminiscent of our first few interactions. "Yes. I think it's about time I take you out on a proper one. Don't you?"

A smile broke out across my face. "I'd love to do dinner."

"And here, this is for you." From his coat pocket, he handed me a long box with a bow on it.

"You want me to open it now?"

"Yeah. I have Legos for Tristan for later, but I wanted to give this one to you in private."

Oh. I untied the ribbon and lifted the lid to reveal a lovely silver bracelet. On it were two charms. One was Tristan's birthstone, and the other was a sun.

"It's beautiful." My throat was closing with emotion as I dared to feel hope for the future. Someone didn't get a person a charm bracelet without an unspoken promise to fill it up with more charms. Right?

"I'm glad you like it."

"I, um, have something for you, too, but now it seems silly." Because his gift was thought out and had obviously cost more than five dollars bought from a drugstore this morning.

"I'm sure I'll love it."

I shook my head as I put a hand in my sweatshirt pocket. I was having serious second thoughts about how he would take this gift. "I, uh, I only had a pharmacy and convenience store for options to get you something after learning you were coming, so I apologize. And I probably should've gone with the chocolate-covered cherries instead. Although I don't even know if you like those things. But I definitely don't. I mean I like cherries, and I love chocolate, but put them together with that weird liquid center, and eww."

He chuckled, holding out his hand, palm up. "You're adorable when you get nervous. Now hand it over."

Ha. Guess it was good he thought so. I gave him the small box I'd hastily wrapped. Watching as he opened it, I bit my lip.

He held up the key chain which said, *"I like my girls Southern, Sassy and Sweet."*

"It probably should say crazy at the end, and it's stupid but—"

He cut me off, flashing me a grin. "I adore it."

After dinner was over, the last of the gifts had been opened, and Tristan was ready for bed, I walked Mark out to his rental car. The day had been more than comfortable. My mom and stepfather had engaged Mark in conversation, and Tristan, loving the Lego set Mark had bought him, had then wanted to show him all of his toys.

I fought disappointment when, instead of pulling me close for a kiss that showed how much he'd missed me, he only pecked me on the cheek and told me he'd pick me up tomorrow night.

Although slow wasn't a favorite speed of mine, I couldn't help being excited about the prospect of a real date.

———

OUR FIRST OFFICIAL date the next evening included dinner at a local steakhouse at a quaint table for two and a subject I wasn't expecting. "Brian mentioned he was asking you to do a toast at the wedding reception."

I almost choked on my mashed potatoes. "What's that, now? What toast?"

A grimace came over Mark's expression. "Shit. I thought by now he would've asked."

"He said that when he got back from vacation next week he had a favor to ask for the wedding. I thought perhaps he wanted me to help with setting up something, not actually speaking in public. Good grief, what is he thinking?"

Mark chuckled. "He's thinking how better to entertain a crowd? He also mentioned that it was you who told him Sasha was the one for him since the day she started working there. That you used to do recon on her for him in the beginning. That should make for a good story."

"True, but you know how I get when I'm anxious. Stuff starts blurting out in an inappropriate fountain of too-much-information. Guess I'll have to be sure to remain sober and write it down so I don't go off the rails." I was truly honored to give a toast. But given my propensity for embarrassing moments, I didn't want to saddle the bride and groom with the kind of speech that had people talking for weeks.

"There is no doubt in my mind that everyone will love you."

Did that include him? I knew it was only a figure of speech, but the ultimate question didn't ever leave my mind. Would he ever be able to say the words? And since we were on the subject of the wedding in a few weeks, how would he act around me there, surrounded by all of our friends? Would it be awkward as it had been for Catherine's party? Or would he be okay with showing people we were a couple? Hell, half of them already knew. So many questions, yet going slow meant learning not to push things.

After dinner, he walked me to the front door of my mom's house.

I leaned in toward him, wishing he'd invited me back to his place instead of dropping me off.

"So, how do you feel about me coming back down for New Year's?" He took my hands in his.

"Yeah. Only if you want to." Cluck. That sounded a lot like insecurity.

He leaned back and cupped my chin. "I definitely want."

God, so did I. I met his lips, hungry for the taste of him. But he pulled back the moment my arms snaked around his waist to draw him closer.

"I don't want to push this. This is too important to rush things."

I didn't want to sound desperate, but I'd missed him and the physical contact. "Yeah. I look forward to New Year's."

"I'll be counting the days."

"Me, too."

He sighed regretfully. "Good night, Jules."

Yep. I tried to remember that slow was good. Slow was necessary. Oh, who was I kidding?

After our kiss—slow seemed like an impossible speed to maintain for long.

Turns out the best time I ever had on New Year's Eve didn't involve getting dressed up, going out, or even staying up until midnight. Instead it was the night I spent with Mark. He'd reserved a hotel suite a few miles away from my mom's house and invited Tristan and me over for a Disney movie marathon. Mark thought of everything from champagne for us adults to sparkling apple cider for Tristan. We ordered up room service and made it through three movies before Tristan fell asleep.

After we'd put him in the bedroom, I snuggled close to Mark on the couch while he found the New Year's countdown on TV. Unable to help myself, I let my hands wander along his strong arms, stroking and feeling his skin. I inhaled the scent of him, shifting so I could get up on my knees beside him. As I kissed him behind his ear, I ran my other hand through his silky hair. I'd missed him.

"Jules. You're making this hard."

"Mm. Guess that means I'm doing it right, then." There was something really appealing about being the one to initiate sex for once. Something empowering.

But he wasn't having it. Instead, he flicked off the television and stood up abruptly. "Um. How about I'll take the couch, and you can share the bed with Tristan?"

He stood there with his hands in his pockets while I fought the insecurity over being rejected. "Sure. Happy New Year."

I got up, intent on making a beeline for the bedroom, but Mark snagged my waist, pulling me into him.

"Wait." He breathed into my neck as if struggling with restraint. "This is more than sex. I want you to know that."

"I've always known that." He wasn't exactly the type to sleep around.

"I want the next time I make love to you to be perfect. I don't want to rush or worry about waking up Tristan or me having to catch a plane first thing tomorrow morning."

"Okay. I guess I get that." Waiting would make it worth it right? Except that I wanted him now. Then again, the idea of having him all night without trying to be quiet and waking up with him in the morning sounded good, too.

"What are your plans for the next couple of weekends?"

"I have a lot happening with the house and stuff." I was moving, planned a garage sale, and closing on the house.

"I should be able to make it down again in two or three more weeks."

It wasn't like I could expect him to travel to see me every weekend, especially when he'd just done the last two. "That sounds good. Or maybe I could come up if my mom can watch Tristan." Although I was unsure when it would work for her.

Suddenly it felt as though progress was at a standstill.

"I NEED to figure out how to seduce Mark."

I dumped these words on Sasha the Monday after New Year's. There was slow, but then there was completely stopped. That's where I felt Mark and I were at the moment. And since I didn't want to wait weeks to be intimate with him, I was thinking of getting my mom to babysit and fly up there for a night if I needed to. Clearly, I'd developed a one-track mind.

From across her desk, Sasha eyed me with an arched brow over her coffee mug. "As much as this may sound weird, you may be better off talking to Brian about this kind of stuff."

I laughed out loud. "Uh, we're close, but you're right, that would be weird. Seriously, you exude—" I waved at her. "—sexual confidence in spades. I need, like, an ounce."

She lifted a brow. "First off, it's not me who originally did the seducing in my relationship; it was your boss. I have no game in the bedroom. Well, I guess I do now, but back then—"

I put my hands over my ears in exaggerated form. "TMI."

She laughed. "You started this conversation. Plus, I thought you and Mark were taking it slow."

I flopped down into her guest chair. "We are. And it's wonderful. But he has this idea of everything being perfect for when we, you know—"

"Have sex again."

"Exactly." I should probably be able to say it out loud before I went and tried to seduce someone, but I wasn't used to having this kind of discussion. Not even with my girlfriends. "He said he wants a night with only the two of us, but with the move and everything else, I'm not sure when we can get a weekend away. I don't want to wait another week or weeks until your wedding weekend. Especially since he didn't hint at attending together, which is another problem in and of itself."

"Well, there's a definition of slow for you."

"Excruciatingly so. He's thinking he needs to show me it's not just sex, but I get that." God knows, we had plenty other hurdles to overcome, but this wasn't one of them.

"We talk every night. And he continues to meet with Dr. Mac, but don't you think intimacy might be important, too?"

She grinned. "Of course I do. But what's this really about?"

Leave it to my friend to get to the heart of it. "I think it's about me taking control. From the beginning, he's been the one furthering our, um, physical relationship. I love that take-charge side of him, but maybe I have something left to prove when it comes to my sexual confidence. I realize he's afraid of hurting me, but I need that intimacy with him again, much more than I need it to be perfect. Because without it, I start to get anxious. You could say it's an important connection for me to have. And I don't want to wait any longer."

Since I'd been through a relationship where I'd stopped having any sort of intimacy, it made sense that I now craved that as an integral part of my new relationship. And yes, I could simply tell him, but the idea of showing him sounded much better.

The more I thought about it, the more I realized that while Mark was facing his demons, I had a couple more to conquer. Sure, I'd let him see me naked and had been vulnerable with him, but I'd yet to initiate sex with him. I'd yet to be the one who took control. Right now, that was all I could think about.

"In that case, we need to go shopping, and I'm about to spoil a surprise."

"What are you talking about?"

She sighed. "Mark planned to be here next week. He found out from Brian that you have the day off next Friday for your home inspection. Mark wanted to come down as a surprise in order to help with everything. He even called your mom to arrange babysitting for that Friday night. My guess is he intends to take you out. So if you want to seduce him, I suggest you make some plans of your own."

I grinned. "Okay. Operation Seduction has commenced. And the first order of business is not to tell Brian."

Learning that Mark had wanted to surprise me fueled my self-confidence. I intended to hijack his plans and make some of my own.

CHAPTER TWENTY

*B*rian looked taken aback to see me walk into his office on Friday morning. "What? What are you doing here? I thought you had the day off for your home inspection."

I had to fight my grin and not blurt out my plan. "I realized I didn't need to be there. My realtor will go to represent me and give me a copy of the report in case we have any repairs to make. Matter of fact, I brought in donuts today for everyone. I want to get back to doing that on Fridays."

So what if half the office had made a New Year's resolution to lose weight? I hadn't. If anything, my resolution was to stop beating myself up for every little indulgence and focus on being healthy instead. You know…starting tomorrow after I had a glazed donut or two.

"How are you feeling, by the way? Only a few more weeks till you're a married man."

He smiled, more eager to tie the knot than any guy I'd ever known. But then his expression changed. "Uh, I'm good. But you don't need to be in the office. Why don't you take the day?"

I put my hands on my hips, unable to resist giving him a hard time. "Is it a problem for me to be here?"

"No, but you're welcome to take the time off anyhow. I'm sure you have a lot to do for the garage sale."

Yep. Tonight I hoped to seduce Mark, and tomorrow I was selling off virtually every piece of furniture in my home. All that I was keeping were the things from Tristan's room or anything with sentimental value. Simply put: it was time to rid myself of the memories. Time to close that chapter.

"My mom and I already tagged everything. And I don't enjoy spending time at the house if I can help it. Why? Are you trying to get rid of me?"

His face started to turn red, which said a lot. Brian wasn't the type to embarrass or frazzle easily. "I'm not. It's just that—"

We both glanced up when Sasha came through his halfway-open office door, her eyes on me while she fought a grin. "Hey. I heard Mark is here with Josh. Have you seen him yet?"

I turned my faux-narrowed gaze on Brian. "Is that why you wanted me to go home?"

He had the decency to wince. "I'd told him you wouldn't be in the office today and—"

"So he figured it would be safe to come in? You planned this with him?"

"Juliette, it's not like that. He wanted to surprise you."

I drew myself up to my full five-foot-two frame and turned toward Sasha. "Are they in the large conference room?" It was the one with all of the glass. He would be able to see me walk by in the hall, fitting directly into my plan.

She nodded. "Yep."

Brian was starting to sweat it. "You can't go in there right now. He and Josh are meeting with someone."

"Oh, I'm not. I'm simply going to walk by on my way to get a donut from the kitchen." Glancing down at my hunter-green sweater dress paired with knee high boots, I was thankful Sasha and I had gone shopping. I was looking exceptionally put together today.

"You're not planning on doing anything crazy, are you?" Brian asked with trepidation.

I lifted a brow, happy to tease him a bit more. "Yes, I figured I'd start chucking donuts at the glass, causing them to stick and then slither down slowly. Meanwhile, I'd blare eighties music from my phone on top volume until he notices me."

Brian raised a brow. "That was scarily vivid. The problem is I know you well enough to believe there's a ten percent chance you'll actually do that. Then again, if it were my sister, the likelihood would be more like fifty percent, so I guess I should be grateful."

"If you're taking suggestions for music, I vote for Whitesnake," Sasha quipped. "Ooh, or Poison. And don't waste the chocolate donuts; those are my favorite. Use the glazed ones."

"But I love the glazed ones."

"Hm, maybe the jelly-filled ones then. Those can go."

Brian shook his head, exasperated with the two of us discussing which donuts should be sacrificed. Turning to Sasha, he lamented, "You're only feeding the crazy, honey."

Because there was real fear in his expression, I couldn't help it. I burst out laughing.

Sasha was quick to follow.

"Okay, either you two are certifiable, or I'm totally missing something here." His glance bounced between the two of us.

"Don't you know better than to keep secrets from me, Brian Carpenter?" I teased.

It only took a moment before he figured out our game and turned toward Sasha. "You told her, didn't you?"

She shrugged. "For a good reason."

He quirked a brow. "Such as what?"

"Operation Seduction," I supplied.

He put his head in his hands, forearms on his desk. "Jesus. I had to ask." He took an exaggerated breath. "All right. What, um, what do you need me to do?"

Now if this wasn't the definition of true friendship, I don't what was. "It's simple. When he comes in here, tell him I heard he was here and that I'm in my office. And do not spoil my counter-surprise."

He looked up with a grin. "As if I would go against the two of you."

Sasha went over to plant a kiss on his lips. "Good answer." Turning toward me, she smirked. "You ready for your drive by?"

I nodded, feeling the nerves jump up. "Yep."

She smiled. "I'll go with you."

I moved by the conference room windows with Sasha by my side, using Baywatch slow-mo speed, minus the cleavage and the swimsuit. I had to force myself not to look into the windows. Instead, I laughed at something random she was saying. Loud, but not too loud, just enough to hopefully make him aware I was here.

After doing a second pass, donut in hand, I went to my office. Sasha smiled and took a seat in my guest chair. But I was no longer smiling, suddenly second-guessing the whole thing.

"Watch. His back will have been turned away from the glass, and he didn't even notice me either time. Love has officially made me stupid and regressed my maturity level."

"It's not stupid. It's human. You simply want what every woman does, which is to make her man take notice of her. Plus, on the scale of crazy, this is pretty tame. However, if you started chucking donuts at the glass while Whitesnake blasts in the background—I've gotta say, that would be epic craziness."

I scoffed. "Please, we both know I'd be blaring Metallica." What could I say? I was a sucker for eighties rock bands.

We both laughed until I posed the question. "Was this a stupid idea? Maybe instead of pushing, I should let him set the pace of things. Wait for him."

"You're aware patience isn't my strong suit, either, right? And why shouldn't you both get a say? You want sex and intimacy with your man, so go get it. Just wait until after his meeting."

"Okay, but if you hear the sound of fresh donuts hitting glass in an hour, you'll know he still hasn't noticed me, and I've gone to new levels of desperation in my plan."

THANKFULLY, I didn't have to go anywhere or resort to desperate measures. Mark came directly to my office fifteen minutes after I'd walked by. And damn, did he look good in his suit and tie.

I hoped my voice sounded more nonchalant than I was actually feeling. "What brings you to the Charlotte office?"

He shut the door before answering. "I realize how this must look, but I was planning to surprise you. Your mom is babysitting tonight so I could take you to dinner. And Brian said you were out of the office today, so I was doing these meetings and then—"

I smiled, cutting him off. "I know."

After standing up from my desk, I walked around to close the blinds. When his brow lifted, I had to steady my heartbeat as I considered my next move.

"What are you doing?"

"Ensuring privacy."

"For what, exactly?"

"This." I put my hands on his chest and then trailed them down his dress shirt, feeling his muscles jump at my touch.

"You knew I was going to be here today?"

"Mm, I may have gotten a hint." Our gazes locked. My fingers itched to touch the warm skin beneath his clothes.

He sighed. "I swear Brian can't keep a secret."

"Mm, wasn't him." I loosened his tie, loving the harsh breath he expelled when I undid the first few buttons of his shirt.

"Jules…"

I let out a squeal of disbelief when he lifted me onto the edge of my desk, his hands resting at my hips. Wasting no time, I pulled him down by the tie for a searing kiss. The kind that had our lips frantic, tongues tangling, and me wanting him inside of me now.

He pulled back after a moment, looking completely caught off guard. "Jesus, what are you doing to me?"

"I would think it obvious. I'm seducing you."

His eyes were dark with lust. "But what about our date tonight and—?"

"You gonna judge me if I put out before it?" I locked my legs around his, pulling him closer into the apex of my thighs.

He grinned. "Hell, no, but I didn't want to rush this. Didn't want you to think this was only about the sex."

Now it was time to get serious. "I've never thought that, but I miss the intimacy between us. A lot. The connection is really important to me—despite the fact that we're still working through the other stuff. I don't need perfect timing or the perfect date. I only need it to be with you."

His gaze stayed focused on mine. "Why didn't you say something sooner?"

"It took a while for me to figure it out. Plus, now I prefer the idea of showing you. I haven't ever seduced a man."

My fingers undid two more buttons.

"Here? Now?" His voice had gone up a full octave with his questions.

"Why not? Don't you have some fantasy about the office and a desk with me on it?"

He inhaled deeply. "I definitely do now. But what if someone hears us?"

Tugging on his tie, I pulled his lips back to mine. "Don't tell me my dirty-talking alpha man in the bedroom is suddenly shy about the possibility of office sex."

He shifted his kiss to my neck. "There's no way the entire staff wouldn't hear us with what I have in mind."

I'd never grow tired of the way he could spike my libido with simple promises like that one. "How about a little preview, then?" My hands slid to his belt buckle.

His quickly covered them, keeping me from my intention. "Do you have any meetings the rest of the morning?"

"Nope. Brian wasn't even expecting me in today."

"Okay. Let's go."

He lifted me off my desk to my feet and grabbed my purse for me.

"Go where?"

"My hotel room is two miles from here."

"We're going to have an office nooner? I've always wanted one of those."

He was shaking his head at me while fighting a grin and trying to button up his shirt. "Shh. Straight face. We're going to talk."

Uh-huh.

Taking my hand, he led me down the hall and into the lobby. Josh, Brian, and Sasha were all standing by the conference room as if waiting to see what would happen with us.

"We're, uh, going for coffee to talk. I'll have her back in an hour." Mark managed to get this out while looking serious, despite the buttons not matching properly on his shirt, his mussed hair, and my lip gloss still shiny on his lips.

"Actually, maybe make it two hours in case I need more than one cup." It was out of my mouth before I could stop it and served to make Mark turn red.

Brian, being the friend he was, gave some helpful advice. "I'd hate to rush coffee. In fact, take all the time you want."

Mark was already grabbing my hand and leading me out the door and to his rental car.

We stopped on the passenger side of his sedan. Suddenly, I was pinned against the door.

I smirked at him. "Guess I'm just really excited about coffee."

He put his lips to my ear. "What should I do with this mouth of yours?"

I had some delicious ideas, but I had to ask the burning question first. "Did I embarrass you in front of our friends?"

He took a moment, tucking my hair behind my ear before he whispered in it. "Not at all. It's not like they didn't know exactly why I was rushing you out the door—even before you mentioned you might need two cups. Now get in the car before we give the office a show in the parking lot."

I grinned and climbed into the passenger side, shimmying out of my panties once he put the car in gear.

"What are you doing?"

"Taking off my thong. It's gotten awfully wet."

My normally reserved, careful Mark turned into a speed demon during the short distance to the hotel. By the time we made it to his door, I wasn't sure if I was more out of breath from anticipation or from being led through the hotel lobby at breakneck speed. My short little legs in high-heeled boots had to struggle to keep up with him.

After fumbling with the room key, he pulled me inside and was on me before the door clicked shut. "I've missed you. So much," he got out between kisses down my neck. Meanwhile, his hands reached the hem of my dress and pulled it up over my head in one swoop.

"From now on, I need the bedroom to be the exception to taking things slowly." I barely got the words out as his palm cupped my wet center, rocking the heel over my clit and driving me crazy with need.

He chuckled. "Deal."

Nimble fingers moved to undo my bra, which let the weight of my breasts fall into his palms. "Gorgeous."

He lavished attention on one side and then the other, eventually moving down my stomach. Since I'd already removed my panties in the car, I was left standing there in only my boots.

"Your turn to strip. Because I have some plans for you."

He quirked a brow but quickly worked to remove his clothing.

I licked my lips in anticipation of tasting him and didn't bother to wait until he'd pulled his trousers all the way down before I hit the carpet with my knees and dove on his cock. Wasting no time, I took him to the back of my throat, cupping his balls with one hand and working his shaft with the other.

"Christ, woman, you're going to make me come like a teenage boy if you keep doing that."

Music to my ears. I doubled my efforts, gripping his ass and bobbing up and down on his length while relaxing my throat to allow him even deeper. The salty taste of him hit my tongue as his roar filled the room. I swallowed him down, milking every ounce of him.

After he helped me to my feet, he didn't hesitate to kiss me. "There are no limits with you, Jules." I knew he meant more than sex by the way he looked deeply into my eyes.

"Get on the bed."

I loved the way he looked caught off guard by my demand.

"Not done?" he asked.

I shook my head. "Not even close."

I wasn't. I took my time exploring every inch of him, flicking his sensitive nipples with my tongue and then sliding it down his impressive abs. I made him hard again in no time, but he'd had enough of my teasing.

"I've been dreaming of when I'd get to taste you again." He flipped me over on my back. After positioning his broad shoulders between my knees, he kissed up my quivering thighs to the very heat before devouring me completely.

"I, oh......" I couldn't finish the thought. My eyes rolled back in my head while an all-consuming orgasm roared through me. But he wasn't content to let me down from the wave that had rocked me. Instead he was pushing me to the edge again with his unrelenting tongue on my clit and his fingers deep inside me, pumping in and out.

"Again. I need to feel it again."

My body didn't disappoint. It felt like someone hit me with a live wire. Every nerve ending was on fire. While the white heat rolled over me, I realized Mark's gorgeous face, now sans his glasses, hovered over mine.

"You all right?"

I nodded mutely, making him grin.

"A speechless Juliette is always a high compliment indeed. Now let me get these off of you."

He unzipped each boot and then peeled down the stockings underneath, leaving me completely naked before him.

After grabbing his glasses, he stood a moment simply staring down at me from the side of the bed. Once upon a time, I would've covered myself, insecure at being vulnerable and worrying about stretch marks. But the way this man looked at me made me believe him when he said I was beautiful. Because to him, I was.

"This is why the office wouldn't have done it. I needed to see you like this. You're even more stunning than I remembered."

I watched him walk over to his suitcase to retrieve what I guessed was a condom. After he stretched out on the bed next to me, I rolled into his embrace, kissing him with all of the pent-up emotion I'd been feeling over the last couple of weeks. I loved this man unequivocally and had missed him so much.

Framing my face with his hands, he pulled back. "I need to

put on the condom." His gaze searched mine. I imagined he was thinking of the last time we'd made love without one.

"Yeah, that would be good." I surprised him by taking the package out of his hands.

After I rolled on the condom, he positioned himself on top of me and entered me slowly. "Don't close your eyes," he insisted.

The level of intimacy stole my breath as he moved inside of me. He increased the pace and lifted my hips with his arm, which created the right angle to trigger my climax once again. This time I wasn't content to do it alone. My hands ran down his back, pulling him deeper while I clenched my intimate muscles tight around him.

"I love it when your pussy demands I come with you."

As my orgasm crested, I felt his start. I relished the sound of him growling my name as he ground out his climax deep inside of me.

We lay there for the longest time, each unwilling to sever the connection. Finally, Mark pulled out and got up to dispose of the condom. I'd started on the Pill again a couple weeks ago and was looking forward to being bare with him again in the near future.

When he came back to the bed, he gathered me close. Naked entanglement was my favorite.

"I didn't realize how much I needed this connection with you again," Mark murmured.

"Me, too. And I didn't realize how good it would feel to take charge and seduce you. In fact, I think I'll need to take charge more often."

He chuckled. "I hardly remember the drive over here I was so turned on."

"Good thing the police didn't pull us over." I giggled at the thought of how we'd explain the situation.

"I wanted to surprise you for the weekend. Not only for tonight but also in order to help with the garage sale and moving. I know selling things won't be easy."

His perception never failed to take me off guard. "That means a lot. It'll be difficult, but it's like a final purging of my past. I've selected some things to keep for Tristan: his father's graduation photo, his first badge, our wedding picture. He deserves to know we once loved one another and what kind of man Rob used to be."

"He absolutely does. I realize Brian and Sasha are helping you tomorrow and also your mom. If you'd rather stay home and not watch your things go, I'm certain we could manage."

It was kind of him to offer, but this wasn't something I could do via proxy. "I need to be there and see it through, but thank you for understanding how difficult it will be."

"Where is this new place you're moving to?"

I hesitated, not knowing how he felt about me making plans without him. "It's a small rental townhouse with two bedrooms. It's month to month. I just wanted to get out of my mom's house." Shit. I sounded apologetic.

"It's okay for you to have plans. You couldn't put everything on pause, waiting for me."

I wanted so badly to ask when he thought he'd be ready to give up Connecticut and all of his memories up there. But one step at a time.

He smiled, his fingers finding my most intimate spot. "Now then, since you bought us two hours, I intend on using every minute."

———

I KNEW the garage sale today would be rough, but that was an understatement. Watching strangers haul to their vehicles the living room furniture I'd bought as a newlywed was like an emotional gut punch. But I also knew I didn't want to take those memories with me into a new home. I was even selling the sheets, towels, dishes, and other wedding gifts that had originally set up my old home.

A couple hours in, Sasha came up and studied my face. "You doing all right?"

"Getting there. After closing and turning over the keys, I think I'll be better."

She squeezed my hand and then looked beyond me toward Mark. He was lifting a very heavy box of books for a woman who'd purchased them. "Huh, Mark has muscles."

Brian came up from behind, putting his arms around her. "Nuh-uh, no way. You made your choice. Plus, I have muscles, too. Not to mention I'm really great at—"

Both Sasha and I held up our hands. I laughed. "I really don't need to hear you finish that sentence." I caught Mark's gaze across the room and grinned.

He winked and then helped the older woman out to her car with the box. He'd been here all day, lifting, lugging, and packing.

And so had Brian and Sasha, along with my mother. I was where I needed to be, surrounded by everyone I loved.

By the time it was over, we'd sold all the furniture and bagged up any leftover clothing, kitchen, and garage stuff to give to charity. My mom had left to take her load to Goodwill and pick up Tristan. He'd been staying with my aunt and uncle for the day. Next, Sasha and Brian loaded up their car. They were nice enough to drop off the clothing that Rob's parents hadn't wanted at a shelter that was eager for the donation. Afterward, they would meet us at my new rental to help move some stuff in.

I walked from room to room, gathering up the few little things left and, in my own way, saying a final goodbye. My last stop was the master bedroom. Here I paused, hugging my arms to my body. This particular room had been such a source of happiness in the beginning, but had become a place of bitterness and resentment only a few months ago. Now it only left me sad.

And just when I thought I had no more tears to give him, they came now, most inconveniently.

Strong arms came around from the back and turned me. Soon I was crying in Mark's embrace. He stood there stroking my back and holding me until I had no more tears to shed.

"I'm being stupid. I mean, why now would I cry over this house?"

"Because you loved Rob once, and this house represented your future together. There are good memories here, Jules. And those are hard to say goodbye to."

Now I understood more than ever why Mark hadn't been able to sell his home. He'd been preserving those precious memories all these years. "Thank you for being here and for understanding."

"Of course. I wouldn't be anywhere else. Now, how about I pick up pizzas for everyone and meet you at your new place?"

"Sounds great."

LONG AFTER EVERYONE HAD LEFT, all the boxes had been shoved inside my townhouse, and Tristan had fallen fast asleep in his new room, Mark and I snuggled on my new sofa. Not fifteen minutes before, we'd happily christened it with a new memory.

My fingers trailed down his chest as I enjoyed this lazy cuddling. "This weekend is Sasha's bridal shower, but I was thinking maybe Tristan and I could come up to Connecticut the next weekend. It's the last one before the wedding." It was only fair to take a turn and not make him travel every time.

"Unfortunately, I can't do that weekend."

"Oh. Okay." I wanted to ask so badly what he was doing, but I waited him out to see if he would volunteer the information. Luckily, I wasn't disappointed.

He sighed heavily. "I planned on telling you although I

wasn't sure how or when. That Sunday is the anniversary of Sarah's death."

I let his words sink in.

"I, uh, I spend it with her family."

"Of course. Yes. That makes sense. And I'm glad you told me." Although I absolutely understood, it didn't hurt any less. I'd thought we'd come so far, but this was a reminder that he wasn't yet ready to let go. Then again, how could I ask him to? Being with her family probably gave both him and them comfort during a difficult time. I could never ask him to give that up.

"But I'll see you at the wedding. How's your toast coming, by the way?"

"I haven't started working on it yet, but something will come to me." Hopefully.

CHAPTER TWENTY-ONE

$\mathcal{T}$he mind can go from being completely rational to spiraling out of control and imagining all sorts of scenarios. Those were the extremes I'd gone to over the last few days. Not that I shared the issue with anyone. This time period was about Sasha and Brian and all of the festivities leading up to their wedding day. But I worried Mark would take a step back since the previous weekend had been the anniversary of his fiancée's death.

The fact I hadn't heard from him in days was doing nothing to quell my fears. It was Thursday morning. Four days since the anniversary. Five days since I'd last spoken with him. My fingers hovered over the icon on my phone's screen, ready to dial. Or maybe I should text. Darn. Or maybe I should stop stressing about it. Which led me back to the idea of simply calling him because the only way to stop my anxiety was to hear his voice and ensure we were still fine.

Finally, during my lunch hour when I couldn't wait any longer, I closed my office door and dialed his number. My heart lodged in my throat while the phone rang. Once, twice, three times. Just as I expected it to go to voicemail, finally a click and "Hello."

"Hi, it's me."

"Hey. Um, is everything all right? Tristan okay?"

It was like that now? I had to be calling for a problem? "He's fine. How are you?" *Why haven't you called me,* my subconscious screamed.

"Okay, but I'm sort of in the middle of some stuff here. Can I call you back? Maybe tomorrow? Or I'll see you on Saturday at the wedding."

I fought the hurt. "Yeah. I guess." I could hear voices in the background and wondered if they belonged to Sarah's family.

"Jules, I just need time here. I'm sorry, but I have to go. I'll see you Saturday though and we'll talk then. Okay?"

"Yeah. Okay." I mean what else could I say.

The sound of the disconnect left me cold. Although I didn't want to believe he wasn't ready to move on from Sarah and the memories, it might be time for me come to terms with that reality. In fact, he may always need more time.

MARK HADN'T CALLED. And I had a wedding to prepare for, so I didn't have the time if he had. At least, that's what I told myself because I certainly wasn't going to spend time obsessing over what him needing time meant. Right.

In any event, I was here for my friends today. I certainly wouldn't let things with Mark ruin that.

When I looked in the reflection of my hotel room mirror, I smiled. At least I felt good about myself today. It was the first time in a long while. I'd gone to the salon together with Sasha, Kenzie, Catherine, and Haylee. I'd had my hair done and even a manicure. Then we'd all had our makeup professionally applied. I felt pretty in my red dress. When we'd gone shopping last weekend, Sasha had insisted the color would make me feel cheerful as well as complement my brunette locks. I had to agree. It also felt good to step out of the color black for a change.

It was cold as hell at the February beach wedding in North Carolina. But my two best friends marrying at sunset in an intimate ceremony at Sasha's favorite spot was one of the most beautiful things I'd ever witnessed. The love Sasha and Brian expressed for one another brought tears to my eyes.

I noticed the moment Mark arrived. Although he stood over with Josh and Haylee on one side of the couple while I was with Kenzie and Colby on the other side, he did give me a smile. The nerdy-hot kind that made my stomach do somersaults.

But he didn't make a move to go with us back to the reception hall. And forty minutes later, he still hadn't shown up at the party. By then, I was ready to stab 'hope' along with her friend 'time' with my fork if either of them were mentioned again.

I forced a smile and took a seat next to Kenzie. She excitedly told me about her backup singing gig which started touring in March. Considering I'd practically seen Brian's little sister grow up, I enjoyed catching up with her. Better to do that than pathetically scan the room for Mark.

Matter of fact, I made a decision. Mark could seek me out instead of me stalking the entrance waiting on him. I threw a cocktail back—only one for now because I had a toast to give later, resolving to enjoy myself despite my emotional turmoil.

As everyone took their seats for dinner, I felt a tap on my shoulder. Turning, I gave a smile to the handsome groom.

"Hey, you ready to do your toast?" Brian queried.

At least he made it easy to focus back on the here and now. "You bet. The question really is: are you ready?"

Brian chuckled. "Absolutely."

I got up out of my chair and followed him to the front where —gulp—they had a stage. Someone handed me a microphone.

Then my goofball of a boss did something unexpected. He

turned to me and got serious. "Juliette, you're like the older sister I never had. I hope you know that."

It took a full three seconds for his words to seep in and for me to swat him. "Hey, I'm younger than you. And don't you know better than to rile up the person about to make the speech?"

He laughed but then kissed my cheek. "I was only kidding— about the older part. Thank you for agreeing to do this. It means a lot."

"Are you kidding me? It's an honor. Besides, it was kind of a group effort."

"What?" Suddenly, he started to look nervous.

But it was too late. I gave a nod to Colby, who brought out a wheeled projector. Kenzie meanwhile got the large screen ready on the other side of the room. See, it paid to have a movie producer in this circle, not to mention access to the many embarrassing photos I'd gathered from family and friends.

I watched the lights go down and then the spotlight shine on me. Damn. No pressure. The sounds of clinking glasses silenced the room and the two hundred plus people who'd come for the reception party at the country club.

I glanced over toward the beautiful bride and groom. Emotions got stuck in my throat because of how happy they looked and also because of what they represented. True love.

"Hi, ya'll. I'm Juliette. And I was asked to give a speech tonight about the happy couple. Although I give it five minutes before they may be regretting that request."

A few chuckles from the crowd.

"Now then, in order to get the full picture of this love story, I think we need to go back to the beginning."

Up flashed a picture of Brian at about two years old, naked as a jaybird.

"There once was a little boy who was cute as could be,
Who always had a smile on his face as we all can see."

And so the rhyming story went on through four more awkward pictures of Brian before switching to Sasha growing up.

Then, finally, we arrived at a picture I'd snapped about eight years ago when we'd all started working together. It showed Sasha and Brian at a bar during a happy hour. She had a smile on her face and it was clear he'd put it there. The entire crowd did a collective "aww." I could see by the stunned looks on the bride and groom's faces that they'd never seen the photo before.

"When boy met girl, the question he asked was,
Find out her name and do it fast.
But I did one better, don't you know,
I snapped this picture hoping someday I would show
The moment it became clear to me
That you two together was meant to be."

The final photograph was of them at their engagement party smiling for the camera. There I finished my speech, trying to control the emotion welling up.

"So that's the end of my rhyme as I'm almost out of time. But, uh…"

I glanced down at the notecard with the words in front of me, but I couldn't focus on them. Instead, I chose to go from my heart.

"I couldn't get this last part to rhyme, so I'm just going to say it—" I lifted my gaze to the crowd and saw Mark across the room with eyes on me.

Breathe, Juliette.

"It's rare when you get to see two people more in sync and more in love than these two."

And right there on that stage, it hit me. If anything were to happen to one of them, I couldn't imagine the other one finding someone else. Ever. They were it for one another. What if Sarah had been it for Mark?

"I think the kind of love Sasha and Brian have for one another only comes around once in a lifetime."

I had to fight back my tears and keep from making eye contact with Mark. Because I finally got it. It was sinking in why he couldn't move on. Why he was unable to love me. Because the type of love he'd felt for Sarah wasn't the kind you could ever recover from losing, let alone put a time limit on.

"I love them as my friends, adore them as my coworkers, and think of them as family. So let's raise our glasses to Sasha and Brian and wish them all the happiness in the world."

I held up my glass and watched while the lights came up and everyone toasted. The entire room was clapping. Soon I was engulfed in hugs by the happy couple.

As I turned to step off the stage and go back to my table, Mark immediately came up to me. "That was great. Especially the slideshow."

"Yeah, well, no small animals were harmed, and no embarrassing information shared, so I guess we could call it a win."

He grinned. "Do you have a minute to talk?"

I couldn't do this. Not right now. Not at the wedding in front of a bunch of people and definitely not after my revelation. Luckily, I was saved by the bell, in the form of Brian's mother.

"Mark, can we get pictures of you and Josh with the groom, please?"

He appeared hesitant to leave my side, but I took the out and encouraged him. "Go on."

I stood watching for a few minutes while the three college friends stood for pictures, and then I walked toward the bar. I needed a few minutes of alone time with two cocktails. Slipping out of the ballroom while everyone was busy doing pictures was easy. Luckily, I found the women's lounge upstairs. Gotta love a country club because it wasn't merely a bathroom, but a full-out lady's lounge, complete with plush sofas. Perfect.

Unfortunately, I hadn't even taken a first sip before the door opened. I was unsure about the etiquette of downing two martinis in the ladies' room but wasn't sure I cared. Bracing myself to smile at the stranger, I was surprised to see it was Sasha.

"Oh, thank God it's you."

She flopped down next to me in her beautiful designer wedding gown. "That's my line. I need a moment away from my new mother-in-law. Hey, do you have an extra?" She was eyeing my second martini.

Because I loved her and she was the bride, I handed it over. "Here you go. What happened?"

"Nothing major. But you know me with people. I just needed a little break, and then I'll go back. Brian is out smoking cigars with his friends on the balcony, so it's the perfect time. Loved your speech, by the way. And I want a copy of that photo from the slideshow. It was such a shock to see us from so many years ago."

"Ha. Well, then, you'll be happy with your wedding gift." I'd framed it for them.

"You doing okay?"

Nope. But there was no way I was going to unload on her even a little bit on her wedding day. "Yeah. Everything is good."

She quirked a brow. "As in hiding-in-the-ladies'-room-with-two-martinis good?"

I laughed, about to make some sort of joke, when the door opened again. We both were relieved to see Catherine come in, looking gorgeous in a stunning blue dress.

"What are you girls up to?" She eyed our glasses.

"Hiding from my mother-in-law. Juliette supplied the martini."

She laughed and took a seat on the sofa across from us. "I love these shoes, but they're killing my feet. And since Will is out smoking cigars with the guys, I thought it was the perfect opportunity to take a break."

"I'll text Kenzie to bring backup drinks. Come to think of it, she should just bring the bottle." Sasha grabbed my phone.

I clinked my glass with hers as that sounded like a fine idea. I would return to the reception in a few minutes, but this was nice, hanging out with just the girls.

Haylee and Kenzie must've thought so, too, because they snuck in not only a bottle of vodka and another of champagne, but also managed a tray of the chocolate-covered strawberries.

All of us girls hung out for the next fifteen minutes until there was a knock on the door. We all looked at one another, wondering who could it be. Finally, Kenzie got up to answer.

I heard Mark's voice. "Is Juliette in there?"

Kenzie opened the door wide enough for me to see him. "Yep. Uh, do you want us to give you a few minutes?"

He smiled at her gratefully. "Yes, if that's okay?"

Sasha stood up. "Perfect timing, actually. Break time is over. I should get back."

I watched wordlessly while my friends filed out, all giving small smiles. Kenzie was the exception, asking, "Did I miss something?"

Yeah, good question. When I got to my feet, I realized that three drinks in a short amount of time had me a bit tipsy. Given past experience, this probably didn't bode well.

Once we were alone, he shut the door and moved in front of me. "Hi."

"Hello." Although I'd braced myself for what I was convinced he was about to say, I decided to preempt it. "If you're intending to break up with me, can we please wait until after the reception?"

He looked shocked. "Why on earth would you think I'm breaking up with you?"

"Because I get it now."

"Get what?"

"I had an epiphany during the toast when I tried to imagine

Brian or Sasha finding someone else if anything were to happen to one of them. I realized that kind of love—maybe it does come around only once in a lifetime."

He ran a hand through his hair. "You are completely on the wrong track here. But that's my fault. Last week was difficult, but I should've—"

I shook my head. "No, it's okay. You said you needed time, and it's pretty clear when you avoided me during the reception that you still aren't ready and I'm telling you it's okay because I understand it now."

"Jules, stop. You definitely do not understand." His frustration was showing. "First, I was late showing up to the reception because I went with Haylee and Josh to decorate the bridal suite after the ceremony on the beach. Which sounds a whole lot fucking weirder than it was when I say it out loud. Basically, Haylee wanted to do it, she roped in Josh, and he begged me to come, too, so he wasn't the only one tossing rose petals on the bed."

A smile tugged at my lips at the thought of them making the wedding night hotel room romantic.

"As you're probably imagining, it was ridiculous for Josh and me to be helping, but obviously it's for our friends, and Haylee asked. Anyhow, when I arrived back here, I ended up having to go way over to the far side of the lot to find parking. Then, when I came in to the reception room, I got waylaid into a conversation with Josh's mom. I haven't seen her in a while. After that, Catherine and Will. Before I knew it, you were up there giving your speech, and I hadn't had any time to talk to you. Then when I got tied up with photos, you disappeared. But I was not avoiding you."

"I guess that explains where you went."

"As for last week, I should've called, but I wasn't in the right frame of mind. I had a lot going on, which I want to tell you about. But maybe not now because it's a lot. Especially since

Brian told me they're cutting the cake in ten minutes. Is it okay if we talk later? Promise you won't take off on me?"

"I won't take off, but maybe you could give me a clue about the ending of this talk. Because the last few weeks my mind has been going through this pinball game of emotions. I mean, the silver ball gets launched and is high at first, but bam—It goes right, then left, pinging around to we're good, we're great; oh, no, it's moving lower and we're not so good now because you need time, but how much time before the ball goes down the hole because I can't save it with those flapper thingies—? Ping, ping, ping."

I was making hand gestures to illustrate my words when he cut me off with a kiss. "God, I fucking love you."

I pulled away in shock. "Wh-what did you just say?"

He cupped my face, letting every one of his words sink in. "The peek at the ending is that I love you, Jules."

"But Sarah is the love of your life."

He sighed. "She *was* the love of my life, but that is not my life any longer. Although twenty-something-year-old Mark loved Sarah more than anything, I'm no longer him. Instead, I'm the man standing before you. A different person than I was all those years ago with a different life. And the man I am now loves you more than anything."

"But—" I didn't mean to argue with him; however, I was having a hard time believing this turn of events.

"But nothing. You are the love of this life. And instead of just filling a void in it, you give me the reasons to live it."

My eyes instantly filled with tears.

He reacted to this as every guy does. He panicked. "Whoa, whoa. Jules. I didn't mean to make you cry. Hey. What's going on in that beautiful head of yours?"

I swallowed past the ball of emotion in my throat and shook my head. "I love you, too. But during my toast, I thought—God, I thought I was letting you go tonight because I finally got it."

"No. It's me who finally got it. I'm only sorry it took me this long and that I made you doubt my feelings for you. And I certainly didn't want to make you cry at our friends' wedding reception." His thumbs wiped my tears.

"These are happy tears. I promise."

He looked skeptical. "Yeah, well, happiness is sort of running away with your mascara, so you'd best take a minute to fix it before we go back in there and everyone thinks I made you cry."

A giggle escaped my throat. "Afraid of being punched by the groom?"

He grinned. "Um, to be honest, I'm more afraid of the bride if she sees you with a splotchy face."

We both smiled at the thought. Sasha wasn't called fierce around the office for no reason.

"So how about we return to the reception and talk more later?"

I nodded. "I think that sounds like a good plan."

After I touched up my makeup, we went back to the reception hand in hand. At my table, our friends had saved two seats next to one another. Mark not only made a show of pulling out my chair, but he also settled his hand on mine in plain sight of everyone.

I hadn't realized how much I'd needed the validation in front of others until now. This public display was also a huge step for Mark showing he'd overcome his guilt to the point he could allow our friends to see him happy again.

Later, when he pulled me out onto the dance floor, I felt myself truly relaxing for the first time in weeks.

"You're awfully quiet," he whispered.

"Weird, huh?"

"I tend to think of it as a compliment. Like maybe the pinball machine is on pause?"

Huh. He was right. I only tended to talk constantly when I was anxious. At the moment, I was feeling peace. Peace in us, peace in me, peace be with you. Yep, a whole lot of clucking peace. "I find it funny you picked up on that before I did, but yes, the game is quiet right now with all the balls where they belong."

He chuckled. "Good. You look beautiful tonight in this dress and your sexy shoes."

The pinching of my feet was worth the small amount of pain they caused as they elevated my height. And the shoes weren't the only thing I'd purchased.

"Wait until I show you what I have on underneath. Here's a hint. The color is the same as this dress." I couldn't quite believe I'd spent that much money on a scrap of lacy underwear and matching bra, but now was glad I had as I was anxious for Mark to see it.

A low growl reverberated through him. "Would it be rude to drag you off this dance floor and back to our hotel room right now?"

"Our hotel room? Didn't you get one, too?"

His face scrunched in confusion. "No. I assumed we were sharing, and since you made your reservation before I did, I didn't bother to get one. Because why would we get two rooms?"

Why, indeed? "I think we still have some work to do on the communication front. I should've asked instead of assuming."

"I think it's safe to assume we'll be sharing rooms from now on. So, was that a yes, I can drag you back to the room?"

I checked my watch. "In thirty more minutes. I'm in charge of sparklers for the happy couple's send-off." Brian had thought of little details that I was happy to help carry out.

"You know, for not being in this wedding, this is a lot of work."

He was joking I could tell. "It's what friends do. Now, back to you wanting to drag me off to the hotel room. Maybe you could tell me in detail what you have planned."

Because I did love his filthy mouth.

"If I do that, then we won't make it to say goodnight to the couple. Plus, we have some more things to talk about before we get to the good stuff."

I felt like a kid who'd been told to do my math homework before I could go outside to play. Then again, since I already knew the ending to whatever he intended to tell me, I felt less anxious about what he had to say.

"Did you call your mom to check up on Tristan, by the way?"

Because the wedding was in Sasha's hometown, we were five hours away from Charlotte. My mother was babysitting there overnight. "Yep. He's down for the count after having watched the movie *Cars*. And nice try with the distraction."

"It's for both of us. Never tell Brian or Sasha this, but I can't wait for this reception to be over."

I grinned. "I won't, especially since I feel the same. And I'm sure they'd understand."

After staying until the end of the party and then, outside the club, sending off the happily married couple with a gauntlet of sparklers, Mark and I headed back to our hotel room a few miles away.

Once there, I slipped off my shoes before zipping down the side of my dress. Let's hear it for side zippers as I didn't need assistance.

"Wait. Leave the dress on. I do need to talk to you about this last week."

Thanks to the wonders of champagne, I'd pretty much forgotten that he'd wanted to talk first. "Is everything okay?"

"Yes. But if you take off your dress, I'll be distracted with your gorgeous body, though I do plan on enjoying it soon."

He cupped my face, more solemn than I'd ever seen him. "I meant what I said earlier. I love you, Jules. With all of my heart. I can't and wouldn't change that it first belonged to Sarah or that she'll always be part of my past. But I want you to believe me when I say I've moved on, something I'll hopefully show you every day. You're my future. You and Tristan."

Cue the liquid happiness running down my face again. "I love you, too." The words came out muffled against his chest since he'd crushed me to him, giving me the type of hug that envelops the soul.

"I'm sorry I needed time last week, but there was a lot happening. It was emotional, to say the least."

I pulled back, needing him to understand he didn't have to say he was sorry for it. "It's okay. It wasn't easy not hearing from you, but don't apologize for needing this time. Did you, uh, hang out with her family all week?" I was genuinely curious if he'd spent it with her family, sat huddled in the dark crying his eyes out, or what.

"Some of the time. Yes. But most of the week was spent packing up my house."

"WHAT?" I practically shouted, stepping back and staring at him in disbelief.

He gave me a small smile. "Sarah's parents and sister came over and took the items they wanted, such as pictures and mementos. We were going through photos when you called, so again, I'm sorry I wasn't ready to talk. Anyhow, I put some other things in boxes that I'm not sure will ever see the light of day again, but I wasn't ready to let go of them. And the house will go on the market after I finish making a couple needed repairs."

"Holy shit." Not only was it the first time he'd freely spoken to me about Sarah in conversation, but he was also selling his house. I took a seat on the bed, completely in disbelief. "Sorry, give me a minute here to say something better. More profound."

He chuckled, taking a seat beside me. "You owe a dollar in the jar. But I think your response just now was the only one I needed to hear."

"Why this week?" The anniversary of Sarah's death seemed

an unlikely candidate as a time for him to come to these conclusions.

He expelled a long breath, taking my hands. "It had been building for a while. There was a reason I was spending every night at my office instead of going home to a house full of reminders. Although it's a sad time each year, I was tired of being sad—if that makes sense."

He tucked my hair behind my ear, taking a breath. "It sank in on that Sunday when I went over to her parents' house like I do every year. We visited her grave, we went through pictures, and I went home. Then on Monday I drove back over, finally admitting to her family that I'd felt responsible. After all these years, I blurted it out. And you know what? They already knew that she'd come there because we'd disagreed about the wedding. She'd told them. And they'd discussed how postponing actually did make sense. They said that when she'd left the house, they all knew we would be fine. That we'd simply postpone the wedding until after the bar exam. I only wish I'd brought it up sooner so I could've known."

Although it was usually Mark who was dealing with guilt, I couldn't help feeling a measure of my own now. I felt sad she'd died and that things hadn't worked out for them and yet happy he was with me now. It wasn't comfortable to dwell on it. "It was closure for you?"

He nodded. "Long awaited. And then I told them about you. About you and Tristan."

"You did?" I was floored. Holy crap, when the man said he needed to "talk," he wasn't messing around. The surprises just kept on rolling.

"I didn't want to hide it any longer. It was important they know I found love. They're happy for me. In fact, they want to meet you. Someday. When you're ready. And I'd love for that to happen. Not because I seek their validation or need their opinion about you, but simply because they're like family to me."

The last thing I wanted to do was be a wedge between him and people who clearly loved him. They even wanted to maintain a relationship with him despite him having a new woman in his life. "I'd love to meet them. Although you do know how I am when I get anxious, so please be forewarned that I'll have buckets of nerves. You may find it adorable, which for the record could speak to your level of crazy matching mine, so—disclaimer and all."

He smiled. "Duly noted, and think of it this way. If you weren't that way, I wouldn't have ever discovered how much my fingers turned you on at the rooftop party the first time we met."

I giggled, thinking back to that disastrous night. In the end, it was turning out spectacularly. "Two-fingered-orgasm-inducing fingers, if I recall correctly."

He threw his head back, laughing. "It's a good thing you didn't have the same reaction to Dr. Mac."

Now I was laughing, too. "Wait, if you're selling your house, does that mean you plan on moving?"

He started kissing behind my ear. "I hear North Carolina is nice. Pretty girls there."

"Depends on where you go. For instance, Charlotte is probably best. I hear the girls there are kind of kinky."

"Thank cluck."

I pulled back, framing his face and smiling. "Did you just mommy-modify the F-word?"

"I figured I'd better start if I want to make a case for moving in with you anytime soon."

"You're going to contribute to the jar?"

"You bet. Or if moving in right away is too fast, especially since you got into your new place only a couple weeks ago, I can get one close by, and we can wait."

"It's not too fast, but you're the one whose life changes drastically when you move in with me and a toddler. Are you sure you're ready?"

It wasn't a small task to go from a bachelor who worked from home to a guy living with a mom and child.

He didn't hesitate with his answer. "I want early mornings of waking up with Tristan and letting you sleep in while we quietly make you breakfast in bed. I want getting up in the middle of the night because maybe someday he'll call my name when he's afraid of the dark. And I want family dinners, bath nights, and homework. I want dinners out with our friends. Holidays split between our families and anything else I'm not thinking of. I want it all with you."

The man was perfection. "I want it all, too. And I'd love if you moved in."

"Would it be too presumptuous if I did it tomorrow? I brought my stuff with me."

I stood up and stepped out of the dress, enjoying the way his eyes narrowed with desire at my red lacy thong and matching bra. "It's not too presumptuous. And I hope you packed the toy bag."

He pulled me to him, hugging my waist. "Have I mentioned how much I love the girls from Charlotte? Now, let me look at you. You're so fucking sexy."

I arched a brow at his failed attempt to avoid profanity, which made him chuckle.

"I think this swear jar may end up being a new form of fore-play. Come to think of it, I'll put in a twenty right now for what I have planned."

I squealed when he swept me off my feet and onto the bed. "Hell, if that's the case, then I'm putting in another twenty."

He grinned, hovering over me. "How do you feel about taking credit card payments?"

I matched his grin. "I think that can be arranged. In fact, we should probably take some time off work soon because, at this rate, Disney World, here we come."

EPILOGUE

*T*en months after I moved in and started contributing to the 'swear jar,' we were finally going to Disney World. It was a toss-up who was more excited about it: Tristan or Juliette.

We could have done the trip sooner, but we'd wanted Tristan to be old enough to really appreciate it, and Jules had wanted to see the place all decorated for the Christmas holiday.

"You ready to get on the road?" I asked.

Juliette smiled.

I would never grow tired of putting that expression on her beautiful face. Nor would I get tired of seeing my ring sitting comfortably on her left hand. We hadn't set a date for the wedding yet. Instead, we'd discussed that she wouldn't take my name until Tristan could have the same one. I more than understood. It was my hope that someday, once he was old enough to decide for himself, he'd want me to be his dad. Then they'd both take my name, enabling us to become the Hines family. It was also our plan to add to it someday. But all in good time. As it was, we were now about to go on our first of many family vacations.

"I'm ready, but are you? You must be tired since you just flew in."

For the last couple days, I'd been up in New York with Josh for business. I'd only returned this morning. The travel had been strategic as I had an early Christmas surprise to show Juliette, and I was anxious to see her reaction to it. "Yep, got plenty of sleep last night, so I'm well rested for the drive."

If you'd told me over a year ago I would ever have been this happy, I would've called you a liar. But Jules brought me back to life. Gave me a reason to live it and thank God for every day I had her in it. Her and Tristan. I might not be Tristan's biological father, but I loved him more than I ever thought a heart was capable of loving.

"You said the condo at Disney has a washer and dryer in it, right?"

I smiled because she'd already asked me these questions. But how could I fault her for wanting to ensure everything was organized? At least one of us was that way. "Sure does."

"And Internet?"

"Yep." I knew it was important because she continued to take classes. I was so proud of her for sticking with it. Not because it made a difference in how I felt about her if she had a college education, but because I knew how important it was for her to complete her degree.

"And it has a kitchen, so we can get groceries. I already packed the snacks you bought for the drive. And last week I loaded a couple of movies onto Tristan's iPad to keep him entertained."

"You're always good with this stuff. Too bad you're still a slob, though." She kissed me playfully.

We'd moved into a larger townhome and made the basement my office. And, well, with that space—old habits die hard. I was in fact a slob. "Only my desk is a mess. And maybe the floor next to it."

"If I ever wonder where all the glasses and mugs have disappeared to, I only need to go downstairs. But I cleaned it up while you were gone. Hung a picture on the wall above your desk, too."

"What picture?"

She busied herself putting the last of the smaller bags by the door. "Tristan drew you one, and I framed it. It's your Christmas gift from him."

I looked toward the couch where Tristan was working to put on his tennis shoes.

He had his Mickey Mouse shirt on in addition to a Disney World magic band around his wrist. He'd evidently slept with both, anxious to get down there.

"Did you make me a picture, bud?"

"Yep. It's a surprise." At three-and-a-half, he was starting to string together complete sentences. It was adorable.

I bent down and helped him with his last shoe. "Do I get to see it before we leave?"

He hopped down and took my hand. "Yep. Come on, Mommy. You come, too." He waved his hand for his mom to follow.

The first thing I noticed was that Juliette had indeed cleaned up my desk. I smiled as I remembered the first time she'd organized my files in Connecticut. I'd been absolutely mesmerized by her.

She flicked on the light, and I could see the anticipation on Tristan's face. As I studied the eight-by-twelve frame holding the hand-drawn picture above my desk, I expected to see an animal of some sort. Those were his favorite to draw. Instead, I saw three stick-figure people.

First was me, the tallest with glasses; then came him in the middle, holding my hand; and Juliette stood on the end with long brown hair. But when I looked closer, I realized they were

295

labeled with letters in crayon. *ME* was below him, *Mommy* below Juliette, and *Daddy* was written below my likeness.

My eyes hit Juliette's.

She answered my unspoken question. "He drew it and then asked me to write the words to go under each person. He wanted yours to say Daddy."

I swallowed hard as I bent down to lift him up. "I love it."

"Mommy said I gotta ask you."

"Ask me if I want to be your daddy?" My voice was thick with emotion. This little boy and his mom were my everything.

"Yep." With his adorably serious face, he was so matter-of-fact and sure with his one-word declaration.

I glanced toward Juliette; her cheeks wet with tears. "And you'd be okay with that?" Although I knew she loved me as much as I loved her, this was a whole other level of trust. I wanted to respect that in asking for her blessing in this pivotal step.

"Yes. I know you said you wanted to wait until he's old enough to decide, but I think he has by drawing this picture."

"Can I?" Tristan asked, putting his little toddler hands on either side of my face.

"I'd be honored."

He scrunched up his little face with confusion at my words. "What?"

I laughed at my mistake in phrasing it that way for a three-and-a-half-year-old. "I mean yes. Yes, you can call me Daddy. That would make me very happy."

He hugged me to him. "Me, too. Momma said I have two. One in heaven and you here with me."

I appreciated the way she had explained this to him. I never wanted to lie to Tristan about his biological father. But some day when he was older, I would sit him down and tell him this was the day I became his dad. Just as his mother had captured my heart, so had he. "That's right. I love you, Tristan."

"I love you, too, Daddy."

Oh fuck-cluck. I was going to lose it. I handed him off to Juliette, who was quickly becoming a mess of tears herself. "Uh, here. Why don't you two go upstairs, and I'll be up in a minute?"

She led him up the stairs.

I was grateful for a few minutes to myself to get a handle on my emotions. Toddlers didn't always understand happy tears, so I didn't want him wondering why his picture had made me so emotional. Taking the frame off the nail it hung on, I studied it closer. There was no way I was leaving it here for the next week. Nope, it was making the trip with us.

When I went up to the main level, Jules and Tristan were waiting by the door. Both looked curiously at the fact I was holding my present under my arm. "I want to take it with me, so I can have it all week. Then I'll bring it back and put it above my desk again."

This appeared to make Tristan very happy as he grinned from ear to ear.

As we started on the road south toward Orlando, I couldn't help smiling. Obviously, I hadn't been the only one with a big Christmas surprise in mind. I took Juliette's hand across the console, and we spent most of the trip talking about the new house we would start building in the new year. I'd purchased the lot next door to Sasha and Brian, who were almost done constructing their house. I'd surprised Juliette with it when I'd proposed last month.

After the eight-hour drive with a couple stops, we got checked into our hotel and put Tristan down for the night. I'd relished it when he'd wanted his 'daddy' to brush his teeth, tuck him in, and read him his bedtime story.

Finding Juliette in the bathroom removing her makeup, I came up behind her and put my arms around her waist. I hugged her to me.

"You okay?" she asked.

I nodded, meeting her gaze in the mirror. "Better than that. You really blew me out of the water today with the family picture. Thank you."

She smiled. "For what? I only provided the frame."

I shook my head, moving her hair off her neck in order to land a kiss. "No. You gave life to that little boy, and now you're sharing him with me. There is no greater gift."

Her eyes went misty. "That was beautiful. I can't think of anyone who will make a better father than you."

I turned her around and kissed her softly, appreciating how amazing this woman was. But when her hand rubbed my chest, I stepped back with a wince.

"What's under your shirt?"

Her head was quirked to the side, causing me to smile. "Something I can't wait to show you."

She lifted a brow. "Is this another 'if you show me yours, I'll show you mine'?"

Ah, she was referring to the way I'd got her to slowly reveal her body in the beginning and shed her insecurities. "My favorite game. But this is your surprise."

"What kind of surprise?"

My girl loved surprises, but only if she could find out what they were quickly. But suddenly I was nervous. I unsteadily fisted the back of my T-shirt and pulled it over my head, holding the soft cotton in front of my chest.

"If you don't like it, then I can get it changed. Although I guess it's a little late for that, but I could always get it removed. Maybe I should've asked you whether you were all right with changing it before doing something permanent. But that would've ruined the surprise." Ironically, I was the one rambling instead of her.

"Get what changed?"

I dropped the T-shirt and watched her curiously take in the square bandage above my heart.

"Show me," she whispered.

I peeled it back, revealing a J-U-L-E before the S which had once stood alone.

She gently ran her fingers over the raised skin, which was still a bit red and tender, and around the black cursive letters. "When did you get this?"

"Two days ago, in New York."

My gaze didn't leave hers as I watched and waited for her reaction. "Please tell me you don't hate it."

She shook her head, whispering the words, "Not even close."

"I wanted a way to show you that although the past was there first, the future is there now too."

She continued to remain stunned.

"Say something."

She lifted her eyes to mine, so full of emotion. "The symbolism is everything. I can't even put it into words what it means to me. It's incredible."

I let out the breath I'd been holding. Thank God, she loved it. "I love you so much."

"I love you too."

"Marry me?"

She giggled. "I believe you already asked that question on one knee in the grassy field where we're now building our house, and I said yes."

I grinned. "You did. But you make me want to ask you over and over again. Because now that I've found forever, I'm just anxious for it to start."

Her hands framed my face. "The fact that this mouth can say the most beautiful, and yet the most deliciously dirty, things will never cease to amaze me. And I won't ever get tired of saying yes. In fact, I hear Vegas is real nice in March."

"You'd be okay with getting married in a few months?" If I was being honest, it was taking everything in me not to rush things. But I hadn't wanted to remind her of our first botched attempt, when I'd pushed things quickly for the wrong reasons.

"Mm. Absolutely."

I dipped my head, taking her lips in a searing kiss and backing her up to the edge of the bathroom counter. I lifted her up, quickly taking off my glasses so I could pepper her neck with kisses.

"Now it's your turn to show me something."

She giggled. "Oh, I'll show you something—"

"Mama. Mark—I mean Daddy?"

I grinned in the crook of her neck, giving her earlobe one more tug for good measure before turning.

Tristan was standing there in his PJs, shielding his eyes from the bright light.

"What's up, baby? Why are you out of bed?" She hopped down to kneel by him.

"Why were you hugging?"

She winked up at me. "Uh, it's what mommies and daddies do. It means we love each other."

Thankfully, Jules was quick with her explanation because I was still working on an appropriate response.

"Can I hug, too?"

I lifted him up. "Sure thing, bud. Big group hug."

Jules and I both squeezed him tight. In glorious fashion, he giggled between us and said the sweetest words I'd ever heard.

"I love my family."

I couldn't have said it any better.

If you love office romance, check out my next series, the Without Series! Peyton and Simon's story is up next in Without Apology.

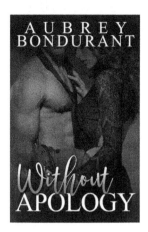

ACKNOWLEDGMENTS

Some of you have been anxiously awaiting Mark's story since book one and I have to say I put it last because I knew just how emotional it would be. Not only because of what he and Juliette had to go through, but also because it's the end of the series. Saying goodbye to this group of friends is really tough for me. That being said, never say never for future characters…because I may already have something in mind that allows us to check in down the road! And as you read above there will be a Series Epilogue that is exclusive to those who have signed up for my newsletter!

I hope you enjoyed this book and the four that came before it as much as I did writing them. I set out to create a series that not only featured imperfect women who lifted one another up with their friendships, but also write my favorite types of romance. Each of these books and the characters mean so much to me and the greatest compliment is when someone tells me how they have related to them.

I want to give a big THANK YOU, shouted in all CAPS to my loyal, amazing readers for sticking by me throughout this amazing journey. You know someday I'd love to do this full time, but in the meantime, you've been so patient for the next book. Every tag you make, every share, every person you recommend my books to means so much! It's for you that I happily stay up late at night typing away!

To my family: Thank you for the continuation of encouraging the dream and putting up with the balancing act that doesn't always go perfectly!

To my editor, Alyssa Kress. Once again you keep me on track, push me to do better and encourage me to keep going. It's truly a pleasure to work with you since day one!

To Lori who requested Mark be a dirty talker. I love the way you think my friend! I only hope I did him justice!

To all of the amazing bloggers, some of which I actually got to meet this last year! When I say I wouldn't be doing this without you, I really mean it! You've been unbelievably supportive in sharing, promoting and supporting me, I can't thank you enough!

To LB: Lastly, but not least: When an author finds out that her good friend has been cheated on and lied to by her shitty husband, what does she do? She names Juliette's ex after him and of course happily kills him off. (Insert the clink of the champagne glasses toasting.) Sorry it wasn't more of a torturous scene my friend! And although Juliette's story is not yours by any stretch, I know your Mark is out there for you someday!

Made in the USA
Las Vegas, NV
06 September 2021